DARK HOLLOW

Book One

of the

Hidden Heritage Series

Enjoy the Book

Tara Winters

Tara Winters

PUBLISHED BY WINTERMOON PUBLISHING

Visit Tara Winters' official website at www.tarawinters.com
for the latest news, book details, and other information

Date of first printing: July 2014

Editing by: Sue Ducharme of Textworks
Cover Design: www.coveryourdreams.net
eBook formatting: Guido Henkel, www.guidohenkel.com

Printed in U.S.A.

For Joe and Samantha

Once the box of secrets is opened, it can never be closed again.

—Pandora

CHAPTER ONE

THE MAN SAT WATCHING FOR HER, AS HE DID MOST DAYS; he knew her schedule better than she did. A ring of smoke slipped from his lips, and he let the cigarette dangle from his hand, browned by sun and sea spray. He squinted through the morning sun as it began to burn off the fog hugging the coastal New England island. Dampness seeped through his jeans, and he brushed the early-morning dew from the arm of the bench and let his gaze drift up the hill, knowing she would appear from around the corner.

He did not have long to wait. He recognized her dark ponytail streaming behind her as she navigated the familiar island streets on her bike. A small smile curved the man's thin mouth as he watched her spin down the hill toward the village nestled at the harbor of Porta Negra. Her body was lean and lithe from pedaling around the island, but it was her face that captivated most men upon meeting her. Her silver-gray eyes—almond shaped and fringed with dark and sooty lashes—high cheekbones, and sensuous mouth were all framed by a thick wealth of raven hair that hung down her back.

He knew her story and he knew her secrets—even those she was not aware she kept. He had watched her and kept vigil for eighteen years, waiting. Porta Negra was a small island, and the year-round islanders were all too familiar with the air of mystery that hovered around Tabitha Devins.

He stood as he watched her slip through the park and wind her way toward the café that hugged the pier. Standing, he let the cigarette fall to the ground and then stamped it out. He stretched and headed back toward the less tourist-laden side of town.

Tabitha Devins felt pavement give way to cobblestones as she wound her way down the narrow streets to the tiny café nestled at the end of the pier. The sun was just rising over Porta Negra, and the warm smell of fog burning off promised a sunny day for the kick-off of the Memorial Day weekend. She leaped off her bike as she rolled behind the café and then slid her backpack off the handlebars. As she secured the bike to the cement pole, she glanced around the dumpster, looking for her newly adopted moocher. The elegant stray waited for her on the mornings she opened the café, his tail held high as he mewed for a quick morsel and a scratch under the chin. Tabitha suspected the resourceful little cat was also working most of the other shop workers along the pier for a quick meal or two.

She glanced around, pursing her lips to call him, when she heard a plaintive wail from behind the dumpster. She saw that the cat had dragged himself back to the dumpster but could move no further. Tabitha lowered herself onto the ground next to the tiny animal and felt tears sting her eyes as she sobbed. As she gently lifted his body into her arms, blood flowed from wounds on his back and legs. He had been in another fight and this time had come out worse for wear.

Tabitha gently cradled the dark cat as she promised, "I'll get you to the vet. Hang on!"

Her fingers warmed, and a tingle seemed to ease up her arms. Tabitha drew a breath as heat spread from her fingertips up her arms. She calmed her nerves, almost afraid to try...Could she? Was it even possible?

Tabitha let the heat engulf her; her arms began to pulse, and her fingers seemed consumed by fire. She felt as though she were slipping into a warm cocoon, and through her lowered lids she could see a pale glow creep up her hands. With barely a whisper of breath, she let her eyes close. She began to sense the cat's wounds. Bones started to knit, and warm blood began to flow through veins and arteries again as they closed up and began to heal. Muscles knit together, and slowly the edges of skin inched closed. Tabitha watched the process in her mind's eye, as though watching a surgery through glass. Her hands seemed to hover over the wounds on their own; her mind allowed them to move as they would.

Without knowing how she had released the healing or at what point it was completed, she suddenly snapped into awareness. The cat leaped from her hands. After a quick rub against her outstretched fingers, he trotted back toward the locked café doors, glancing back at her expectantly. Tabitha kneeled on the ground, in awe. Her eyes dropped to the bloodstains on her legs, the only proof remaining of the cat's injuries.

She felt herself begin to shake, and a chill permeated her body. Her belly burned with a hot hunger, and as she licked her dry lips, her tongue caught in a painful sting.

She leaned forward, clenching her belly as fear rippled through her body.

Tabitha.

His voice seemed to come out of nowhere, echoing through her mind. It had been years since she had spoken to him. What had caused him to reach out to her now?

Are you all right? The warm timbre of the voice, so familiar, was deeper, more mature than she remembered.

With a cry, Tabitha ignored his call and ran to the café. With shaking fingers, she unlocked the door and slipped inside. She tried to regain control of her quivering muscles as she hugged herself and sank to the floor of the dark shop. She slid her head into her trembling fingers and gasped. How had he known something was wrong? How did he always know to reach out when something was happening to her?

That voice in her head, his existence, was another secret that she kept from the world.

The back doorknob jiggled once and then again, and Tabitha moaned when she heard keys opening the lock.

"Hey, Tabs, let me in!" her cousin Callie called. The door swung open, and Callie entered, her blond head appearing as she struggled to remove the keys from the door. "Why did you lock the door? You knew I was opening with you, right? Tabitha?"

Callie dropped to her knees and grabbed Tabitha's chilled fingers. "What's wrong? Oh God, Tabitha, you have blood on your legs! What happened to you?" Callie gasped and fell back on her haunches. "Tabitha! Your teeth..."

Tabitha lifted horrified eyes to her cousin. "What?"

Callie shifted back and slid a finger up to her own teeth. “They are…I mean, you have…fangs.”

Tabitha lifted a shaking finger to her mouth to feel the long pointed fangs jutting from her incisors. She let out a long wail and tried to leap to her feet, but her legs would not support her. She tumbled back to the floor.

Callie pushed her back so Tabitha was sitting on the floor facing her. “What happened? The blood? The teeth?”

Tabitha shook her head. A sob bubbled out of her mouth. “Callie, it’s not mine. It’s the cat’s.”

Callie’s warm brown eyes were calm. “Tell me what happened.”

“I got to the café this morning and looked for that little stray that has been hanging around,” Tabitha stammered, her heart pounding. “I found him and saw he had been in another fight. He was all torn up. Badly. I mean real bad, Callie.”

“And? What happened?”

Tabitha whispered, “I healed him.”

“Healed him? As in fixed him? As in stitched him up?” Callie prompted.

“Callie. I healed him,” Tabitha whispered. “As in, he is like it never happened.”

“Oh my God, Tabitha. Have you ever done that before?” Only Callie knew about her cousin’s abilities, but this one was new.

Tabitha shook her head and tried to get up. Her legs were still trembling, but energy seemed to be seeping back into her body. “Never. I never even tried. I had no idea I could do it.”

Callie stood back and leaned against the counter, staring at her cousin in disbelief. "And the teeth?"

Tabitha shook her head. "I don't know. This has never happened to me but..." She swept her tongue over the pointy fangs. "When I was done I was so thirsty that I could not stand it."

"And this has never happened before?"

"Never."

"Tabitha, you have got to talk to your mother."

Tabitha stepped behind the counter to stuff her backpack under the counter. "Just drop it, Callie. I don't even want to talk about it."

Callie stowed her purse with Tabitha's backpack and tied her apron around her waist. "Tabitha, this is getting serious. I mean, you can't just have fangs erupt out of your mouth. It may be time for you two to have a really serious discussion. Those little things you have always been able to do are one thing, but it's like little abilities are now starting to just...s-pill out of you."

Tabitha glanced over at her cousin, not missing the note of fear in her voice. Callie was right. Her abilities had been increasing. As a child, she had always had special abilities. Tabitha was able to hone what little she understood about them into something like control as she grew. But this one, this new ability that seemed to emerge when needed, had shaken her to the core.

Talk to her mother? Tabitha could not even imagine starting that conversation. Doni Devins had evaded every question about Tabitha's father since childhood. Her father was the deep, dark secret that haunted the family.

"What makes you think she is going to start confessing now, of all times, who my father is and where she went twenty-two years ago when she disappeared?" Tabitha walked over to the line of coffee pots set up the night before and started them to brewing. Perhaps the normalcy of work would settle her humming nerves.

Callie used tongs to lift the pastries that had been delivered into the case. "Well, maybe it is time for her to come clean. To not tell you about your father or where the hell she went those years ago is one thing. But a lot of people want to know what happened, and she refuses to say a word. Everyone on this island thought she had been kidnapped or murdered or who knows what." Callie pointed the pastry tongs to accent her point. "She just up and disappeared one night. Walking home from a party. On an island. How do you disappear from an island? My mother says that people were crazy with fear, not to mention that the police and FBI were all looking for her. And then she shows up four years later with a baby and refuses to say anything?"

"Thank you for the recap."

"Tabs, explaining is the very least she can do. She has to stop being so damn delicate and start telling you where she was and what happened," Callie retorted.

"And I just go home tonight and ask her?" Tabitha demanded. "And then what? Watch her fall apart...again? Wait until she gets out after yet another trip to the asylum and then ask her again?"

Tabitha headed back to set up the cash till. The coffee pots hissed, and Callie finished filling the last of the row of thermoses. Despite the unexpected events of the morning, the café was ready for business. The sunshine warmed the windows, drying the evening's moisture from the panes. Tabitha noticed people starting to wander down to the pier.

"What about Greg?" Callie asked. "Does he know about any of this?"

Tabitha glanced up. "Seriously? You think I would have told him?"

"Does it have to do with why you broke up?" Callie persisted.

"Partially. I mean let's face it, we're both heading off to school in the fall. He's going to North Carolina and I'm going to Boston—"

"Don't remind me," Callie grumbled.

"So why spend the summer waiting for the inevitable? I don't want to dread September because we will be going our separate ways."

"I don't understand why you had to break up at all."

"Not everyone has what you and Derek have, Callie," Tabitha said. "I mean, you two are perfect for each other and happy together. You have your job at the hotel, waitressing down at Outrigger's and working here. Derek works construction with his dad. You two have it all figured out. You know what you want, and you will probably both live and die on this island. Callie, sometimes, I am so envious of you."

"You could have the same thing, Tabitha. You just have to stop hiding."

"Hiding?" Tabitha retorted. "How can I ever have what you have? How can I ever do anything except hide? What do you think Greg's reaction to what I just did would be?"

"You think he would judge you?"

A bubble of dry laughter escaped. "I think that he would think I was some kind of freak. I think he would be worried about what I could do. Not to mention waiting until we are on our honeymoon to whip out the fangs."

Callie walked over to the door and pointed to the open sign. "You good?"

Tabitha ran her tongue over her teeth and verified they had receded. "Yeah. Open up."

Callie flipped the sign.

"So you kept him in the dark, and now you are breaking up with him because of your quirks?"

"No, I broke up with him because we are going off to college after I work three jobs for three months to save as much money as I can. I broke up with him because I don't want a four-year long-distance relationship."

As if on cue, the tiny bells above the door jingled.

"Hey. We missed you last night." Greg grabbed a cup and headed for the hot thermoses of coffee.

"Hey, yourself. I had to get up early—it was a long night," Tabitha commented quietly. She noticed that Callie had slipped into the back room. She slid her gaze over Greg's golden head as he stirred his coffee. She watched that familiar tilt of his head and observed the strong grip of his hands. *Why couldn't I just fall in love with him? Settle for life on the island, get married, and have children like Callie plans to do?*

He turned toward her, and his same old smile tugged at her belly. As Greg approached, Tabitha tried to turn and continue her work, but the tasks suddenly seemed unfamiliar, and she could not remember what to do with her hands.

It had been her idea to breakup—she had insisted—but Greg could still turn her inside out, make her lose her grip on stability.

"You around tonight?" he asked before sipping his coffee.

Tabitha shook her head and turned toward the safety behind the counter. Greg reached out and drew her back to him. "Tabs, I get it. I know that we broke up."

Tabitha would not meet his eyes; the pain in them would wrench what little self-control remained. Greg had been with her all through high school, her boyfriend, the name linked to hers in conversations and invitations: Greg and Tabitha. But the dark secrets she hid had become walls between them. How could she give herself to someone when she had to hide her true self behind a veil of normalcy? Greg had no idea that he only knew the small part of her that was visible. The rest of that iceberg was hidden beneath some very dark water.

Greg lifted her chin until she had no option left but to meet his eyes. "I am not asking for anything from you. All I want is to be with you. I know we are leaving at the end of the summer. But that does not mean we can't see each other, even once in a while, over the summer."

Tabitha tried to move her eyes from his. The pain reflected in them was too much. "Greg, it will only prolong the inevitable. It can hurt now or hurt in August. I don't want to spend the summer dreading the end, some final scene."

"It doesn't have to be like that," Greg said softly, leaning down until his mouth was a breath away from hers. "Maybe you might discover that absence *does* make the heart grow fonder."

Tabitha opened her mouth to retort, but his lips covered her protest, and the familiar sweet taste of his kiss emptied her head of all thoughts. As he slipped his arms around her waist, she knew all was lost.

The jingle of those damn bells over the door interrupted. Greg's uncle laughed as he entered the café. "Sorry to interrupt, but I need some coffee if I am going to make it through the day with Romeo here."

Greg reluctantly released her, and Tabitha slipped behind the counter. She grabbed a coffee pot and emptied it into Greg's uncle's thermos.

Greg grinned at her over the counter. "Tonight?"

Tabitha fought to keep the smile off her face as she handed the full thermos to his uncle. "I am working at Outriggers tonight."

"No problem. I'll get Derek to set me up bussing tables. I'll work with you, and then we'll go out when you get off." He winked and waved as he followed his uncle out the door.

Greg always had a way of setting her off-kilter. *He does not deserve to be involved with the local nut case*, she mused.

She glanced up and noticed one of her regulars entering. "Hey, Kayle. Going out today?"

The older man walked over to the thermos to fill his cup. He glanced over at her with one of his rare half-smiles and shook his head. "Nope, engine's out again on the *Stormy Seas*. Going to spend the day getting her running."

Tabitha nodded and watched him fill his cup with hot coffee. Kayle was one of the island fishermen, and although she had known him all her life, she knew little about the man. She would have to struggle to guess his age; his face was sun-lined, but the gray eyes that peered out from under slashed brows were youthful. His dark hair, heavily shot with gray, was tugged back into a long ponytail that hung down past his shoulders.

"You want your usual?"

"No, ma'am. I am going to take a break from the bagels. I will just have some fruit this morning." Kayle patted his flat belly and snatched a banana from the basket.

Tabitha laughed as she put his cash into the register. "Yeah, I was going to say you were looking a little hefty."

Kayle smiled and nodded. "Gotta watch that!"

She smiled and watched him head toward the door. His tall frame was muscular and lean in his dark tee shirt and faded jeans. His work boot caught the door and pulled it shut it behind him. He gave her a last wink, on his way to the pier.

Refocused, Tabitha went back to work, tucking her thoughts back into the vaults of her mind, where they belonged.

CHAPTER TWO

TABITHA LAY IN BED LATE SUNDAY NIGHT, HER MIND playing and replaying the argument with Greg the night before. Their words had been harsh, and she beat herself up with guilt over her part in their fight. She could not take all the blame, but she knew that her desire to keep him at arm's length both physically and emotionally had played into their arguments. She threw her arm over her eyes, wanting to block out his angry accusations.

She tossed onto her side and, with a huff of frustration, rose to open the windows to capture the breeze wafting off the ocean. Her third-floor bedroom offered an unobstructed view of the ocean and caught the cool breezes that swept up from it. The familiar lull of the waves calmed her churning nerves. She let the light wind still her thoughts.

Taking a deep breath of the salty air, she became aware of the sound of a quiet conversation drifting up to her. She wondered who could possibly be speaking on the back porch at this hour. Her mother was all but reclusive, and her great aunt retired early with her TV. A line-up of reality shows usually blared from behind her closed bedroom door. Tabitha leaned out the window to get a better view of the porch jutting from the back door. As her eyes adjusted to the darkness, she saw two people on the porch.

One person walked quietly away from the other toward the railing. There was no mistaking the long silver tresses of her mother. The breeze picked up her silken hair, and it drifted around her shoulders as she turned to face her companion.

Tabitha propped her arms against the sill and concentrated her abilities to hear what was being said.

"—but how would it have been opened? It could not have been…" Her mother's lilting tone rose up to her.

"Every time you go through, you weaken the bond. How could you have been so careless?" a man's gruff voice growled.

Tabitha strained to make out the tall form as he approached her mother. *Kayle?*

"I am sure I closed and sealed it the last time," her mother insisted.

"You've got to stop, Doniella. It gets weaker every time. One of these times, you'll be followed."

Her mother laughed lightly. "Be serious. Even if someone tried to follow me, they couldn't possibly get through. The net is too tight."

"Don't be so sure. You have to remain diligent. It is time you stopped going over. One of these times, he is going to be waiting, and you won't be able to make it away."

"I have to go. He is dying," her mother stated.

Tabitha struggled to follow the discussion. Who was dying, and who would be waiting? Where was her mother going, and what had been left open?

When she turned her attention back to them, her mother's face was staring up at her open window. Tabitha opened her mouth, but before she could speak, her mother waved a graceful hand and everything went black.

Tabitha woke to find herself wrapped in her sheets, the window securely shut, the bright summer sun flowing in through the open curtains. She rose stiffly and stretched, her mind going back to the dream from the night before. It had been vivid. She could still remember the conversation she had dreamed between her mother and Kayle.

She showered and tossed on a tee and a pair of shorts before she trotted down the two flights of stairs to the kitchen. She set the coffee to brew and was popping bread in to toast when she heard the creak of the stairs as Aunt Trude descended the steps. Tabitha glanced up at the clock in surprise. Trude was a habitually late sleeper. To have her come down before eleven in the morning was a novelty.

"Trude, you are up early—are you sick?" Tabitha called as the woman made her way down the hall toward the kitchen.

"I could not sleep, you little wise-ass mongrel," Trude growled. She bounced the kitchen door off her arm and entered the kitchen.

Tabitha laughed as her great aunt hip-checked her out of the way and grabbed her favorite coffee cup, an enormous mug painted with huge, colorful, tasteless clowns. Trude grabbed the coffee pot and filled the mug before shooting a sour eye in Tabitha's direction.

"Why are you so chipper this morning? I heard you coming in at some God-awful hour last night," Trude commented as she and her flowered robe settled into a corner chair. Huge clumps of her dyed-red hair stuck up in every direction.

"I didn't wake you, did I?"

"No, I was already awake," Trude grumbled.

Tabitha glanced over her shoulder at her great aunt. "I had the strangest dream last night."

"Oh, yeah? Tell me about it. Dreams can have a whole lot of messages in them."

Tabitha relayed everything she could remember about seeing her mother and Kayle out on the deck.

"Hmm...Well, your mother out talking to anyone seems strange to me as well. You know she avoids people from town as much as she can. And Kayle? Another recluse if I ever saw one," Trude mumbled.

"I know. Strange, right? I mean, I have never seen them speak before. What would she be talking about leaving open?" Tabitha mused before she bit into her toast.

Trude shrugged and brushed it off. "Wouldn't think much about it. You're probably just thinking too much. Maybe that registered letter she got had something to do with you thinking crazy things."

Tabitha stopped chewing. "Registered letter? What registered letter?"

"Didn't she tell you? She got a registered letter. They dropped it off Saturday. Strangest thing," Trude grumbled.

"Who would ever send her a registered letter?"

"Who knows? I thought that was why you were dreaming about her having midnight conversations with one of the locals." Trude chuckled as she stood to refill her coffee.

Tabitha crammed in the rest of her toast and swallowed a last gulp of coffee. "I am off to deposit my tips. Need anything?"

Trude shook her head. "You working tonight?"

"Yes, at Outriggers."

"I have a tarot party to do over at McCall's. Check in with your mom before heading to work."

Tabitha nodded and grabbed her backpack. She grinned at the thought of her aunt's tarot parties. Trude made her living as a psychic, reading tarot cards and palms. Her repertoire would include the occasional séance if the price was right. With her larger-than-life frame and dyed and coiffed bright red hair, Trude—or Ruby, as she was professionally known—knew how to give them their money's worth.

"And for God's sake, Tabitha, take my car or your mother's car when you work the late shifts at the restaurant. I hate the thought of you out there on that bike late at night."

"There is so little parking around town this time of year. I would rather take my bike." With a slam of the screen door, Tabitha was off on her errands.

The night air swept a pleasant ocean breeze across the deck at Outriggers. Tabitha delivered the steaming seafood to a table of hungry tourists, taking a moment to refill their water glasses and check that everyone had the right meals. She turned toward the door, setting chairs to tables and straightening as she headed back inside. She made her way absently back to the bar. She was standing at the end, absently playing with a stirrer, when Derek wandered over.

"You okay?"

She shrugged. "Yeah, what's not to be, right?"

"What'd Marcy want?"

Tabitha gave a short laugh, recalling the visit earlier in the evening from a high school acquaintance. "She's asked Greg out and wanted to make sure that we were not an item any longer."

"Well, that was nice of her." Derek snorted. "Could she have waited until the dust settled? Jeez, like she was circling him with her fin sticking out of the water."

Tabitha laughed a little laugh at the image. "She didn't exactly have to ask me if we were over. I thought that was pretty big of her."

"Can see her point, just making sure you are out of the picture before she moves in. Like a vulture."

Tabitha reached out and squeezed his hand. She knew he could care less if Marcy asked Greg out. He was more concerned that Tabitha would regret her own decision.

"Wrap up there, buddy. If I am not mistaken, the little wife will be looking for you."

Derek shook his head as he poured himself a cup of coffee. "Not tonight. She's catching the early ferry with her mother. They are going over to the mainland for the day. I could use an early night anyway—get to work early for once."

The phone cut off her response. Derek leaned over to pick it up as Tabitha went back to her last table. She was just clearing their plates and taking a coffee order when Derek called out to her.

"Tabs, phone!"

Tabitha gestured to the busboy to finish clearing the plates and headed to the bar. Who would be calling her at work?

Derek handed her the receiver, a strange look on his face.

Aunt Trude's frantic voice cut off her greeting. "Tabitha, you had better come home."

Her heart froze. "Why? What's wrong?"

"It's your mother. She's gone."

Tabitha scrambled out of the car door when Derek came to a halt in the driveway. As she raced up the back stairs, she heard him call that he'd put her bike in the garage. She crashed through the door into the kitchen. Trude's hair was tugged free of its coiffure, her eyes frantic.

"Trude, where is she?"

"I don't know, Tabby Cat. I don't know." Trude rose from the table. "She's been gone for hours. I knew she would do this. I knew someday she would leave again. I just knew it."

Tabitha ran to the woman, grasping her arms in a frantic grip. "Where, Trude? Where is she? What do you mean you knew she'd leave one day? And go where?"

Trude pulled herself free of the fingers on her arms as she wailed, tears coursing down her face. "I don't know. She got that damn letter—she wouldn't talk about it. She left this afternoon and never came back. I got home from my appointment and she was not here. She had not come back. She does not stay out after dark."

Tabitha tried to make sense of the information assailing her. Derek came in through the back door. "Is there anything I can do?"

Trude spun on him and shrieked, "Of course not—get out! This is family business. The last thing we need is one of you damn people starting to talk about her again. Leave us alone."

Tabitha stared at her aunt in amazement. "Trude, stop! He is a friend. Have you called the police?"

"And tell them what, Tabitha? That she has disappeared again? What do you think they are going to say?"

Tabitha felt her head pound as she struggled with what was happening. "Trude, we have to call the police. What if she isn't gone? What if she had an accident?"

Her aunt glared at her and shook her finger in Tabitha's face. "She left a note this time."

"What note?"

Trude glanced at Derek, turned her back on the doorway, and returned to her seat. Her pursed lips were set in a determined line; Tabitha read the message all too clear. Trude was not saying more until the "outsider" was gone.

"Derek, thank you for the ride. I will try and find out what is going on." She ushered him to the door. "I promise I will call you if I need you."

He glanced uneasily over his shoulder. "You sure? Do you want me to drive around, look for her? Stop at the police station? Call Callie or her mom?"

Tabitha shook her head and attempted a smile for his benefit. "I am sure everything is all right. I will try and get to the bottom of this."

Derek nodded, and with a final uncertain glance over his shoulder, he trotted down the steps back to his car. "You have my cell if you need me."

Tabitha nodded and shut the door. Back in the kitchen, she confronted her aunt. "Okay, what note? Show it to me."

Trude rose and glanced at the window, watching the headlights reverse down the driveway. She pulled an envelope from her pocket and handed it to Tabitha.

She saw her name scrawled across the front in her mother's handwriting. Tabitha tore open the envelope and tugged the sheet out, letting the torn envelope slip to the floor.

Tabitha,

Please do not worry about me. Your grandfather has taken gravely ill and I have gone to offer my condolences to your father and his family.

I will be home soon. Please do not concern yourself. I am fine.

Mom

Tabitha lowered the simple message and dropped into the seat across from Aunt Trude. How could this be? After eighteen years of silence, not a word about her father or where her mother had been during those years she had disappeared, now this? A simple note? Her mother had gone to see her father?

Her eyes locked on the envelope on the floor at her feet. A thought nagged at her, and she suddenly glared up at her aunt. "Where is the note she left you?"

"I don't know what you are talking about."

"This note was sealed. How would you have known she was gone if she didn't leave you a note as well?" Tabitha snarled.

Trude rose to her feet, but Tabitha was in front of her, blocking her. "Where is it? You have to tell me what you know."

"All right, dammit, here it is."

Tabitha snatched the note from her and read the lines scrawled there. "Where did she go? She doesn't say anything more in here except not to tell me anything and to make sure I don't try and find her. Trude, you have to tell me. She cannot refuse to tell me anything about myself and then just take off, for Christ's sake. Trude, tell me."

"Tabitha, I don't know. Do you think she told me any more than she told you? She never said a word. All I know is that she is trying to protect you."

Tabitha threw her hands into the air in frustration. "Are you kidding? You expect me to buy that? Trying to protect me? By leaving me in ignorance and confusion? Not telling me anything about where I come from? About who my father is? And then one day I find out that I have a father and he is out there somewhere with a family that she is going to? To offer condolences?" Tabitha ran her fingers through her hair in frustration. She felt rage swell up in her. "Are you kidding me?"

"Tabitha—"

"She told you not to tell me anything. She had to ask you not to tell me anything. That means you know something, Trude. I am not an idiot."

Trude lifted a hand toward her niece and began to speak, but Tabitha cut off her comment with a raised hand. "You had better be preparing to tell me what you know. If anything but the truth comes from your mouth, I am outta here. I will find out the truth on my own."

"Tabitha, calm down. Just relax. I tell you, I don't know where she is—"

"*Bullshit!*" Tabitha roared. She lifted both hands, swung around, and let loose a swell of anger toward the china cabinet. The dishes and cups nestled within suddenly burst into shards. She heard her aunt's cry of fear as she lifted her hands again, and the doors of the cabinet swung off their hinges and crashed to the floor.

"You think I might need to know who my father is? You think that just maybe it might concern me that whoever my father is apparently gave me quite a legacy?" Tabitha shouted, grabbing her backpack and her mother's note off the table. "When you are ready to tell me what you know, call me. In the meantime, I am going to find her."

Tabitha raced from the house, tears streaming down her face, and the door slammed shut behind her. She swung the garage door open and grabbed her bike, hefting her bag over her shoulder. She swung a leg over the bike as it rolled down the driveway. She could hear her aunt crying as she began to pedal down the driveway. A moment of regret sent tears pouring down her face, but the rage bubbling in her stomach propelled her feet forward as she pedaled away from the house along the dark street.

CHAPTER THREE

THE MORNING SUN PENETRATED HER EYELIDS, and Tabitha squinted her bleary eyes tighter against the rays. Sounds emerged from Aunt Ellen's kitchen. Tabitha tugged the worn blanket closer around her shoulders and snuggled deeper into the den couch.

She had not known where else to go. Aunt Ellen's home had always been her sanctuary from her mother's insanity and Ellen could sympathize with the strain her younger sister put on Tabitha. She had ended up crying hysterically with Callie and Ellen trying to soothe her. Tabitha knew that they were worried about Doni, and Tabitha's fury had done little to help the situation. Ellen had come back into the room after calling Trude, a cup of tea gripped in her fingers. Tabitha could see from her face that Trude had told Ellen about her enraged display of power. Tabitha dropped her eyes guiltily; she had little doubt that neither woman knew what to make of it.

Tabitha tried burrowing her head deeper under the pillow, willing the sun out of the sky, wishing that sleep would take her away, even temporarily. Just a few minutes of peaceful not-thinking, waking with a clear head. Is that too much to ask?

She could hear her uncle's voice as he wandered into the kitchen, no doubt asking about the late-night visitor and the wild tales from his in-laws. Ellen's husband Frank was a warm and kind man who used words infrequently and took most things in stride.

He quietly peeked into the den, and Tabitha feigned sleep to avoid dealing with the questions yet. Another set of feet pounded into the kitchen. Tabitha hid a smile as she heard her aunt hiss for the younger girl to walk quietly. More whispered comments followed, and the voice of her younger cousin, Roni, rose a decibel in surprise.

Tabitha sighed. She had to face the day sooner rather than later, and she might as well get up. The enticing smell of coffee seemed as good a reason as any. Wearing a borrowed pair of sweat pants and a tank top, she slipped off the couch and padded across the den in her bare feet.

Roni turned as Tabitha entered the kitchen. "Do you think— Oh! Hey, Tabs!" Tabitha adored her younger cousin, but right now the thirteen-year-old's viral imagination was too much for Tabitha's fragile nerves to endure.

Tabitha walked over and slipped an arm around the young girl. "Go ahead, say it. Don't hold back on my account."

Ellen waved a finger at her younger daughter. "No, I won't have random speculation. This is Tabitha's mother—my sister and your aunt—we're talking about. We don't know where she is, but we have enough to worry about without your ideas filling our heads with all kinds of images. Worry is useless."

Tabitha grabbed a coffee mug and poured herself a cup from the fresh pot. Frank slipped past her and dropped a kiss on her forehead as he reached behind her for a bowl. That gentle gesture was more consoling than any words he could have uttered.

Callie walked into the kitchen. Tabitha sighed as she remembered her cousin's plans for the day. "Oh, Cal, I am sorry. I didn't mean to ruin your day off. You were going off to the mainland, weren't you?"

Callie brushed off the apology as she grabbed a piece of toast off her dad's plate. "Never mind that. We need to stick together on this. We can stay here and help."

Ellen turned to look at her daughter. "What did you have in mind?"

"Hey, if I can say something? She did ask that no one try to find her. Shouldn't we at least consider that?" Roni piped up.

The four adults in the room turned quiet eyes to stare at the young girl. Her face blushed scarlet as she realized what she had said.

Ellen shook her head, her short hair slipping from the headband. "You were listening at the stairs last night when Tabitha got here, weren't you?"

Roni shrugged guiltily and had the good sense to look sheepish. Ellen stared at her youngest daughter until Roni could do little more than hang her head and slip to the chair on the far side of the table. Tabitha hid a grin. Ellen could pack quite a lot of scolding into one of those glares.

"We'll talk about your eavesdropping later." She turned her sunny face back to Tabitha. "What are you thinking? How can we help? I confess that I have no idea where she could have gone."

Tabitha sipped her coffee, thinking about her next steps. “Well, first I can go back to Trude’s and see about that letter Mom received. Knowing my Mom, I can’t imagine she would have left anything lying around but the envelope might be at the house. It might give us a clue about who sent it.”

Callie nodded. “If not, the post office might be able to tell us where it came from.”

Uncle Frank snorted. “What makes you think that they would give you that kind of information?”

Callie shrugged. “Who knows? But it can’t hurt to ask, right?”

“Well, we can assume she left the island, right?” Ellen asked as she emptied the dishwasher. Her hands were always busy, no matter what task was at hand; Tabitha knew the woman had to be doing something. Activity seemed to allow her mind to work quicker.

“Would have had to have left on the ferry, right?” Tabitha mused. “I wonder if Sean was working yesterday.”

Sean, Greg’s older brother, was just back from his second year at college and working aboard the ferry for the summer.

“He might be worth checking with. Maybe he saw Doni. Maybe he’d have an idea where she was headed.”

“But where would she have gone from the ferry landing? You said her car was still at home, right?” Callie asked.

Tabitha nodded. “Yes, good point. If her car was at home, she was either going someplace close to the ferry or—”

"Or maybe someone was picking her up?" Ellen interjected.

All eyes turned to her as she hefted a pile of plates into the cabinets. The room was silent while everyone mulled that over.

"Who could have picked her up, and why now, after all these years?" Tabitha mused.

Callie shrugged. "Well, the answers will start with that letter. We have to find something about who sent it."

Tabitha nodded and stood. "I am going to shower, and then we can see what we can find out." Activity and the sense that they had a plan seemed to alleviate some of her frustration.

The afternoon crept to a close. Tabitha headed back to Ellen's house, frustration brimming over in her mind. She'd had little luck tracking down any sign of her mother. The ferry office could not recall seeing her, and she had not been able to find Sean to ask if he had seen her. She clutched the return envelope in her hands, an attorney's name in the upper left corner. She slammed the car in park and picked up the envelope.

"Richmond and Adams, LLC, Attorneys at Law," Tabitha murmured. "I just do not understand any of this. I mean, why a law office in Boston, after all these years? And why would she not say one word about where she was going?"

Callie slid up next to the window. "Any luck?"

"I have the envelope, but no luck with the ferry office. I will have to try and track down Sean when he gets off work."

"You going to call the attorney's office?"

"I did. They wouldn't tell me anything." Tabitha pushed the door open and slid out. The two girls walked into the house.

"But?"

Tabitha gave a long sigh and dropped onto the couch. "I did get to speak to the attorney who sent the letter."

"And?"

Tabitha lifted her silver eyes to her cousin, a thousand emotions running through them. "She took my call, but she wouldn't give me any information. She is going to contact her client, and if he says it is okay, she will tell me what the letter said."

"Her client?"

"That would be my father." Her words came out in a soft croak, and Tabitha let her face drop into her hands.

After dinner, Tabitha drove over to Greg's house. She was thankful that his car was not there. Tabitha knocked on the door. Greg's mother, Sheila Doherty, came to the door, surprise registering on her face.

"Tabitha? I am surprised to see you. Greg had said..."

Tabitha nodded and smiled as Sheila struggled with the words. "I know. I am not here to see Greg, actually. I was hoping Sean was home. I called, but your phone was not answering. I just wanted to ask him something."

"Oh. Oh, well. Come in." She moved aside to allow Tabitha into the kitchen. "Is there anything wrong?"

Tabitha was tempted to just spill the whole story and cry on her shoulder, but that was not fair. Sheila needed to get used to the fact that Greg and Tabitha were not a couple. "No, I just have a question about the ferry yesterday. It's important. I need to try and catch him as soon as I can. I left him a voicemail on his cell but didn't hear back from him."

Sheila laughed and gestured towards the countertop. "No, of course not. His phone has been here. He is not allowed to carry it at work, and by the time he gets home, he always seems to forget it. He just leaves it plugged in right there."

"Well, do you know where he is?"

Sheila hesitated and shuffled her feet nervously. "Well, he is at the Landing having dinner with Grace. I am sure they won't be getting back late if you would like me to have him call you."

Tabitha headed for the door. "That won't be necessary. I can swing in there. It won't take me a minute to ask what I need to know."

Sheila looked alarmed as she bid Tabitha good night.

The Landing, a small restaurant in town, was on her way back home. She planned to stop in and talk to Sean before heading back to Trude's to try and make amends and offer some kind of explanation for the display she'd put on last night at her aunt's home. After living with Trude for eighteen years, she was sure her elderly aunt would have some choice remarks. She did not even want to think about what she'd destroyed.

Tabitha circled the block a couple of times until she found a space to tuck the car into. She rummaged through her purse for some change for the meter and trotted around the corner to the restaurant. The thick smell of fried seafood assailed her nose as she tugged the heavy wooden door open. It took her eyes a moment to adjust from the sunlit evening she had just left to the darkness in the small restaurant. She glanced around and caught sight of Sean over in the corner, his arm around his on-again, off-again island girlfriend, Grace. Another couple sat at the table with their backs to her. As she approached the table, Sean was laughing at some comment and just lifting his beer to his mouth. He glanced up and caught sight of Tabitha approaching.

His smile dropped. Tabitha frowned at the odd look crossing his face. She and Sean had always got along well. *What would cause him to look so alarmed to see me?* she wondered briefly.

Then Tabitha stopped short, realizing why Greg's mother as well as Sean looked so horrified. Greg was sitting across from his brother, his arm draped over Marcy's shoulder. Greg glanced up, and his mouth dropped in surprise when he saw her standing at the table.

Marcy was the last to glance up. She shifted guiltily away from Greg and attempted a smile at Tabitha.

"I—I am so sorry," Tabitha stammered, her face reddening. "I had no idea you were all together. Sean, your mother told me you were here. I just wanted to know if I could talk to you for a moment? I promise it won't take long."

"Uh...Sure, Tabs." Sean rose from the table to follow her.

Tabitha led him out of the restaurant, groaning loudly as the door shut behind them. "Ugh! Sean! I had no idea! Why didn't your mother tell me? I feel like such an ass!"

Sean scratched at his head as he watched her, puzzled. "Well, I mean...this is a little strange, you just showing up here."

"I must look like some kind of stalker. I tell Greg to get on with his life and then show up when he is on a date... Eehhh!" Tabitha buried her face in her hands.

"Yeah, I must admit, Tabs, this is a pretty weird." He shifted his weight from one foot to the other. "So what is so important?"

Tabitha pulled herself together and tried to put her embarrassment behind her. "Sean, were you working the ferry yesterday?"

"Yeah, I was on from eleven to seven. I got off the last ferry when it docked. Why? What's up?"

"Was my mother on any of the ferries?"

His eyes widened. "Your mother? Doni?"

Tabitha nodded.

"On the ferry? You mean leaving?"

Tabitha nodded, swallowing her disappointment. From his surprised questions, it was obvious he had not seen her.

"No, and I was taking tickets, Tabs. I would have seen her. It was not like the ferry going to the mainland on a Monday afternoon was wicked busy."

Tabitha shook her head in frustration. If Doni had not been on the ferry, how had she gotten off the island?

"Did she disappear again?" Sean asked.

Tabitha inhaled deeply. How much longer could she continue to cover about her mother? How many other stories would they have to concoct to hide her erratic behavior?

Just as she was about to respond, the heavy door swung open and Greg walked out and joined them on the sidewalk. Tabitha felt her stomach clench as the mortification came crashing back. Hands on his hips, he glared at her.

"What is this all about?" he demanded.

"I swear, Greg, I had no idea you were in there. I stopped at the house to see Sean, and your mother said he was here. I never dreamed you would be here too, on a date."

Sean excused himself with a mumbled "Sorry" to Tabitha. Greg waited until he was back in the restaurant to begin. "What the hell were you doing looking for Sean? I mean, c'mon, Tabs. You tell me to screw off, that you need some space and want to take some time off, and as soon as I try to, you show up with some lame excuse about having to see Sean."

Tabitha turned away from him, emotion raking her nerves raw. She tried to pull herself together. The past twenty-four hours had taken a toll on her, and she discovered that she was not ready to see Greg with someone else, even if it had been her idea.

"Greg, I am not trying to play head games with you. I called Sean, but he never called me back. I just had to ask him something." The words sounded hollow in her ears, and she could not imagine him believing a word of it.

"What? What was so fucking important? Or can you not tell me, now that you have excluded me from your life?" His voice rose in a harsh snap, and passersby on the sidewalk turned to watch them curiously.

Tabitha tugged his arm and pulled him around the corner, away from the prying eyes. "Will you stop? I do not want to drag you into any more of my drama! You don't deserve it, Greg."

"Tabitha, Christ—for once, drag me in! For the two years we were together, you tried so damn hard to not tell me anything. I am not going to make you feel like a nut! Why the hell won't you trust me? Have I ever done anything to give you the impression that I think you are crazy? Do you really not know how I feel about you, crazy family and all? I can look beyond all that—why the hell can't you?" He leaned over her, one arm propped against the brick wall, cornering her against it. "For once, Tabitha, tell me. Tell me what the hell is going on. Just once, trust me, and just maybe I will surprise you."

Tabitha inhaled deeply. "I needed to know if he had seen my mother on the ferry yesterday."

"Your mother? And…?"

"She left. She got a certified letter from some attorney in Boston and then she disappeared with only the clothes she was wearing. She left me and Trude a note." Tabitha exhaled, trying to control her trembling. When her eyes hesitantly met his, the intensity of his gaze shook her. She could feel tears spilling from her eyes. "She only left a note saying that my grandfather was ill and she had gone to him."

"Your grandfather? But he's dead." A moment ticked by. "You mean, as in your father's father?"

She nodded, turning her face, trying to hide the tears that coursed down her face. Greg opened his mouth, and

Tabitha could hear the unspoken questions swirling around her. He didn't even know what to ask. Tabitha wished he would not even try. He sighed and slipped his arms around her. Tabitha wrapped her arms around him and clung, sobbing.

When her tears were spent, Tabitha pushed away from him, the memory of what she had interrupted nagging at her. Poor Marcy was undoubtedly wondering what had happened to Greg and probably thinking the worse.

"Greg, you have to go back," she whispered.

"Tabitha, do you need me? I am here if you need me." His face was pressed against her hair.

She shook her head. "I need to figure out where she is and what is going on. And you need to get back in there, I have done eno—"

The end of the word dwindled off. His warm mouth was moving over hers in a soft kiss. She could not help but respond. She wrapped her arms around his waist as he pressed her against the wall.

With an effort, she tugged her lips from his, but he moved to nuzzle her neck. It was all she could do to pull herself out of his embrace.

Greg sighed heavily, his eyes hot with desire as he stepped back, trying to regain control. Tabitha leaned against the wall, letting the cool of the stone seep into her back as she tried to steady her pounding heart.

"Why can't I get you out of my system?"

"Because every time we try to get away from each other, we end up kissing." Tabitha pushed herself off the wall and ran her hands through her hair. "Physical attraction was never our problem, Greg."

He laughed bitterly. "Will you call me later to tell me what's going on?"

She nodded. He put his hand on the small of her back and guided her out onto the sidewalk.

She headed back toward the car. As her nerves began to settle, Sean's words began to sink in. Doni had not been on the ferry.

How had she gotten off the island if she had not been on the ferry?

"Maybe a private boat?" Callie suggested, snatching a chip from the open bag in front of her. "Maybe she hopped a ride on one of the fishing boats. Tabs, she has been on the island all her life, and reclusive or not, she still knows everyone."

Tabitha opened a bottle of water and leaned her hip against the counter. "Yeah, but, Cal, think about it. The local guys go out do their fishing or lobstering and come back. They don't make runs over to the mainland and drop people off."

"They do if they are selling the catch over in Gloucester or Rockport," Callie pointed out.

"Yes, but she would have had to spend the day aboard the boat. Besides, she was here in the morning. Trude didn't miss her until that night. No one goes out in the afternoon," Tabitha argued.

"Any number of sailing ships or pleasure boats goes out all afternoon. She could have hired one."

"With what money? She didn't have time to get to the bank, and it is not like she has access to a lot of cash for hiring a boat. And the pleasure boats all have set agendas; they don't drop people off on a whim." Tabitha paced the kitchen. *What am I missing?*

Callie shook her head. "You are forgetting the obvious: that letter may have included arrangements to pick her up. She could have easily been picked up at any number of piers. Someone could have come over. I mean, who knows what that letter said?"

Tabitha chewed on her lip thoughtfully. "Or it could have come from someone already on the island."

"Who sent it certified through a lawyer in Boston? From the island to Boston, only to send it back here, certified? For chrissakes, they coulda just as easily have stopped over when Trude and you were out."

Tabitha opened her mouth to respond and her phone rang. She grabbed her bag and rummaged, the melody of her ringtone muffled as she dug through her bag looking for it. After what seemed an eternity, she grabbed the phone and answered with a breathless "Hello."

"Tabitha Devins?"

"Yes."

"Hold, please." The phone clicked; Tabitha held her breath. "Miss Devins?"

"Yes."

"Ah, this is Victoria Ristucci. We spoke earlier this afternoon in regards to a correspondence sent to your mother, Doniella Devins."

"Yes. Hello. Do you have any information? Do you know where she went?"

"I do indeed. I have something to send to you. Is your address the same as Doniella Devins's address?"

"It is. What are you sending me? And from who?"

"I have a package for you from my client, Antoine Montfort. It is something he would like you to have."

Tabitha's breath left her in a rush, and she sank to a chair behind her. "Umm. Who is Antoine Montfort?"

There was a pause. "You are Doniella's daughter?"

"Yes."

"Born March first? You are eighteen years old?"

"Yes."

"He is your father." The attorney paused again. "You did not know your father's name?"

Tabitha's voice shook. "I don't know anything about him."

"I would have given him your cell number, but I apologize. He is in a place where he cannot call you," Victoria stated.

"Can you tell me where that is?"

"I am sorry but I cannot. I hope this package will help you, though. Perhaps when you receive it, you can use the information to go to your mother." The attorney paused. "Would you prefer to come to my office and pick it up?"

"In Boston?" she paused. "Yes. I can be there in the morning."

"Excellent. Please have me paged when you arrive. You have the address?"

Tabitha confirmed and hung up. Her eyes were haunted as she looked at her cousin. "I am going to pick up a package from my father."

As the ferry pulled away from the dock early the next morning, Tabitha clutched her coffee and walked along the railing, wanting to watch the land ahead come in sight instead of the island she was leaving behind.

Across the island, the man dropped the wrench he was holding, and his head snapped up. He extended his senses and swore as he jumped out of the boat shed. Tabitha was leaving the island.

Damn!

CHAPTER FOUR

A LONE *TICK* SEEMED TO REVERBERATE THROUGH THE small room. Tabitha sat, her leg bouncing in time with the irritating noise, as she once again glanced at the time. She had been waiting for twenty minutes for Victoria Ristucci. She watched the heel of her shoe tap against her foot to that annoying *tick*.

"Miss Devins?"

Tabitha whirled to see a smartly dressed young woman at the door. She stood to follow the woman down the hall. She barely topped five feet and her delicate build made her seem childlike, but her slight stature did not slow her pace. She quickly led Tabitha through a maze of hallways. Her features were small and pinched: a small upturned nose and a sharply pointed chin. Her dark hair swung just below her ears in a short blunt cut, her bangs offered a fringe above her large dark eyes for hiding.

A large, polished desk waited, empty. Tabitha guessed that the tiny woman must be the one who worked behind the massive desk. The image of the small woman working behind such an enormous desk seemed comical, and Tabitha coughed slightly to cover the embarrassed laugh that threatened to escape.

The woman showed her to a large set of double doors and rapped sharply on them to announce their arrival. Tabitha could hear a woman's voice bid them enter, and her guide swung open the double doors. The woman stepped aside, gesturing for Tabitha to enter the room.

Tabitha hesitated at the rich surroundings in front of her. Her stomach clenched nervously, but she squared her shoulders with a confidence that she did not feel and entered the office. The first impression that overtook her was the warmth of the morning sun streaming in through the floor-to-ceiling windows ahead of her. Boston's Back Bay lay sprawled before her, the twinkling ocean behind it. The enormous office was staggering, and Tabitha wondered for a wild moment how long it took people to vacuum the rich carpet each night. The walls on either side of the long, sparkling windows held veneered bookcases filled with legal textbooks and files. A large desk stood straight ahead of her.

Tabitha tore her eyes from the room to study her host. The woman was tall and willowy, with long black hair that hung in a straight curtain down her back. Her face was long and angular, her large dark eyes fringed with long lashes. She stood as Tabitha entered and came out from behind the desk with her hand extended.

"I apologize for your wait. I am Victoria Ristucci." She took Tabitha's hand in a firm grip and indicated a chair in a seating area.

Tabitha took a seat in a dark leather chair and Victoria sat across from her. The small elegant table between them held a colorful Tiffany lamp that gave the area an almost cozy feel.

Tabitha's tiny guide brought them two bottles of mineral water with glasses of ice and small porcelain plates with lemon slices stacked on them. She quietly placed them between the women and slipped unobtrusively from the room.

Victoria sat back in her seat. Her unwavering gaze never left Tabitha's. "I am curious. Your mother left with no indication of where she was going?"

"She left a note stating that my grandfather had taken ill and she had gone to express her condolences."

"I see."

Victoria leaned forward and poured the mineral water into her glass. She gently squeezed the lemon over the dancing ice cubes and delicately placed the used rind on a tiny plate. Tabitha squirmed at the woman's deliberate movements and her delay in responding.

"Do you mind if I ask you something? Did your mother ever tell you about your father?"

Tabitha shifted, uncomfortable. "No, she never told me anything. I assume you know the circumstances behind my mother's disappearance."

"Of course. Few people in this area do not know of the story of the island cheerleader who disappeared one night. Her face was in the news for months. Speculation ran wild with theories of what could have happened to her. Abducted? Raped? Murdered? Aliens?" The woman's voice was silky as she described the horror that was Tabitha's legacy.

"Yes. I have heard it all. So I can assume I do have a father and am not the daughter of an alien?"

"No, you are decidedly not the daughter of an alien. Your father is a very normal man and quite successful in his area."

"Can you tell me anything else about him—Antoine Montfort? Is he local? Why would my mother have disappeared and never mentioned anything to me about him?"

Victoria shrugged delicately. "I do not have any of those answers. I only know what my client wishes to divulge.

"Will you tell me something? Anything?"

"If I share something with you, will you answer a question for me?" Victoria finally said.

"Ask away."

"Were you born with any outstanding abilities?"

The question shook her. Tabitha fought her instinctive urge to lie. "Yes."

Victoria cocked her head and studied her. "What abilities?"

"First tell me something."

"You look like your father."

"I have some slight telekinetic abilities."

"As does your father."

Tabitha inhaled deeply. "Wow. Okay. So that explains something."

Victoria's eyes narrowed slightly as she continued her perusal of the girl in front of her. "Have you ever had any contact with anyone at all? Any abnormal contact with anyone that would lead you to believe that your father is, in some way, in a place of great distance?"

Tabitha stared at her, confused at the question. "I am not sure I understand your question."

Victoria nodded slowly and waved a hand. "Never mind. If you had understood it, you would have known how to answer the question."

For a brief moment, a thought slipped into Tabitha's mind, the barest hint of an idea—a memory that she kept hidden deep in her mind. *Is it a clue?*

"Well, then, I think it's time that we close our meeting, don't you?" Victoria's attitude shifted back to cool professional. Tabitha was aware for the first time that she had cracked that shell somehow.

As Tabitha gathered her purse, she could hear Victoria behind her, going to the desk, opening a drawer. "Well, I assume you are curious what your father asked me to give you."

Tabitha turned to face the desk as Victoria pulled a small package from a drawer and walked around to hand it to Tabitha.

"One final question? Do you hear much from your brother?"

"You brother? Are you kidding?" Callie asked in amazement.

"I must have looked stunned because she quickly took it back, saying she had confused me with another client." Tabitha spoke loudly into the phone over the sounds of the ferry as she headed back to the island.

"I cannot imagine where that came from." Callie paused, and Tabitha could almost hear her mind whirring. "Do you think it could be true? Aunt Doni was gone long enough to have had two children. It is possible. But why would she have left another child and just brought you back to Porta Negra?"

"I don't know. I just do not understand anything. I mean, the longer I look for her, the more questions I have. And now I have actually met someone who knows my father. All of a sudden, he is a real person. After eighteen years of having no idea about him, suddenly he is a man with a father who is dying, and he has a lawyer."

"This is so strange. For her to suddenly just up and leave after so many years is just unbelievable. And what was with that question about having contact with someone from where you father lives? Do you think she was talking about your brother?"

Tabitha inhaled deeply, not sure how to respond. She pled ignorance, and with a promise to call when she docked, she hung up the phone. She sank onto a bench and pulled the package from her purse. She had torn it open when she got into her mother's car and had stared at it in wonder. The small box held a polished black stone on an empty key chain. As the stone swung before her eyes, she tried to make sense of why her father would give her a key chain. It was similar to any number of key chains in the gift shops all over Porta Negra—just a polished black stone.

The only other thing in the package was a single square of paper with the typed words: Dark Hollow.

A shiver went up her spine, and she pushed the note back into the package. Was this supposed to be a joke or some strange message of foreboding? Dark Hollow was a wooded area in the recesses of Porta Negra, a swampy, dark place where local legends told of strange happenings. People claimed to see a burning ring of fire in the depths of that darkened wood or told of mysterious disappearances. It was where Tabitha's mother had disappeared some twenty-two years ago. Doni Devins was the only person to have disappeared from Dark Hollow and reappeared.

Dark Hollow.

A black stone on a key chain and a note with only the words Dark Hollow: after eighteen years and no word from a father she was not even sure existed, the only correspondence was this? Tabitha blew out a deep breath and put her head back, letting the sun warm her face. She replayed the conversation with Victoria Ristucci. The seed of an idea took root. Tabitha watched the curl of the sea spray around the hull of the ferry as she considered for the first time that she might have had contact from some other place. Was that where her mother had gone? Was Luc the key to all of this? It had been so many years…

She had first heard his voice when she was six years old. For a brief time, her mother had taken up with a summer tourist, a man living in one of the many seaside cottages for rent for the summer season. Doni had moved in with the man and had halfheartedly taken her young daughter with her. Tabitha had hated the cottage and had spent much of her time at her Aunt Trude's or with Callie at Aunt Ellen's. But on occasion, her mother would insist that Tabitha spend time with her and William.

One afternoon, the pouring rain had driven her into the house. William was in the back room working, and her mother was running errands, leaving her to try and find some entertainment. William would not allow the TV to be on, and Tabitha had read every book she had brought with her. Her crayons were scattered across the coffee table, but even coloring lost its appeal after hours on end. Boredom took its toll, and Tabitha meandered into the kitchen to try and find something to eat. Her stomach rumbled, and she remembered that she had not eaten since early that morning. Checking up on Tabitha's meals was not something that Doni did often. Tabitha could no longer fight off her hunger. She saw the jar of peanut butter in the cabinet and the loaf of bread on top of the refrigerator. Both were out of reach, but Tabitha's stomach was growling and there was no other accessible food.

She could hear William on the phone and knew it was now or never; her hunger outweighed her fear of the man. She dragged a chair over and climbed up to take the bread off the refrigerator. The cabinet was not too far to reach, so she stretched over and grabbed the cabinet door. It swung open easily enough, but it swung toward her, blocking access to the jar. She held her breath, afraid to further alert William by dragging the chair over. She stretched on her toes, and her fingers brushed the jar. She leaned one knee onto the countertop and was able to grab the jar with one hand. As she started to lift the jar off the shelf, she felt the chair with her one foot on it slowly begin to slide away. As her weight shifted, the chair spun away, and Tabitha crashed. The jar smashed next to her.

She cried out. As she struggled to sit up, her hand pressed down on a piece of glass, and she felt the deep piercing slice as the glass plunged into her palm. Tears coursed down her face. Sobbing, she rose onto her knees. Blood coursed down her hand. She suddenly noticed the dark shoes next to her knees. Terror rolled through her as she lifted her eyes and saw the anger mottling William's face. Red splotches colored his cheeks, and his eyes were fairly burning in fury. His hands balled into fists. He burst into a rage. She could not remember much except curling on the floor in a fetal position while he rained blows down upon her. He shouted at her, something about being on some important call before her tumble had forced him to hang up.

After what seemed like an eternity, William had dragged her by the hair to the cellar door and flung her down the stairs into the dark and dank basement. She was dazed and only half-conscious as she pulled herself into a sitting position, hugging her knees to her chest as she sobbed, trying to keep the sound from escaping the basement. She waited, terrified of the dark basement as much as her fear of him opening the door and coming down to beat her again.

Why are you crying?

Tabitha had looked up, but her eyes could not penetrate the darkness. *Who said that?*

Fear traced icy fingers down her back, and she imagined a ghost speaking to her. Panic began to well under her ribs, and her breath was expelled in short gasps as she shook in terror.

I didn't mean to frighten you. Sorry.

The voice spoke softly in her head. Her flood of tears momentarily halted as she gasped back a sob. "Who are you?"

Why are you crying? the voice asked.

"I broke a jar. I was climbing in the kitchen," she responded quietly.

Ahhhh. And now you are being punished? The voice was a boy's, older than her, she guessed. His soft tenor was a warm caress within her frightened mind.

"Yes, I am locked in the basement." she admitted. "I'm afraid." A fresh stream of tears slid down her cheeks.

I will stay with you.

"Who are you? How can you speak to me in my head?" she inquired, more curious as her alarm began to diminish.

My name is Luc, he responded. *We should get you out of here.*

"I can't. I can't see anything, and I can't go back up the stairs. He is still upstairs."

If you can hear me, I would assume you have some abilities?

She nodded. "Yes. But I cannot go back up there…"

Okay, okay. What happened to make you so scared?

"He beat me. I was only trying to find something to eat!" Tabitha replied hotly.

Beat you?

"Yes, beat me. I am bleeding. My hand hurts, and my back. He kicked me," she mumbled.

I will help you get out of here. When you are out, do you have somewhere to go?

"Yes. But I am scared," Tabitha said softly.

I am with you. I will not let anything happen to you. Once you get to where you are safe, I will make sure he does not beat you again.

Suddenly the voice seemed to be gone, and Tabitha wondered if she had dreamed it. Then she heard a *click*, and the door behind her swung open. Tabitha froze and slowly turned to face the widening doorway, half expecting to see William standing there. But he was not. No one was there. The door swung open and let in low gray light. She stared. And then suddenly, she heard a creak and a groan and the sound of metal clanging when the steel doors of the bulkhead swung open. Rain pattered on the cement stairs. Tabitha hesitated only a moment before getting to her feet and sprinting for the outside.

I will stay with you. Now get to where you are safe.

Tabitha ran as fast as her legs could carry her, ignoring the pains shooting through her bleeding hands and the bruises on her legs and back. She felt a calming presence as she sprinted towards Aunt Ellen's house. The boy stayed with her until she found her aunt. Tabitha raced toward Ellen with a blood-spattered face and clothes that were torn and dirty, finally burying her face in her aunt's shoulder.

Much later that night, she lay in a bed in her aunt's house, warm and drowsy from the pain medications the doctor had given her. Her hand was stitched and bandaged, and her bruises were just dull aches. She started to drift off to sleep, but she heard the sound of women shouting.

Callie came into the room, and the voices grew louder as she opened the door and then muffled again when she shut it behind her.

"Tabs, you okay?"

"Yes. I am fine. Who is that yelling?"

"My mother. Your mother just got here, and my mom is giving her a butt whipping for letting this happen to you." Callie chuckled. "I guess your friend William has left the island. When he saw your mother, she said he took off. She could not imagine what had scared the crap out of him, but he said he was never coming back and he high-tailed it off. The police will be following him."

"He is really gone?" Tabitha asked groggily.

"Yeah, Tabs, he is gone. Get some sleep." Callie snuck back out the door.

Tabitha watched the sliver of light disappear when the door shut behind her.

Thank you. She sent the thought out, wondering if he would hear her.

Get some rest.

Tabitha spoke with her new friend many times over the summer. He was two years older than her, and he said he lived somewhere close by but not close enough for her to get to. They talked and became friends. But after taking to Callie, Tabitha learned that most people did not have friends who spoke to them in their heads. Callie had cautioned her about telling people that she had a friend that only she could hear.

It was years before she heard from her mysterious friend again. She had been riding her bike home from school when a surprise deluge caught her unawares. She pedaled with all her might as the rain pummeled her. She had not expected the vicious storm that swept the small island or comprehended its intensity until she took that last turn and felt the brunt of the wind as she pedaled along the windward side on the long, snaking road that ran beside the rocky shore.

She struggled to maintain her forward pace and fought the wind and the driving rain toward the final sharp curve that would be her salvation. The trees there would shield her from the worst of the wind after she made it around the curve, and then she could walk the rest of the way. She put her head down and concentrated on staying on the white line at the edge of the road, one foot following the next as she pedaled forcefully toward the protection the woods would lend her.

The curve loomed just ahead. Tabitha groaned, thrusting her legs to the limit to push up that last bit of hill as the howling wind shoved her back. The bike handles shimmied desperately in her grip as the wind drove against the handlebars and threatened to propel her off course again and again. She refused to look down at the surf crashing angrily against the rocks below. One wrong move could send her and the bike careening over the edge. She knew there was no way she could fight that storm surge if she plunged into it. The wind screamed in her ears as she battled her way toward the shelter of the woods.

When she saw the curve ahead, Tabitha focused her might into getting around that last bit of road. Just as she attained the edge of the curve, a car came careening around the corner. Headlights dazzled her vision for a moment, and she stared in horror when the car's tires spun on the slick road. The driver did not seem to see her. Tabitha looked desperately for a way to avoid the skidding vehicle.

Tabitha leaped off the bike, and the car swung into the guardrail just feet from her. The fender clipped Tabitha's bike and sent her and the bike spinning through the opening that the car had just split in the guardrail. She could hear her terrified scream as she felt a sharp thud and then a bounce. The world seemed to spin before she saw a flash of rock and felt a faceful of seawater, and then all went black for just a moment before Tabitha heard the rage of the waves below her. Her foot was tangled in a wheel, and the weight of her bike pulled her toward the pounding surf.

Tabitha grabbed a boulder, but her fingers could not find a solid hold on the slick surface. Her vision was blurry, her eyes burning with rain and salt water.

She felt the bike sliding toward the waves, dragging her foot along behind it. Her fingers began to slide along the edge of the rock, finding little to hang onto.

"Help me!" she cried out, hoping that the driver of the car had seen her and had stopped to help. She shook her hair from her eyes, trying to get a clear view of the edge of the road above her, but the rain blinded her and she could see little beyond the twisted metal of the guardrail.

The bike slid another foot. Tabitha tried desperately to yank her foot free from the spokes, but the weight of the bike dragging at her was making it impossible to pull her foot free.

She cried out again as she slid another couple of inches, the rock's wet surface scratching at her belly as her shirt slid up. Her other foot hung in air, and she tried to find a foothold to get some leverage. The harder she struggled, the quicker the bike seemed to slip toward the waves.

Stop struggling.

"Luc?"

Stop struggling. You are going to be dragged in if you don't stop struggling.

"Help me, please! I don't want to fall—"

Hold on. I need you to just hold on as tight as you can. Hang in there. Try to give me some room to work.

One hand at a time, she explored the boulder's surface, trying to find a hold. She felt the tiniest crevice with her right hand and clung to it for dear life. With her left hand, she swept the surface and tried to find another spot. She found a small outcropping and clung to it, the jagged edge tearing into her palm.

"Okay, I have a grip. Hurry, Luc, My bike is going in."

Just hold on. His voice seemed older, but that warm rich timbre that she remembered from so many years ago remained. She clung to the rock, not feeling fear, only purpose, her job to hang on as tightly as she could while Luc helped her.

She could not hear him but she could almost feel a presence beside her. She shook the wet hair from her eyes and strained to look around; there was no one there. But she could feel him, sense that he was with her, and it kept her from panicking. She felt the pressure of the bike slowly, ever so slowly, begin to ease off her foot. She lifted her arm as much as she could and strained to look down to her foot. The bike was edging back up, the spokes ever so slowly easing away from her foot. Tabitha twisted her foot slightly.

Stop. Not yet. Hold still.

She froze. The wheel spun just a bit; she felt the pressure ease and then her foot was free. She pulled it back, and the bike crashed against the rock and slid down. Tabitha dropped her face against the cold, wet stone.

Don't look down, and don't move too quickly. Just listen to me and do as I say.

She was sprawled against the rock, one leg hanging precariously over the edge of the dangerous surf, but now nothing was dragging her down.

I want you to gently pull your right leg in, very slowly. Once your foot is on the rock, I want you to roll to the left.

Tabitha drew in a deep breath and fought down her nausea and vertigo. She began to draw her leg in from the precipice. With an effort, she dragged it back and rolled over to the left. She lay spread-eagled on the rock, the rain pouring down on her.

Okay, now you can start to crawl back up toward the road.

Exhausted, out of breath, she nodded, wondering if he could see or sense her response. The world seemed to spin around her, and she inhaled deeply before rolling one more time up onto her knees.

Stay with me. Don't stand, just try to crawl forward.

It was not a long distance, but the slick surface and her chilled hands made it a difficult climb. She gently crawled up the tumble of large rocks that made up the coast. When she grasped the guardrail and dragged herself onto the road, she stood and stared back down at where she had come from.

The small rocks along the roadside gave way quickly to large stones and boulders that spilled down to the ocean. Tabitha could see the place where she had been, a large flat rock, angled toward the ocean. She must have bounced off the large one above it and landed on that platform. Her bike would have simply gone over had her foot not been tangled in the spokes.

As the cold from her soaking clothes began to seep into her, she slid her arms around her middle and hugged tightly.

You need to get home.

"My b-b-bike..." Her teeth chattered as she stared at the twist of metal that was being pummeled by the surf.

You need to get home, Tabitha. You have to get out of those clothes.

Luc was relentless. He coaxed and persuaded and nudged her toward the street. She could feel herself being propelled, shaking and trembling, the shock making her lethargic. Later, looking back, she could not remember how she had got home, just that he had gotten her there.

Trude saw her approaching and ran out of the house to get her. Somewhere between Trude's reaction and Tabitha's onset of tears, Luc had vanished.

Tabitha had not spoken to him since. The only other time she'd heard his voice was on the morning she had discovered her healing ability. She had panicked, and his voice had asked if she was all right. But she had not responded.

And now she was wondering if Luc might hold the answer to the questions nagging at her. Was he somehow the key to her mother's disappearance? Her abilities?

CHAPTER FIVE

THE FERRY BUCKED THE WAVES AS IT MOTORED towards Porta Negra. Tabitha struggled with the pieces to the puzzle her mother had left. She tried to make sense of it but it was as though the picture would shift every time she asked another question.

She assessed what she knew and realized that it was precious little. Twenty-two years ago Doni had disappeared and been gone for four years. Doni had never told anyone where she had been or shared any clue as to who had fathered her child. She had simply disappeared from Dark Hollow one summer night and showed up four years later with a baby.

Dark Hollow.

What was the connection to her mother's disappearance and the stone? Dark Hollow had always had a morbid fascination for Tabitha. It was rumored that teenagers would have parties down in the depths of the Hollow, away from prying eyes. Tabitha had heard the story of how her mother had broken up with a boyfriend and stormed away from the Hollow that night and not been seen for four years.

As Tabitha stared at the curling waves, something clicked. *Vanished without a trace. Off an island.* How does one vanish without a trace off of an island and then four years later show up again? No one had seen her. No one had seen her on the ferry. There was no airport on the island.

What if she never left the island?

Tabitha stared at the black key ring in her fist.

"I don't understand." She lifted the black stone and dangled it before her eyes.

If her mother had not left the island, where was she? Was she still within a couple of miles of home? And why suddenly reappear with a child after four years?

And apparently her father had abilities like Tabitha's. The only other person she knew to have some kind of abilities was someone she had never met, the one who came to her when she was in trouble. Someone she knew only by his voice.

Luc seemed to know where she was, and he was able to find her. When she had her bike accident, he had been able to return her home. So he must know the island?

She shoved the stone back in her bag and exhaled loudly.

She lifted her head and noticed that the crowd returning on the ferry this afternoon was fairly light. She had been so engrossed in her thoughts that she had barely taken any notice of the ride. She glanced at her watch. When she looked up, she saw a man standing at the railing watching her intently.

He had dark hair and dark eyes and wore a light tee shirt and jeans. When she caught his eye, he smiled and slowly approached. A vague sense of foreboding came over her as he advanced. His smile was friendly enough. He looked to be about her age, but she could not shake a sense of concern.

"Hi."

She glanced around to see if anyone else was close by. "Umm...Hi."

"Sorry if I was making you uneasy. I just couldn't help notice you." He smiled.

She glanced around again, observing that Sean was near the off ramp, preparing for docking.

"I probably should get down to my car. We'll be docking soon." Tabitha stood to leave.

"Hey, what's your rush? I mean, we have about ten minutes left before we dock. Come on, give me ten minutes to try to convince you to meet me for dinner."

Tabitha tried to brush off the request. "Sorry, but I am seeing someone, and I really should be going."

He held his hand to his heart, as though he was having a heart attack. "You are killing me! It took me almost the entire ride to get the courage up to speak to you. The least you can do is give me a couple of minutes. Maybe grab a cup of coffee upstairs?"

"No. Thanks again, but I really should get to the car."

"How about I walk you to your car? Make sure you get there safely?" He leaned forward and extended a hand to her.

"I am all set, thank you." She started to walk away, heading toward the relative safety of Sean.

"Hey, Tabitha, come on! Cut a guy a break here!"

She turned slowly. "Do I know you?"

He grinned and slowly sauntered toward her. "No, but I know *of* you. I also know your father."

Tabitha gasped. "How? How do you know my father?"

"Make a deal with you. Stay on the ferry and ride it back with me. I will tell you everything you want to know." He smiled and lifted his brows suggestively. "Maybe then you will agree to have dinner with me? What do you say? All I am asking is that you make the ferry trip back with me. I will tell you everything I can."

Tabitha stared at him in shock. The ferry was just reaching the dock. She glanced back and forth between the dock and the man in indecision. "Why don't you just get off here? Then we can talk. You can grab the next ferry back."

He shook his head. "I was hoping to have your undivided attention. We'd be reaching the mainland just at dinnertime, and maybe I can convince you to continue our discussion over dinner?"

"But why can't we just get off on Porta Negra? And why didn't you tell me before this?" The desire to hear about her father was strongly overriding intuition.

"I don't want to see you get off the ferry. I didn't want to waste the entire trip telling you everything I knew because then you would disappear. So what do you say? It's still early. Come with me. We can sit right here—you can ask me anything about your father." His dark eyes enticed her, and he stepped closer, hand extended.

She shook her head. "Can you call me? I need to know anything you can tell me, but I just can't..."

He grasped her left hand when the ferry bumped the dock. His fingers tightened, and he slid his other hand up her right arm. "Listen. I can tell you everything you have been dying to know. I know where your mother was, and I know your father. I know where she is now. You just have to come back with me."

Tabitha felt herself begin to panic as his grip tightened. She felt a strong grasp in her mind. Suddenly she became dizzy; the deck swayed beneath her feet. As her knees began to buckle, Sean ran toward her. The man with the dark eyes tightened his grip, holding her up.

"Tabitha? You okay? Who is this guy— *Argh!*" Sean cried out and suddenly dropped to the deck, grabbing his head in pain.

She gasped as Sean fell to the deck, her vision darkening. Another voice suddenly cut through the darkness.

"Let her go!"

Tabitha heard the voice, but her world was spinning. The man with the dark eyes hefted her into his arms.

"No. I am taking her back with me. Stay away from this, Kayle, I warn you."

"Put her down and back away or you will regret it. You know you can't come onto the island. Put her down and back off."

Tabitha wanted to struggle free of the man's arms, but she felt her body go limp as darkness engulfed her.

Tabitha slowly swam toward consciousness and her eyes fluttered open. As she began to focus, the memory of the dark-eyed man holding her in his arms as Kayle demanded her release came flooding back. She sat up with a terrified gasp. Her vision focused on her familiar bedroom. She was home, lying atop her bed in the clothes she had worn to Boston.

She leaped off the bed, ran for the attic stairs, and hurried down. As she approached the second-story landing, she heard soft voices coming from the kitchen. She slowed and gripped the stair newel, straining to hear who was talking. What if it was the dark-eyed man and he was waiting for her down in the kitchen, talking to...?

Trude? That was Trude's voice. And the other, that deep, rough voice, that was...Kayle? She tiptoed quietly down the stairs and went into the darkened living room. The kitchen lights were bright against the gray twilight hugging the woods around the old house.

"But she is all right? He didn't do anything to her or touch her in any way?" Trude's voice was concerned.

"No, I could see him approaching her as the ferry come toward the dock. They spoke for only a couple of minutes. I jumped him as he grabbed at her," Kayle responded. Tabitha heard the clink of the glass coffee pot against a mug. "Why didn't you tell me she was leaving the island? I should have known. I could have protected her."

Trude's reply was a harsh sob. "I didn't know! We had been fighting! She was so angry that I refused to tell her where Doniella had gone, and then she blew my china cabinet apart."

Tabitha heard him exhale sharply.

"She can't know now. For God's sake, we need to find out what that damn attorney told her. Dammit! If only I had known where she was going. They enticed her off the island

and then sent someone to follow her back. We are just damn lucky that they were not able to grab her before I was got there."

"You think they were following her? What would they have done?"

"They would have taken her back." Kayle snorted. "We will have to tell her something when she wakes."

"How long will she sleep?"

"She'll sleep all night," Kayle responded. Tabitha heard the scrape of a chair leg as he rose.

"And then what? What do I tell her in the morning?" Trude demanded.

"What can you tell her? You can tell her that Sean is okay, that she fell when the boat docked and hit her head. Let her think she dreamed the whole thing."

It was Trude's turn to snort. "And when she sees Sean?"

"I'll take care of Sean."

The room grew quiet, and Tabitha held her breath. The questions kept piling up. But now she had proof that not only did Trude know more than she had ever admitted, apparently Kayle did as well. A local fisherman, someone she barely knew except in passing, and he was in on some secret about her? And he would take care of Sean? What did that mean?

"This was too close. We need to tell her something," Trude said. "She is going off to college in September, Kayle. How safe will she be?"

Tabitha held her breath.

Kayle finally responded. “I just don’t know. If we could just keep her here, encourage her to stay on the island, we could guarantee that...”

Trude blew out a breath. “Forget about it. Tabitha is not Callie. Callie is content here on Porta Negra, but Tabitha...she just can’t stay here. The world is out there for Tabitha, and she deserves to be following her dreams, not sequestered here because of her mother’s mistakes.”

“I know, I know...” Kayle exhaled loudly. “I wish I could shut that damn portal.”

“And leave Doni over there in an effort to protect Tabitha?”

“If need be.”

“But how did that man get here if he can’t come on the island? There must be another portal somewhere, right?”

“Yes, but damned if I know where.”

The kitchen door opened and quietly shut. Tabitha crept back through the living room and slid back up the stairs to her room. According to Kayle, she was supposed to be out for the night. She needed to think. Aunt Trude could not get up the attic stairs anyway, so she had some time.

Portal? Was that what she heard Kayle and her mother talking about in that dream? Something her mother had left open? To where?

Tabitha chewed her nail as she paced her bedroom. They were planning to lie to her again to hide the fact that someone had tried to kidnap her and bring her to “him.” Who would that be? Her father? And what was that about not being safe away at school? Kayle wanted her to remain on the island, staying safe? He said he could have protected her.

The questions piled up. As she tried to pull them together, Tabitha could not get her mind around what she had heard. It was like trying to learn a new language from random words. How could she make sense of this if she couldn't even connect the dots?

Now that Doni had fled once again, Tabitha regretted that she had not pressed her for answers. She regretted waiting for her mother to tell her when she was ready. Foolishly, Tabitha had believed that when she was grown, her mother would stop sheltering her from whatever truth was out there and finally tell her the details behind her long-ago disappearance.

She had a right to know about her father and a right to know where and when she had been born. Her mother had been able to produce a birth certificate listing her place of birth as Boston. But she had never told Tabitha which hospital or offered any details of the birth except the name of her nurse: Gwyn. She spoke highly of Gwyn's warm and gentle smile and unwavering support. Her eyes, her mother had told her, had held such warmth that she was able to break through the pain of childbirth and keep Doni from flying apart.

But Doni was gone now, and Tabitha did not know if she was coming back. And if she did not, all the questions would remain unanswered.

CHAPTER SIX

TABITHA ENTERED HER ROOM AND SAT ON THE END OF her bed. She had slept long enough that the evening shadows had crept across the lawn. The moon was starting to peek over the ocean. She stared out at the familiar scene, but the comfort of her childhood view was not enough to drive the chill from her; the foundation she thought she stood on, everything she thought she knew, was beginning to disintegrate beneath her feet.

She thought over her last conversation with her aunt. They had fought yet again when her aunt refused to tell her more than referring to some "place" that her mother went. Trude had also warned Tabitha to give up the hunt for her mother for her own good and had warned her about getting too involved. She had begged Tabitha to let go of trying to find Doni and to just focus on saving money to get off the island for college. Trude's words had hit a nerve; Tabitha imagined just letting all of the drama go and simply concentrating on having a life.

Tabitha thought back on her conversations with Luc. Had he been a figment of her imagination, as Tabitha had long believed? Had her own powers been the instrument for helping her those times that he had reached out to her? Had she invented him to serve as the catalyst for using those powers, as she had long suspected?

Or was he part of some dark force that Trude had warned her against? Someone from "that place" that Trude had so strangely told her to avoid? Had someone sensed her ability and reached out to her?

Well, neither explanation offered her any kind of comfort. Either she was suffering from some delusion that manifested itself as a voice in her head or someone from some strange and dark place that had driven her mother mad had reached out to her.

Was that what had happened to Doni so many years ago? Had someone reached out to her? Had she followed them down a dark road that ended in madness?

Tabitha walked to the window and flung the huge panes open. She stared out as the moonlight twinkled off the ocean. The unending surge of waves crashing against the rocky beach played a lonely tune that she had been hearing all her life.

Where to go from here? Pursue her mother and whatever dark forces Trude had warned her about to discover the answers to the questions that had plagued her?

At what cost? Her sanity? Her life?

Or take the other road, the one that Aunt Trude had begged her to take? Go to work tomorrow, make money for the summer, meet Greg in an endless parade of breakup agony, and then go off to school in September? Pursue a life away from the island and put all of this behind her? Lead a normal life as just a regular person—no skeletons, no hidden family or missing relatives? Tabitha shut her eyes and pictured herself at school, a normal student with friends, classes, papers due, homework. She added blocks to this image that included a part-time job, living in a dorm room, maybe even an apartment off campus sometime? She need not come back to the island. Callie would come to visit her in town.

She could come back on occasion: Christmas, Callie's wedding. Maybe even try and continue her relationship with Greg once college started? Once school was over, she would pursue her career, find a place of her own, and start her own life.

No Doni, no madness or trips to the asylum.

Her life would be her own, and Doni would be on her own to try and salvage what she could of hers.

The allure was strong. Maybe that *was* her answer—just get off the damn island and make a life for herself. She didn't have to find out about her father. There were plenty of kids who grew up with one parent. She could tell people she had never known him, and that would be that. No one need know the truth. No one need know what had happened.

But it was not that simple. It was not about making up a new life for herself. Her mother had disappeared for four years and had a child who grew up with telekinetic abilities, a child who could shatter windows and furniture in a fit of temper, a child who could heal. Those were not abilities that one could brush off and ignore.

Tabitha felt that she did not know herself. She had spent her whole life living in a void, waiting for someone to explain what and who she was. She had kept people at arm's length for fear that if they knew too much, they would find that she was missing something, some part of herself that she could not even begin to explain. Her identity was missing, and she doubted she could manufacture one without trying to find out where she was from and what had happened those many years ago to produce her, a solitary and confused child.

So this was it? Her decision was made. She would pursue this along the only avenue she could think of. She leaned over and grabbed the black stone on the key chain and swung it before her eyes.

Well, here goes nothing.

She stood tall and inhaled deeply. She had never intentionally reached out to him. It had always seemed that he was there when she needed him the most, and he was the one who had always initiated the contact. With a nervous knot in her belly, she took one final deep breath and extended her thoughts.

Luc?

She held her breath. Perhaps he only existed in her imagination. Maybe this was just some kind of craz—

Tabitha?

In a panic, her breath exploded , and she felt her chest constrict. *Oh my God...*

She heard a warm chuckle; his voice was older, more mature, but Tabitha recognized that resonance, like a soft caress. A warm shiver ran down her spine.

No, sorry, just me. Are you okay?

I don't know. I need your help.

What is wrong?

She released an explosive sigh. *Where do I start?*

Well, for starters, it has been a long time. What prompted this?

You are my last hope. I don't know where else to turn. I need you.

A low laugh. *I am not sure that is such a good thing. But I will do what I can.*

I am sorry, I didn't mean it that way. I just...I guess I am not sure if you are real or some figment of my imagination.

I am not sure how I can help out there, but from my perspective, I am pretty sure I am real.

She could hear the faint amusement in his voice. She smiled. *I am sure you are real wherever you are, but perhaps you are only real because I have invented you. Maybe you only think you are real.*

Well, if that is the case, could you invent me a few things to make my pretend life a little easier?

Tabitha laughed and laid back on her bed. The warm bond of friendship from so many years ago began to simmer back into her consciousness. Just talking to him made her feel better.

Where are you? Can you tell me that?

There was a pause, and Tabitha thought she could hear him yawn.

Yes, but it wouldn't mean anything to you. I am closer than you think but at the same time farther than anyplace on your world.

Tabitha sighed. *Please, no more riddles. I have had people throwing riddles and hints and all kinds of nonsense at me for as long as I can remember. Just tell me where you are. Are you dead?*

Dead? Did you ask if I am dead?

Yes. As in, are you a ghost? Her voice was sharp, and she held her breath, waiting for his response. It was one of her greatest fears; she was almost afraid of his response.

A moment of silence was followed by another laugh. *A ghost? You think I am a ghost?*

I don't know what to think. You telling me that you are someplace close yet very far away does not help! she snapped.

Let me see if I can be more specific. His voice paused, and Tabitha could almost sense him stretching. *I am close by. You are by the water. I am probably about five miles or so from where you are. Physically speaking. But if I were to come to where you are right now, you would not see me. I am in your world but in a different world. Does that make any sense?*

Nope.

He chuckled again. *I know where you are. I can feel you. And I can get to that physical place, but we could share that spot and not see one another. I am in a different world.*

She considered this for a moment, not sure what to make of it. *How do you know this?*

Tabitha felt as though he was right next to her. His rich voice seemed to be in her head, and the sensation of that honey-timbred voice speaking to her so intimately while she reclined on the bed was almost sexy. For a moment, she tried to imagine Luc, but she could not picture a face or any physical characteristics. She did get the impression he was also lying down.

Did I wake you?

He laughed softly, and she once again had that warm sense of his presence close to her. *Uhmm...You did.*

Sorry. I was having a moral crisis and debated whether or not to reach out to you.

And what tipped your decision?

She pursed her lips, wondering what it was that had caused her to make that decision. *I need some answers and some help, and I think you are the only one who can help me. I need to know if there was some way that you might hold the answers.*

So why the hesitation?

Someone said something to me tonight that made me unsure if I was reaching out to nothing more than a figment of my imagination or to something potentially dangerous, she admitted.

Hmm. Well. I am not dangerous. I have no interest in hurting you.

Tabitha laughed nervously. *If you did, you would say that anyway.*

True. I probably would. He seemed to be moving, and Tabitha had the distinct impression he was lying down, propped up on one elbow. *But you chose to reach out to me anyway.*

Tabitha adjusted her position on the bed, rolling onto her stomach, her feet in the air; she propped her chin in her palms. *Yes, I did. Maybe against my better judgment? But I weighed the options, and knowing the truth seemed worth the risk. I am starting to wonder if I am in more danger through my ignorance than in my search for the truth.*

She discovered that she had to extend the thoughts she wanted him to hear, but her inner dialogue seemed immune from spilling over into their conversation.

Seconds ticked by, and Tabitha wondered what he was thinking.

Well, I must admit that this has me curious. So what is so important that you risked yourself to reach out to me, even believing there was some danger?

I am looking for someone.

He laughed again, and Tabitha found that she loved that sound. That warm chuckle sent pleasant shivers through her. *Well, you've found someone. I take it I am not the one you are searching for.*

Well, you are, I reached out to you, but I am trying to find my mother.

And you came to me?

She disappeared. I think she may have gone to someplace other than…here. She finished the thought weakly.

What would make you think that?

A couple of clues led me to believe she slipped away to someplace she could get to fairly quickly, without being seen. It is someplace she has been before, and my aunt has warned me against trying to follow her due to the inherent danger. So tell me…how do you know that I am close by? How can you know of where I am when I have no idea where you are?

We know about your world. We have some contact here and there with it, and we know people can manage to get from yours to ours. It is not frequent but it happens. We even know of people who are in your world and come back and tell us about it.

A surge of excitement swept through Tabitha. She sat up quickly. *Then people can come from my world into yours.*

Yes.

And how is it you can talk to me? You are psychic?

Everyone here is. Well, that is not true—we have humans here as well, but all of my people are psychic, yes.

Luc, how do I get there?

What? He sounded startled.

I need to get there.

Get here? Are you serious?

Yes, please. I have to find her. She may be there. It would explain a lot.

Tabitha, do you know what you are asking?

Luc, please. You are the first and closest thing I have ever found that offers any kind of link to my past. I need to know where I am from and where she is. She stopped, tears welling in her eyes. *I need to find her and know the truth.*

It was Luc's turn to sigh. Tabitha could feel his indecision. She knew he was leaning toward helping her, and a sense of excitement began to bubble in her chest.

I am going to regret this, aren't I?

Tabitha grinned. *I have no doubt.*

Tabitha slipped out of the house, her heart beating in fear and excitement. She had pulled on a tank top and a sweatshirt and yanked her favorite jeans out of the drawer; she opted for warmth over shorts. It might be a warm evening here, but she was unconvinced that the weather would be the same there. Luc had told her it was summer there as well—they were on the same planet and as close to the sun as they would be in her world, just in a different place.

She grabbed a flashlight and headed down Shore Road toward Dark Hollow. Luc knew the approximate location of the infamous portal on his end and told her he was heading toward it to meet her. Her heart pounded with fear, and nervousness clawed a hole through her stomach as she walked down the dark lane. The thought of entering Dark Hollow at night was intimidating; she focused on Luc waiting for her on the other side.

What will happen then? She refused to even think about it. First she had to overcome her immediate fear of walking into that dark and mysterious place. Then she would think about the next steps.

Luc had told her that she would need something to get her through to his world. He had described that when the portals between the worlds opened, a searing heat would mark the ground where the portal opened. The intense heat would burn the rocks or grass or whatever substance was between the worlds at high intensity. So she might find a piece of glass from burning sand or perhaps a rock melted into a small fragment. Whatever it was, she would have to find some such fragment in order to cross the portal. He said the portals opened anywhere, and his people had no idea why or when or how they would open or if they would remain opened indefinitely.

So in order to get over to us, you have to actually pick up something that was there at the time that the portal opened and be at that portal when you touch it, he had explained.

Well, what are the chances that someone would pick up such a piece at that exact portal? I mean, these rocks or pieces of glass must get blown or thrown around, right? Tabitha had asked.

Exactly, which is why people seldom stumble through these portals into different worlds. Otherwise, people would end up here every time they stopped to pick up a unique-looking rock or some-

thing shiny. If they were out walking and happened upon such a shard and picked it up and kept walking, they could conceivably wander over here.

Tabitha was unconvinced. *Do these portals open very often? I mean, if a portal opened up and years passed, what are the chances that those bits or shards or rocks would still be sitting there? And what are the chances that I will find the stone that I need…Wait…*

What?

Tabitha stopped talking and stared at the key chain clenched in her hand. She had been swinging the token back and forth in front of her as she talked to Luc. With a mental *click*, she realized why Victoria had given it to her. *Luc, I think I have one.*

A rock? From the portal? How would…?

It was given to me. I went to the lawyer's office that sent my mother the information about my father. The woman there would not tell me anything about where my mother had gone, but she gave me a silly little trinket. I could not for the life of me imagine why she had given me a key chain with a little shiny black rock on it. But here it is. I bet she gave it to me so I could follow my mother over.

Well, only one way to find out.

CHAPTER SEVEN

AN HOUR LATER, SHE WAS SLIPPING THROUGH THE darkness toward Dark Hollow, wondering how they would be able to find the exact spot. As she stumbled along the unlit trail, Tabitha bit back the fears that assailed her. She was putting a lot of faith in someone she didn't know. She had no idea if she would be able to get back home. For just a moment, she hesitated. She had not left a note or any explanation about where she was. What would Trude say tomorrow morning if she found her gone?

Well, too late now. I will have to decide when I get there. At this point, she didn't even know if she would be able to cross over or not, let alone what would happen when she got there.

Tabitha?

Tabitha stood at the fringes of Dark Hollow when Luc's voice again spoke in her mind. The dense vegetation and tall trees blocked the moonlight, and the ground dipped down toward the heart of Dark Hollow. At the thought of entering this dark place that had frightened her all her life, she felt her breath leave her lungs.

I am here. I am just outside of the place where my mother disappeared.

I am heading down toward the area where I understand the portal to be.

Tabitha inhaled deeply, flipped the switch on her flashlight, and began picking her way through the dense brush that led into the depths of Dark Hollow. The ocean waves were soon blotted out. The sounds of the dense forest engulfed her, as well as swarms of mosquitoes. She waved them off and tried to focus on following the trail down to the clear area in the center of the Hollow.

She thought the woods seemed to be lightening slightly. As she went around a sharp bend in the trail, she saw a moonlit clearing spread out before her. She knew enough about the geography here to know that the potentially treacherous swampy area was past this clearing. Other than the trail she had followed, she had no idea where else to start looking for a portal.

Luc, I am down at the clearing.

I am as well. Now, how do I find you? His voice in her head was clear. After a moment, Luc directed: *Go north. Come toward me.* She could not imagine how he was pinpointing a direction.

Tabitha began walking through the clearing, hoping that she was heading north. She could not detect any sense of his presence. *How are you feeling me? Can you sense where I am?*

Yes, I can. I have always been able to determine where you are, he responded. His voice seemed preoccupied with the attempt to pinpoint her location, to draw them closer together.

Why is that? I mean, why can you communicate with me and obviously sense me? A thought occurred to her, and she felt the slightest twinge of jealousy. *Do you communicate with other people as well?*

Her thought had been sharp, and she heard his light laugh.

No. Now stop talking and let me concentrate. Keep walking north. I can feel you getting closer.

Tabitha walked along edge of the clearing, her flashlight illuminating the ground before her. Her thoughts swirled around what he had told her. The idea that this stranger could detect where she was unnerved her; she was not sure she liked the idea. Greg's face popped into her head, and the memory of some of their more passionate embraces made her blush furiously. She stopped walking and demanded, *Are you telling me that you know what I am doing? Or thinking? Have you been spying on me?*

She heard him sigh in frustration. *No, Tabitha. What do you take me for, some kind of voyeur? I could only detect your presence, not your thoughts or what you were doing. If you happened to physically come close to where I was, it was like I could get a feeling of you nearby. Does that make sense?*

I guess, she grumbled, not sure if she was convinced. Why couldn't she detect his presence? *Do you have other people that you communicate with?*

Not in your world, I don't. I have no idea why I can sense you and reach out to you. No one else I know has that link with someone outside of our world.

So they know of me?

A few—those closest to me.

Tabitha thought about this as she stopped to look for a path. She could not head farther north without going into the brush. She slid the orange beam of light across the foliage and spied a tiny trail between some dense bushes. As she slid between the branches, tugging her hair and clothes free of their grasp, she chose her footing carefully.

His voice in the darkness startled her. *You are getting close to me. I can sense you reaching the portal.*

Can you sense the portal?

No. Some people over here can actually find them, sense the openings. I am not one of them. But as you and I draw closer, I can feel your presence approaching physically through it. It is as though we are in separate rooms in a house, and as we speak to one another, we can hear that we are getting closer to one another. His voice remained a warm inflection in her mind; he did not seem any closer. She could not grasp how he was drawing them together.

She commented on that, and he responded. *I can show you how to do it. I would guess that I may just be better trained in the use of my abilities than you are. We start training very young. If you are the only one you know with your abilities, I would imagine that you have had no formal training.*

She climbed to the top of a small hill and found a rocky outcropping rising out of the dense foliage. She climbed onto it, slightly breathless.

How am I going to find it?

Are you climbing onto some rocks?

Yes.

Head inland just a little farther. We will see if we can find it.

If your world is different, how are you seeing what I am seeing?

Come over to me and I will explain more.

Tabitha felt a twinge at the seductive, beckoning tone of his voice, and a mixture of excitement and fear coursed through her. As she got closer to finding the portal, she realized that he would be real, someone she'd meet face to face, not just some voice that she remembered from her childhood. Her skin tingled. She inhaled deeply, trying to calm herself. With a start, she realized that the tingling seemed to be around her, as though a soft sizzle of electricity were coursing through the air, gently caressing her body like a warm breeze.

Luc, I think I have found it.

Well, this is it. Do you still want to cross?

She drew in a deep breath and slowly extended a hand. As she gripped the black rock, the air continued to sizzle, and suddenly a ring of fire erupted before her. The ring was taller than her, maybe six feet or so, and about three feet wide. She jumped back, and the ring quickly disappeared.

Oh my God! Did you see that?

"I did."

Okay…okay. Let me try this again. Will it burn me?

"I really don't think so."

I am ready…

She lifted her hand again, and the air sizzled and brightened in a fiery glow. She inhaled deeply at the thought of going through. Before she moved forward, two realizations hit her like a thunderclap: the foliage around her was suddenly gone, and Luc's voice was not coming from her head.

She spun around, and there he stood. Her mouth dropped open as she stared. He leaned back against a large rock, his arms crossed in front of him, watching her with an amused grin on his face.

Amazement flooded her. Tabitha could barely grasp that she was no longer standing in the woods on Porta Negra but in another world. And she could not tear her eyes from the man standing before her. He was tall. The moonlight lit up his handsome features; his deep black hair swept casually back from a rugged face. A warm smile lit the curve of his lips. Tabitha stepped forward, her mouth still slightly agape as she stared at him. His eyes sparkled with amusement, and she was taken with the deep blue of them.

Luc?

His smile broadened when he stood and extended a hand to her. "The same. You need not speak mentally, but..." *If you are more comfortable...*

It dawned on her that he had put out his hand to steady her. Her knees began to buckle in shock as the impact of what she had done began to seep into her consciousness.

"Oh my God...I can't believe it..."

His steadying hand was warm on her waist. Tabitha felt herself lean into him, still not talking her eyes from him.

"Are you all right?"

She shook her head and, feeling foolish for gaping at him, tore her eyes away from his face and stared around her. The woods had become a wide grove that dipped down to a moonlit meadow. The topography was similar to the Hollow, except that in this world the swamp gave way to a clear pond abutting a long meadow and the woods were more like a park. She gaped around her trying to adjust.

"Why—" she croaked. She stared around her. She paused and tried to pull herself together. "It looks so similar, but not quite the same."

"Well, it is the same place. Many of the same things happen between our worlds. We are, after all, on the same planet. But we may have a storm or some other form of weather that you will not experience. What you are seeing is the same coastline you have at home but different, because the waves have hit it differently. The winter storms might have been more intense one year and less intense another."

His voice was very familiar. Tabitha took comfort in that warm timbre. His arm rested on her waist, and she let his warmth and strength steady her as she slowly came to grips with having departed everything she was familiar with.

As the moonlight illuminated the grove, Tabitha began to feel as though her legs would support her. She felt self-conscious about leaning against him, and she pulled back, standing on her own as she gazed around her. The forest looked similar, but the sky seemed more bright; millions of stars flickered intensely within the deep carpet of black overhead.

"So many stars!" She turned around, letting the soft breeze caress her as she deeply inhaled the salty air. "And the air—it seems…I don't know. Different."

"It should. It is not the same. We are, after all, in a different place. I will let you see for yourself," he replied behind her. Tabitha felt him step up to her; she could sense his warm presence just behind her, and her body tingled with awareness of him. She could feel a deep blush begin and she wondered how much he could sense from her now that she was right in front of him. Could he sense her attraction? Was he aware how off-kilter his presence set her?

She pivoted and looked up to find him staring out over the grass waving in the dark meadow below them, the breeze fluttering back his silky hair. As she gazed up at him, once again struck by his appearance, his eyes again dropped to her. Her tongue refused to voice her many questions.

His smile was warm and engaging. “Why don’t we get going? We have a long walk ahead of us, so we can talk while we walk.”

“Going? Where are we going?” Tabitha felt momentary panic. Her plan had been to come here and find her mother, but now that she was here, the thought of leaving the portal, her opportunity to go home, struck her as a frightening idea.

“To my home. I thought you came over to find your mother. You won’t find her here. We will have to start looking someplace else.”

His hand was warm in her grip as Tabitha stared around her. Should she go back, tell Trude where she would be? She glanced at the rocks holding the portal as indecision gripped her. *Home? Safety and ignorance?*

She glanced back at the new world and inhaled the fresh, salty air. She nodded and smiled up at him. “Okay, let’s go.”

Tabitha walked along beside Luc, in awe of having slipped out of her world and into another. They walked back through the grove and Luc led her through a pine forest over to the ocean. She followed his sure steps, letting him assist her with his strong grip as she climbed over rocks and skirted along the south side of the island.

“Do you live on the island?”

He glanced back. "It is not an island here but a peninsula. And no, I live about five miles inland."

She stopped, glancing about her. "It is not an island? Are you serious?"

He smiled and helped her drop onto the beach beside him. "I told you, the land is ultimately the same but not exactly. Whatever happened many years ago to turn this point into an island in your world never happened here. So it remains a peninsula."

He was still holding her hand as they walked along the beach, and Tabitha could not think of any reason to pull her hand from that warm grip.

"I cannot believe this. It is just so much to absorb." She glanced up at him, studying his calm face as they walked along the long strip of beach that curved toward the inland. "You don't seem overly surprised by my presence here—or any of this, actually. Do you entice many women from other worlds here for moonlit walks along the beach?" He laughed, and a warm shiver of pleasure ran through her at the sound.

"I must confess that you are the first. In fact, you are the first native from your land I have ever met. I have had no other contact with anyone from other worlds other than you."

"Why is it that you and I communicated? Why were you able to reach out to me that first time, twelve years ago?"

Luc shrugged. His expression became distant as he stared out over the twinkling waves. "I don't know. My father seems to think that perhaps we were at the same physical place when you were in that cellar. Maybe in your distress you were reaching out, and somehow you bridged the gap between the worlds? I don't really know."

"Your father? You told your father about it?"

He nodded. "Of course. He was my trainer. He and I are linked. He would have known something had happened eventually anyway. He could not come up with a reason why you would have been able to reach across to this world. And why this one and no other?"

Tabitha bit her lip and wondered how much to divulge. "Perhaps it is because I may have been born here."

Luc stopped walking and turned to stare at her. "Born here?"

Tabitha sighed and relayed the whole story. As they walked along, she told him of her mother's disappearance and her subsequent reappearance four years later with an infant daughter. She told him of growing up as the island spectacle and of trying to hide her abilities for so long. She told him about her mother's second disappearance and the note, plus her own investigation. She finished with the trip to the attorney's office.

Luc listened silently. Tabitha was surprised that she did not feel the usual trepidation over telling the whole story. He already knew of the two worlds and the possibility of Tabitha's mother being here, so it made sense that her story would not amaze him as it would others. The warmth of his hand as they walked lent her some comfort as she spilled out the whole tale.

Luc was silent for a few minutes as she finished. "So you think your father is here?"

"Possibly."

"Well, that would make sense, I suppose. That would make you half Caskan and half human. And that would explain your abilities. It could also explain why you reached out to someone from this world when you were in fear for your safety."

"Caskan?"

"Yes, I am also half Caskan. My mother was human."

"Was?"

"She died when I was very young."

Tabitha nodded, letting it sink in. Things had begun to make sense. For the first time, she began to feel like she was gaining the slightest bit of understanding. If this was indeed where her mother had gone those many years ago, it made sense that Tabitha would be half Caskan; it now made sense where her ability came from. For once, she began to feel as though perhaps she was not a complete enigma. To be around someone else who shared her background and abilities was therapeutic, and she sensed a small bit of the weight that she had always carried slipping off her shoulders.

"I have so many questions I do not even know where to begin," she said.

He chuckled softly. "Well, we still have a ways to walk. I will answer whatever comes to mind. Once we get to my home, you can get some rest. Tomorrow we can think about how we will find your mother."

Tabitha felt a little twinge of apprehension. "Your home? Do you live far from here?"

"A couple of miles by foot. We will take the beach over to the shore road and walk from there."

"But how did you get to the beach so fast to meet me? You were there just moments after me."

He grinned and tugged her back along the beach. "You can't expect me to tell you all my secrets on our first night, can you?"

She frowned. "What are you hiding? It makes me nervous if I think you are hiding something."

"I promise I'll tell you everything you want to know in time. It just doesn't have to include everything all at once, does it? I don't want to overwhelm you."

"I'll be more overwhelmed if I am worried that you are hiding something sinister," she admitted. Her trepidation over following him to his home mounted, and she wondered again at the wisdom of her impulsive decision.

"Nothing sinister, I promise you." He paused again, looking out over the water. "You are not the only one who has concerns. I wonder what I have brought on myself and my family. You are, after all, a stranger from a strange world who I am bringing into my home. As much as I feel like I know you, I am not willing to reveal all of my abilities yet." He grinned and shrugged apologetically. "I do apologize for that, but I am being honest. I would rather not completely open myself yet."

"You don't have to apologize—I understand," she responded, taking a sidelong glance at him. "We should both be a little more cautious. But I know you did not drive here or take some more conventional method. You did something with your abilities, and that has me curious."

"Well, I will let your imagination get the best of you. You can let me know about your theories." He tugged her up a small dune onto a well-worn dirt road.

"So does your family know that I am with you? Did you tell your father that his son would be out in the middle of the night with some strange woman from another world?"

"He knows. He knew when I was leaving the house. He does not know the details, but he knows where I am and that you are with me," Luc admitted. He turned to step in front of her, walking backwards with a grin. "I think he is slightly concerned that I seem to be taken with you."

Tabitha felt her face redden at his flirting, but she could not help the pleased grin that crept across her lips. "You barely know me."

"That's not true. Even with only the sporadic contact we have had, I can tell quite a bit about you from the link that we have."

"Really? What do you know about me?" she asked, curious.

"That you are brave, compassionate, quite smart, and also very cautious with your true self. You do not let many people close, even those closest to you. You shield quite effectively. I wonder if you know how to lower it though."

"Shield? What do you mean?" Tabitha asked.

"You shield yourself. You have a fairly sophisticated wall around you for someone untrained."

Tabitha took slight offense to his comment. "Untrained? You make me sound like a hacker."

His brows furrowed. "Hacker?"

"Yes, an amateur, someone stumbling along…"

"Well, aren't you? Not necessarily amateur but stumbling along, trying to figure out how to use your abilities, all the while hiding them?" he persisted.

She shrugged, not willing to give in to what she took for an insult. But she had to admit that he was right. As much as she hid them, she *was* trying to figure out how to use her abilities. "You need not be so smug, though."

"And you don't have to be so defensive," he countered. "If I had grown up in a world of humans and was the only one around me with my abilities and forced to hide them, I would imagine that I would act much the same. Had you grown up here, where our talents and abilities are as much a part of us as our sight or sense of hearing, I imagine you would be quite different. Imagine if you had a parent who trained you, taught you, and helped you hone your power. Things would be different."

Tabitha bit back a reply and swallowed some bitter resentment. He was right. For just a moment, his comment left her envious of the possibilities. "So tell me what it was like, growing up with all this training. Are you trained to do most anything? Is it a rigorous program or more lax, so you can just explore your talent, like a creative energy?"

"Well, I would imagine it is no different than in your world. It depends who is training you and on your upbringing. There are those of us who are trained only to control ourselves, so we are not blowing the tops off of mountains every time we lose our tempers. And there are those of us who participate in a more regimented training. And of course, everyone's abilities are different and their talents are as individual as they are, so everyone can do things differently."

"So not everyone has the same abilities?" Tabitha asked. "Are there things you can do that others cannot and vice versa?'

Luc nodded. "Of course. It is like a talent for singing or painting. Everyone has different abilities. Well, let me qualify that: anyone can paint, right? But each person does it differently. And everyone's inherent abilities are different, right? It is no different. What I may find easy to do, another may struggle with, and what another may do quite easily, I may have to learn. It is not just the power that you are born with, it is how your mind works—how you process things, how you work through issues and resolve problems."

He stopped and lifted a rock from the road and hefted it in his hand. With a vague movement of his hand, the rock rose from his palm and floated in the air. With the lightest nudge, the rock spun in a tight circle and then danced up and down. With another slight wave, the rock dropped to the ground. "What I just did is fairly rudimentary, simply lifting and manipulating an object in front of me. This was something I learned very young; it was fairly simple for me. Another person may find that very difficult to learn to do and might struggle with the basic concept of using focus to move another object. Another person may have to stop and consider the weight of the object, how to move it, and what kind of force to press against it. It really comes down to a matter of how you process and understand the nature of things around you."

Tabitha nodded. "So everyone can do all the same things. It is a matter of how well we learn? Like someone being better at math than another?"

"Yes, more or less. And just like everything else we learn, some things are easier than others. Each has their individual talents. Having said that, there are some things that only certain people are born with the ability to do."

"Such as?"

"Locating portals is one example. Not everyone can do that. It is a talent that cannot be learned." He directed her toward the right fork in the dusty road they were following.

They turned a corner and Tabitha stopped to gape at the scenery before her.

CHAPTER EIGHT

THE FOLIAGE HAD LIGHTENED AND THE VILLAGE BELOW was cast in a silvery haze of moonlight. Hills rolled gently and were dotted with what she could only assume were small homesteads. They stood on a small rise and the trees had been pared to reveal small plots of land surrounding little huts that appeared on the countryside. Down in the valley below them, she saw a small grouping of buildings surrounding what appeared to be a common of sorts. The buildings all appeared small and clustered together as though they were built into the very landscape around them.

One of the first things she noticed was the lack of lights in the homes. Very few of the tiny glass enclosures revealed the low glow of flickering lights. She noticed that unlike the cities and towns she was accustomed to, there were no street lights.

"It is so cute, but there are so few homes," Tabitha commented as she gazed at the tiny village. "Our cities are so big and so bright"

Luc nodded and followed her gaze. "I have heard. I sometimes wish I could see your world, experience it. It sounds so different from ours."

"Is this a small town? Are there larger places?"

He nodded. "Yes, but they do not get very large here. We do not have the population that you have."

"Why is that? Are you a younger world?" she inquired, captivated by the small village nestled in the dell. She could not help but compare it to the cities along the coast of Massachusetts or even the center of tiny Porta Negra. Porta Negra center was immense in comparison to the small hamlet quietly nestled in the valley below.

Luc shrugged. "I don't really know. I have never heard how old your world is to compare them. But we do have a very different world here. Our population is so much smaller. Few families have more than one or two children. I hear that you have families with twice that. It amazes me. Many women from my race are unable to give birth to more than one child, and many none at all."

"Really? Why is that?"

"We can't conceive multiple times. Why is a question for God, not me. But it has kept our population and our communities small."

"God? You believe in God?"

He chuckled softly, leading her toward the road to the right, away from the village. "Yes. And tomorrow I can tell you why and answer your questions. But we are almost home. I think I should get you settled for the night. I could never explain our entire culture to you in one night."

Despite the night's adventures, Tabitha stifled a yawn. She staggered with fatigue. "What time is it?"

"I would guess a few hours before dawn. I need to get some sleep myself. I do not have the luxury of sleeping the day away. I have returned to my father's house to help him for the summer. He will expect my assistance this morning."

"So we are going to your father's home?"

"We are. I live here for the summer when I am not studying. I need to take a few months off every spring into the summer to help him with the horses." Luc yawned as they trudged down the road, at last winding down from the excitement of their meeting.

"Hmm…Well, you will have to explain that to me as well."

The road curved away from the village, and the trees became denser. For the first time, they walked quietly together, each lost in their own thoughts. Tabitha stole glances at him, still amazed that the boy she had reached out to and spoken to some twelve years ago was, in fact, a man—and a very handsome, charming one at that. She wondered, not for the first time that night, if she would wake in the morning to find this all was a dream.

They turned a last corner. The lane curved toward a small enclosure made of windows with a small glow of orange within. As they approached, Tabitha saw that it was on the crest of a small hill. The glow, which looked like a fire dwindling, seemed to be coming from the center of the enclosure. She was about to comment, wondering if that tiny enclosure was his home, but Luc followed the lane as it snaked around. They turned off the lane and followed a small cobbled path through a wooden gate set in a stone wall covered in greenery. She could see a small row of bushes. As they approached, the bushes parted to reveal an arch-shaped heavy wooden door set into the hill. Tabitha stopped and stared at the hill and the door hidden in its base.

She observed the hill more closely and with a start noticed the darkened arched windows set into the hill. The small rounded shutters on either side of them and the small, curved wooden arches over them were apparently to protect them from the elements.

"You live here?" she stammered.

Luc laughed softly as he opened the wooden door and stepped aside to allow her to enter. "Yes, I do. At least part of the time."

She shook her head in wonder as she looked around her. "I feel like I'm about to walk into Bilbo Baggins's home."

"Are you accusing me of being a hobbit?"

Tabitha stopped and stared at him in amazement. "You know what a hobbit is?"

He herded her through the door and nodded. "Yes, I know what a hobbit is. *The Lord of the Rings* was required reading in our cultural reading class."

Her questions evaporated as she stared in wonder at the inside of the home. The wooden door opened into a large foyer that led up several steps. She slowly walked up the steps, in awe as the open floor plan unfolded before her. She faced a large round room with a circular stairway to each side that led up to two round hallways that circled the first floor. In the large, circular room, warm wood paneling glowed with a polished finish, and inviting, simple furniture dotted the center of the room. Across the room, Tabitha noticed curved windows overlooking the back of the house. Large rounded doors led to rooms off the main entrance, but Tabitha could barely take her eyes off the beautiful room before her.

As she stepped into the room, she saw a set of doors directly across the room that led outside; moonlight illuminated the sloped lawn behind the house. As she glanced up, she noticed that the staircase continued up for three floors, the top floor an open loft room with a soft glow illuminating the glass cupola that seemed to be the pinnacle of the home. The glass enclosure allowed the moonlight to illuminate the lower two floors. The glow seemed to emanate from the dregs of a fire. Tabitha could smell the smoky aroma of burning firewood.

"It's beautiful!" she whispered. "It's underground!"

Luc nodded as he looked around the room, his eyes shining at her reaction. "Yes, the earth offers natural insulation. It keeps the home warm in the winter and cool in the summer. The houses are actually built freestanding, and the earth is added on later. As the house settles, the earth becomes the walls and insulation."

"Is it heated by that fire up there?"

He shook his head. "No, the heat runs through the walls and the floors. Of course, being the summer, we do not need it now. The fire you see up there is simply for our enjoyment. Most homes have a fire pit in the top pillar. It is great to sit up there, surrounded by the glass walls, with a fire burning. I imagine my father lit it for Sybille. She enjoys a fire at night after dinner."

"Sybille?"

"His wife. My stepmother." Luc turned and locked the door behind them and gestured toward the stairs. "He remarried when I was a small child. She is the only mother I ever knew."

"Did they have other children?"

Luc shook his head. "Sybille is unable to bear children. She has her other children, though."

Before she could comment, she heard nails clicking on the floor. She turned to see a large dog padding down the stairs toward them. He looked like a shepherd mixture, but with a larger and leaner body. Luc smiled and patted his leg, inviting the animal over to him. With a warm gurgle in his throat, the dog leaned against Luc's legs, rubbing his large head against Luc's hands to be scratched.

"This is Polaris. He is Sybille's. I have his brother, Cirrus. She had their mother, but she died last spring." Luc ruffled the animal's fur, and Tabitha put her hand down to be sniffed. The dog sniffed her fingers before rubbing his head against her palm.

"He is beautiful. Is he a German shepherd?"

"No, he is a wolf. We do not have the domesticated breed dogs of your world."

Tabitha stared at the animal in amazement, noting for the first time the long sweeping tail and the intelligent eyes. She had never imagined that a tame wolf would be nuzzling her hand. Although she felt she should be alarmed, it was hard to feel fear for an animal that was lapping your fingers and nuzzling your legs to be scratched.

"You keep wolves?"

"I wouldn't say we keep them. It is probably more that they choose to live with us. Their mother was injured and brought to my father to be rehabilitated. She was pregnant at the time and due to her injuries was unable to go back out on her own. She stayed here with us, and consequently her two offspring adopted us as well. Let's get some sleep. I will tell you more tomorrow."

He led her up the stairs, where another soft gray wolf, this one slightly smaller in size, soon joined them. Luc introduced her to his wolf, Cirrus. The two wolves trotted along the hall with them, walking past several closed heavy arched doors. Luc opened the third one, leading her through into a room in the back of the house. The moonlight lit up the room, and Tabitha gasped at the beautiful view from the two large oval windows set in the back of the room. She walked over and gazed out at the beautiful landscape that unfolded below her. She could see another round hill with large doors just down and to the right of the back of the house, a rail fencing surrounding it.

"Is that a barn?"

Luc came up behind her in the dark and braced his arms on either side of her as he looked out over her shoulder. In the distance, she could make out several other large hills with glass pillars atop them.

"Yes, that is the barn. My father breeds and treats injured horses there. And those houses over there?" Luc pointed to the hills just within sight. "On the right is my uncle's home, and the one behind it belongs to a close family friend."

"It seems so peaceful."

"Most of the time. We have our issues, but judging from the newspapers we see, not as many as in your world."

"You get newspapers?"

"Yes. Not daily, but every once in a while copies are sent around for us to read. I get them more often when I am at school or work. I live in a bigger city there, and we have more access."

"How could you leave here?"

"Sometimes it is very difficult to leave, and other times, I can't wait to get back," Luc admitted softly.

They stood, gazing out at the silver moonlit landscape for several long moments. Luc stirred first and stepped back.

"We need to get some sleep," Luc murmured behind her. He stepped away from the window and walked through a door in the side of the room and reappeared moments later with a white shirt in his hand. "Tomorrow, I am sure Sybille can loan you something to sleep in. But in the meantime, you can sleep in this. Through that door over there is a washroom. You will find everything you need in the cabinet. Sybille keeps it stocked for guests."

Tabitha nodded.

Luc returned to the side door. "I am in here if you need me. Try and get some sleep. We can talk again tomorrow."

"Thank you, Luc."

He smiled, and her heart fluttered. "Good night."

Tabitha turned back to the window to look once more at the landscape before her. It was hard to believe where she was. In fact, now that she thought of it, she didn't even know where she was. She would have to ask him the land's name in the morning. She glanced down at the shirt in her hand, knowing full well it belonged to him. It was long-sleeved, the collar open at the throat, and the material was a soft, comfortable fabric that she did not recognize.

She turned around and surveyed the rest of the room. She had been so taken with the view out the rounded windows that she hadn't looked around. The outer wall of the room curved and the inner wall mirrored that curve. The room was about fifteen feet wide, and the curve made the outer wall slightly wider than the inner wall. A bed was built into the inner wall, with warm wood paneling beneath it and soft curtains pulled back from either end. Tabitha thought it looked like the bunk of a ship. She leaned in and noticed that the bed was about the size of a full size one at home. The soft mattress tucked into the wood shelf was covered with a warm comforter, the fabric as soft and welcoming as the shirt she held in her hand. When she looked closer, she saw little indents in the wood panels beneath the bed, which she tugged gently. The wood panel silently slid open, revealing a set of sheets and an extra blanket tucked neatly within. She tugged on panel below it, and the drawer silently opened to display several sets of warm and fluffy towels.

Glancing around the room, she noticed several indents in the wood paneling. She walked over and tugged one. A vertical panel slid open, the length of wall. Hooks ran along the top, suggesting a storage closet of some kind. Several other indents in the wall proved to be similar long storage units that silently slid out of the wall.

Tabitha wandered over to inspect several bulbs that dangled from the ceiling; a smaller set of them also hung in the bed enclosure. As she touched the bulbs, a soft glow illuminated them. She touched each one, and each glowed with a soft glow. When she touched one again, the glow intensified and with another touch became still brighter.

"Well, how do I shut you off?" she mused out loud to the trio of lights hanging from the ceiling. Upon further inspection, she was amazed to discover that the long stems of the lights were flexible and could be moved and lowered. If she wished, she could tug one over to hang above the rocking chair. After several tries, she found the secret to putting them back into place was a simple tug. She brushed her fingers over each light, and with that last dismissive wave, each light went out.

She decided it was time to explore the washroom. As heavy as the door seemed, it silently swung open with one gentle tug. The room beyond was dark without windows to illuminate the interior. She could just make out another set of the dangling bulbs and turned them on. The room lit up. It was a bright and cheery room, not unlike a bathroom in her world. The toilet, although shaped differently, was at least recognizable. The porcelain sink bowl with its long curved faucet was unique-looking. She had to play around a few times to find the way to turn on the water. Once she got the hang of it, she could adjust the warm and cold water flow. In a small jar on the edge of the sink was a soft and fragrant soap with a beautiful scent that she could not seem to place. In fact, the more she sniffed at the warm suds in her hands, the more she realized it was not even familiar.

After she had washed her hands and face, she continued her inspection. Opening the drawers, she found a small, strange implement with a curved handle next to a small jar.

She picked up the jar and noticed a tiny picture of teeth on it. Toothpaste? Was the small implement a toothbrush?

She shrugged and figured it was worth a try. Obviously, these people must have effective dental care. Luc's white teeth flashing in his disarming smile quickly came to mind. Tabitha felt herself blushing again at the impact that grin had on her. Anyway, they must have some kind of dental care for him to own such a bright smile.

She shook her head at her own musing and dipped the brushed end of the implement into the jar. With a slight feeling of trepidation, she tried it on her teeth. To her pleasant surprise, the bristles on the handle seemed to curve to fit the shape of her teeth and the white cream had a very pleasant taste. Her teeth seemed no worse for wear after the brushing and felt clean.

That finished, Tabitha went over to peek around the corner of a small half-wall. Behind it she saw a large saucer on the floor in the corner. For a moment, it's purpose had her stumped until she glanced up and saw what appeared to be another kind of faucet coming from the wall above it. *A shower?* she wondered.

Fatigue plagued her, so she decided to wait until morning to try and figure that out. She swept the lights off in the washroom and went to slip out of her clothes. She lifted Luc's shirt over her head and enjoyed the feel of the soft fabric as it slid over her torso. She slid the comforter back and climbed into the bed. As the comfortable bed embraced her, she felt as though she had drifted into a warm cocoon. Her concern over not being able to sleep was unfounded. She slipped off into a deep sleep as soon as her head hit the pillow.

CHAPTER NINE

AS SUNLIGHT CREPT INTO TABITHA'S DREAMS, SHE slowly rose from the encompassing embrace of deep sleep. Her eyes fluttered open. It took a moment for her to place her surroundings and remember the night's adventure. Then for a few moments, she lay still. The experience of the day before was unbelievable, and she still could not fathom that she had found a way into a whole different world.

She slid from the bed and padded over to the window. Bright sunshine poured in. Tabitha had to assume that it was late morning, judging from the height of the sun. She could see the barn at the base of the hill. A multitude of horses milled about in the various fenced pastures on its far side. A silver streak of water wound through the pastures, and several of the horses meandered back and forth for an occasional drink. Heat seemed to shimmer off the ground.

Tabitha left the window to solve the puzzle of the shower. She emerged several minutes later, dressed and feeling better than she had in days. She had found a comb in the washroom and tugged it through the tangles in her hair, enjoying the fragrance from the cleanser she found in the shower. She was winding her hair into a knot and searching for her shoes when a light knock on the door startled her.

Tabitha? Are you awake?

Come on in. I am just looking for my shoes.

The door opened and Luc peeked in at her. "You slept well?"

"Yes" she laughed. "Apparently world jumping wipes you out."

"Well, I will try to remember that should I ever come to visit you. You hungry?"

She nodded and followed him into the hallway, apprehensive about running into anyone. He trotted down the stairs with a comfortable and energetic gait. She admired his graceful steps as he leaped down the lowest couple of steps and turned to wait for her to join him. She admired his long, muscular body dressed in a pair of worn pants and a soft, dark, short-sleeved shirt. Dust seemed to be gently puffing off of his work boots, and Tabitha could only guess he had been working with his father. The sun had kissed his skin to a warm golden tone, and his sapphire blue eyes sparkled with warm light as he watched her descend.

Tabitha felt her face blush under his regard. She slipped her damp hair behind her ears, trying to think of something to say to alleviate her awkwardness. Nothing occurred to her.

"Come on. My father and Sybille are waiting to meet you."

At the bottom of the stairs, Tabitha froze, but Luc took her hand and gently led her through the large open room toward a set of heavy wooden doors. He pushed on one of the doors, and it swung in with a soundless sigh. He tugged her into a large and bright kitchen. Sunlight flooded in from a large set of windows across the room. A man and woman rose as the pair entered. Tabitha fought the urge to hide behind Luc.

"Tabitha, my father, Bertòn DesChamps and my stepmother, Sybille."

Tabitha was immediately struck by the similarities between Luc and his father. She could easily see where Luc got his rugged good looks. Bertòn stepped forward, extending a hand in greeting, and Tabitha felt her mouth go dry. His hair was the same deep onyx as Luc's but shorter; gray touched his temples. His face was very similar to Luc's: the same bronze skin, slim nose, and handsome mouth. His eyes, however, were a deep black as opposed to Luc's vibrant blue, and they lacked the mischief in Luc's eyes. Bertòn's were dark and serious but not unkind.

Tabitha took the offered hand. The smile he sent her was slow and enigmatic. Before he could comment, Luc grinned, and Sybille gently pushed her husband's arm. Tabitha became aware that some communication had passed between Luc and his father.

"You forget yourself, Bertòn. It is not polite not to include your guest in your conversations," the little woman scolded. Sybille stepped forward and nodded to Tabitha. Tabitha was immediately relaxed by the shy smile the tiny woman shared with her. As tall and muscular as her husband was, Sybille was petite, her head barely up to his shoulder. Her deep black hair hung in a long, straight curtain down her back. Her face was small and round, her nose tiny and upturned, her small mouth delicate. Her eyes were radiant silver, and her skin was pale, as opposed to the golden tones of the two men. She hardly appeared to be old enough to be Luc's stepmother.

Bertòn laughed lightly as he took Tabitha's hand in his own. "I apologize, Tabitha. I did not mean to be rude. I was simply telling Luc that his description of your beauty did not do you justice."

Tabitha laughed, her face reddening at the compliment as well as the intensity of his dark gaze. "Thank you, and thank you for your hospitality."

Luc led her around a long kitchen island with plates set for four. Tabitha took a moment to glance around the enormous room. Dark beams of wood were set across the ceiling and continued down the walls in the room, giving it a heavy, rustic feel. Behind the kitchen island stood a long, heavy wooden table with eight chairs grouped around it. Long windows ran across the walls behind what she assumed was the dining area. She followed Luc around the island and climbed into the high-backed rustic wooden chair that he held out for her, facing the large kitchen in front of her. Luc went to assist Sybille, and Tabitha was amused to see the tiny woman swat him out of her way.

An assortment of copper and cast-iron pots hung from the ceiling beams. Across the room, long rows of herbs and dried flowers dangled from hooks in the ceiling. A large stonework fireplace was set in the wall between the great windows. A huge worktable separated the kitchen area from the fireplace, and Tabitha could see a collection of earthenware bowls under the shelves. Behind Sybille was a porcelain bowl sink with that same long faucet as the washroom. A large cast-iron monstrosity was set against the wall, and Tabitha could only guess it was the stove or some kind of cooking surface.

Sybille placed a mug in front of her. Bertòn poured Tabitha a tall mug of water, and Sybille placed a basket of bread and some bowls of hot stew in front of them before the pair came to sit at the counter. Tabitha caught Bertòn's gaze on her.

"Luc has told us that you came over from your world in search of your mother. I hope we can help you. Please consider this your home while you are here," Bertòn said.

"Thank you. Yes, I am here to try and find my mother. I am wondering if you have heard of her? Or know of anyone who has a guest who may be a stranger?" Tabitha asked, wondering not for the first time how she would begin looking for her mother in this strange land.

Bertòn shook his head, glancing over at Sybille, who did the same. "Tell us what you know. Any information might be helpful. Maybe it will offer some clue."

Tabitha relayed the whole story as they ate. She told them every detail she could recall, wondering if any hint of her mother's location might be gleaned from some minor detail or potential incident.

"And this attorney's name? Victoria? Victoria Ristucci?" Bertòn asked, rolling the name with a slight accent.

Tabitha tasted the stew and was pleasantly surprised at the light and fragrant flavor. She thought it was some type of fish and vegetables, but for the life of her, she could not be sure what anything was. "If I may say, she looked a little like all of you. She's a beautiful woman with long black hair and the very same dark eyes. I know that sounds a little ridiculous, but I thought that when I first saw the three of you together. I guess there is something in your features that reminds me of her."

Luc took a spoonful of stew and seemed pensive. "Perhaps she is an emigré."

"An emigré?" Tabitha asked.

"One of us who lives in another world. There are several. They live over there, share new things, bring back news and occasionally something that we may request," Bertòn responded.

They finished their meal, and Luc rose to carry his bowl to the sink.

"May I ask how it is that we speak the same language? And you seem to use the same measurement standards. Luc told me in miles how far you were from where I entered. You speak of months, years, and days." Tabitha put down her spoon, amazed at the similarities in their worlds. For a brief moment, she wondered if she had actually crossed into another place or if this was some elaborate hoax. "How is it that we have the same frame of reference?"

Bertòn smiled and leaned back in his seat. He handed his bowl to Sybille, who carried it over to Luc at the sink. "Well, I guess before we get into more details about your missing mother, perhaps it is not a bad idea to answer questions about our world." He leaned forward with a grin. "And when we have answered most of your questions, perhaps you will entertain and enlighten us with details about your world."

"But you seem to know so much about my world."

"Yes, but it is different to speak to someone who lives there. Imagine a place that you have always wished to visit, where the lifestyle is so different from your own, when all you have are artifacts, pictures, and written accounts. You may have bits and pieces of that world in hand, but they do not carry you there. We can only imagine your world from the papers and accounts that we have from those who have visited or the occasional lecture from someone who lived among you for a while. But to meet someone who has lived there all her life and has experienced no other life than that world—is a rare treat for us," Bertòn explained.

Tabitha replied, "It is really not as interesting as it may seem. But tell me, how are we so similar? Your references are so much like my own—your language ...everything."

Luc came back and settled beside Tabitha, his chair next to her and his arm around the back of hers. She could not help but feel as though he were being protective of her. She caught their glances and wondered what communication was passing from father to son.

"Our people, the Caskans, were the original people on this land. We are a magic people and have lived in harmony with the land and loved and prospered with our mother, the Earth. We have always been a peaceful people, content to live on the land, the animals beside us as our brothers, taking what we need but never more," Bertòn said.

"Occasionally someone has found their way through a portal. We've had tales throughout the years of people who would wander through and acclimate into our society. Several generations ago the frequency seemed to increase. The portals were opening more often, and when they did, they were swallowing whole sections of people. Whole villages of your humans suddenly appeared every once in a while. Stranger still, these portals closed immediately after swallowing these people."

He took a long drink from his mug and studied her. "It was through this acclimation of your race into ours that we became more like your world. We began to adopt many of their ways of living, as they adopted ours. Many intermarried, and we have now people of both races, as well as full humans and full Caskans. Most of these mass inductions of your race happened in the past couple hundred years. They brought with them their God and the Bible, and we taught them of our love for the land, the Earth, and respect for our planet."

"Where did these people come from? I mean, I would imagine we would have historical knowledge somewhere of large groups of people just disappearing." Tabitha was puzzled.

"You do—we have seen them. Roanoke, Virginia," Luc offered.

"Jamestown," Bertòn added.

"The people that were found on the ocean, from that ship—what was the name?" Sybille glanced up shyly.

"The *Mary Celeste*?" Tabitha asked in amazement.

"Yes! That was the one!" Sybille grinned before quickly returning to the dishes she was putting away.

"Those are a few that come to mind. They are probably some of the most prominent in this part of the land. Our people knew of several portals still open, small ones that never swallowed anyone and seemed to stay active for years. Through these, we discovered the ways through to your world. We would venture through to learn more of your world. In this way, we adopted many of your advances, learned what you were experimenting with, and very cautiously took what technology we deemed advantageous without countering our way of life. We chose to ignore your industrial revolution, but your more recent advances in electricity, especially in the solar and wind technology, are more fitting to our manner of living. We have opted to not adopt coal burning and your gasoline inventions. We see how it is killing your atmosphere and your world, and we have chosen as a people to keep our land pure and our air and water clean."

Luc and his father seemed to exchange silent comments before Luc continued. "We have a small percentage of your population. Our needs are much smaller. One city in your world will have twenty-five thousand people, where one of our provinces might be home to twenty-five hundred on twice the land. Our trains are used to move trade cargo and people longer distances. We use horses and..." He grinned. "Many of us have other modes of transportation. It has never occurred to most of our population to find ways to travel distances because we were always able to do that."

"How? You mentioned last night that you have ways of moving with your power. What is it? Can you blink yourself somewhere else?" she asked, excited over the potential talent building.

Luc's smile broadened and he nodded. "I will show you how we do it and teach you. With most of our population being non-humans, finding modes of transport was never a priority. And since our villages are smaller and closer, we seldom require the amount of travel that you do in your world. Most everything we need is made locally; we can trade or buy pretty much anything we need around our homes."

Tabitha shook her head in amazement. "This is incredible. Why would anyone who comes here ever leave? Why would my mother have left here? It is like utopia."

"We are not perfect, just different. We have our conflicts and we have our problems," Bertòn admitted with a sad shake of his head. "To many, the old ways are outdated and archaic. Some want to modernize our world to be more like your world. They wish to bring more of the technology back. As more portals are discovered and more people explore your world, it is a constant struggle."

"So tell me—the newspapers, the books that Luc referred to…how much do people bring back here? I thought that you could not carry much over the portal except more or less the clothes on your back," Tabitha asked.

"Very little. Only clothes and maybe one or two very small things close to the skin. We are not a culture of writers or painters, so books are a very sought-after commodity from your world. We have all read your classics. We love to study your writings and your ways with words. We, as a people, do write our historical documents, our laws, and our news. We tend to write textbooks of theories for study, but your love of fiction is something that captivates us. We can order things like that, and people will bring them over every couple of weeks," Bertòn admitted.

Luc leaned forward, and Tabitha watched as a small frown crossed Bertòn's face. Bertòn nodded and stood. "Tabitha, we can speak again this evening. I have much work to get done. If you would excuse me, we will leave you to Sybille."

Tabitha nodded and thanked him for his time. As he rose, Luc winked and followed his father out the back door out toward the barn. Tabitha watched them walk together, wondering what had caused them to apparently disagree on some point.

Sybille glanced up and wiped her hands on a towel. "I would love some company if you would join me. I have a workshop downstairs. We can continue talking while I work. I would love to hear more of your world."

Tabitha nodded and stood. "Lead on."

Sybille led her down a set of curved stairs to a workshop deep below the kitchen. Tabitha learned that Sybille made the soap and shampoo that she had found in the washroom. She showed Tabitha through a glass door out to a garden filled with sweet-smelling flowers and colorful plants climbing up and over trellises. The smell was hypnotic. Tabitha could not recognize the flowers she saw blooming along the cobble walkway. The garden was hemmed in by a sturdy fence of cable-like plants with long tendrils that twined and curved among themselves, forming a natural enclosure. Sybille broke off the arm of one of these long tendrils and showed Tabitha the smooth gel that she scraped from within. She explained she would mix the gel with different plant and herbs to make cleansers and poultices.

Inside the workroom, Sybille showed her the flowers and the rows of scented extracts that she made. She drew a short block from a wooden box near the door and tossed it into a cast-iron stove. She lit the block, and Tabitha watched from her perch on a tall stool as the block began to glow. Heat began to radiate from the stove. Sybille set a pot on the stove and dropped a large bowlful of the white gel from the stems of the plants into the pot. As she left it to boil down, Sybille tugged out a board and began to cut various flowers and petals into small chunks that she explained she would then put in a small press to extract the pulp.

Sybille told her of their lives and explained more about the land they loved. The world as they knew it was called Caska. It stretched far to the north into what would be Canada in Tabitha's world and down along the East Coast to the tip of Florida. Their population generally lived along the coast. Farther inland toward the central area were large tribes and bands of Caskans who had stayed more true to their traditional way of life. They lived predominantly as nomadic tribes, moving from one area to another during different seasons. As with their coastal neighbors, they also built homes within the ground, surrounded by earth for natural insulation. Because they were nomadic, the homes were grouped in tighter communities and were well hidden from sight.

"I am told you can actually cross a nomad settlement and never even realize you have walked across one of their villages. It's as if they are not there. They build such communities to be able to seal themselves off in the event of attack," Sybille explained.

"Attack? Who would attack them?" Tabitha asked, taking a sip from a large mug of tea.

Sybille shrugged. "We have had wars—fights over land, as any other civilization. We have lost much of our heritage and some talents due to our fighting. As peaceful as the Caskans try to be, they are warriors at heart. The humans have been lucky in the years they have come into this land that they have been able to acclimate, unlike some other races. I think they are not a threat. But if some have their way, the land will once again be at war. We are already seeing the signs of unrest. Various factions are fighting over our way of life."

Tabitha watched the woman, curious about one comment. "Unlike some other races?"

"Over the years, we have lost races due to the true Caskan's aggression. As humans came over and began to teach them the way of settling in villages, they became a more peaceable people. But it is a new peace for them, and groups of them threaten that peace." She sighed as she stirred the pot and replaced the cover. "We had hoped that the peace would last, but I fear it is not to be."

"But what do they fight over? From what you have told me, there seems to be plenty of land for all. I mean, if they do not agree on a way of life, they can move somewhere else."

Sybille smiled sadly. "It is not so simple, I fear. But I speak of things best left for another time. I did not mean to sadden you. Let's talk of other subjects. How are we to find your mother?"

Tabitha lifted a shoulder and shook her head. "How do I go about finding someone in this land?"

"Well, the horse auction is in three days. Perhaps when the people gather for that, we can ask around. Many of our relatives and neighbors will be here the night before, and we can ask if anyone knows of her," Sybille suggested.

CHAPTER TEN

TABITHA SPENT THE NEXT TWO DAYS WITH SYBILLE OR watching as Bertòn and Luc readied the horses they would be auctioning off. Sybille's warnings of the unease in the land seemed a distant memory. She found her hosts to be gracious and charming. She began to notice the differences between their natures. Bertòn was very stoic but always elegant and polite. He did not smile often, and his dry wit often took Tabitha by surprise. Sybille was shy and reserved, usually more content to be listening than leading the conversation. Luc, much like his father, had a reserved edge, but Tabitha observed playfulness and an easy grin that Tabitha could only assume were attributes from his human mother.

Sybille's business seemed to thrive, and Tabitha was pleased to be able to help prepare the jars of soaps, shampoos, and creams that were piling up in preparation for the auction days. Typically, Sybille sold her wares through the village, but the influx of buyers from all over the province would bring a steady sales stream to the house over the three days of the auction.

Tabitha learned that the horses were bred by Bertòn but the herd also included injured horses that were unable to live in the wild any longer. Caska was, it seemed, largely an undomesticated land, and wild horses roamed free over the land. When a horse was injured, it was brought to Bertòn, who would nurse it back to health to set it free if possible. Those horses that could no longer live on their own would be cared for and then auctioned off to homes. Horses were not only a source of transportation but were also valued pets and highly prized possessions.

The Caskans did not eat the meat of animals nor did they wear leather or hides. After learning this, Tabitha found herself glancing through the house, looking for evidence of any animal product and found none. Their diet seemed to be highly rich in fish, eggs, dairy, fruits, and vegetables. As their source of food was always local, processed foods were uncommon. They did, however, ask her many questions about foods they read about, curious about the unusual eating habits in the strange world from which Tabitha had come.

Tabitha was content in her days at the horse farm but suffered an occasional pang of guilt when she thought of Trude's reaction to her disappearance. She had little doubt that her aunt knew where she had gone, and she relied on that theory to ease her troubled conscience.

If she were being honest with herself, she would have to admit that she most enjoyed the time spent with Luc. When he was not working with Bertòn, he spent his days with her, walking through the woods and showing her his world. She would wander down to the barn and perch on a fence railing and watch him work. There were no saddles, and the bridles were simple padded bands around the horse's muzzles rather than the steel bits in the bridles of her own world. Luc's strong legs gripped the sides of the horses, and she would sit and watch, fascinated by the casual ease with which he rode, an extension of the animal below him.

The three days of the auction coincided with a local village fair, and Bertòn had assured her that the populace arriving for the auction would be many and widespread. As the days crept by, Tabitha found herself wishing the auction would never arrive, the people would never come, and she would not have to start the process of searching for her mother. If she did not have to look for Doni, she could stay here and spend her days with Luc, watching him and talking to him with an ease she had never found with anyone else. Even Callie was not as close a confidante as Luc was becoming. He understood her; he knew what it meant to be half human and half Caskan. He had not had to hide his nature as she had, but he had grown up in a predominantly Caskan world and considered himself a half-breed.

"What do you remember of your mother?" she asked him one evening as they sat outside after an enjoyable dinner with Sybille and Bertòn.

"Nothing, really. I was about two years old when she died. My memories seem to be made up of stories I've heard from my father and my Uncle Rhys. He and my cousin Daniel live in the next province," Luc commented, his head resting back against the back of a heavy but comfortable carved wood chair on the cobbled patio in the back of the house, outside the kitchen. The sun was slowly setting behind the trees, and the pleasant summer evening air casually caught his hair and ruffled it back.

Tabitha sat sideways in her own chair, her feet curled beneath her as she watched him. His eyes were closed. She enjoyed the opportunity to study him unawares. "And your uncle is human, and his son?"

"Mmm hmm. They are. My mother, Yolanda, had a sister who married Rhys. When my mother died, I used to spend a lot of time down there with them. As I grew older, my father insisted I spend more time here to work on my training. I was fairly resentful. I wanted to stay there with them. Daniel was like a big brother to me. My aunt Gisel made it seem more like a home than being here. They were so different from my father. He was so serious. When I was at Rhys and Gisel's with Daniel, they would laugh, enjoy each other. I guess I made it a little difficult for my father."

"When did he marry Sybille? Was it more of a home then?" Tabitha asked.

"He married Sybille when I was maybe six. So they have been married for..." He was lost in thought as he tried to remember. "Almost fourteen years."

"And when you first reached out to me, you must have been eight?"

Luc turned to look at her. "Yes, and you were six. And you reached out to me."

She smiled. "I was terrified! How did you ever hear me?"

"I have no idea. It unnerved my father, to say the least. To have someone reach through to me from another world was unheard of. We still cannot figure out why you and I are linked."

"You and your father are linked. Do you have other links? Sybille? Anyone else?" she asked.

"I do not have a link with Sybille. She and my father have their bond. It is actually a breech of conduct to have a link with a woman who belongs to another man," Luc commented, glancing over at her

"'Belongs to another man'? Did you just say that?" Tabitha teased.

Luc shrugged and rested his head against the seat, closing his eyes once again to enjoy the last vestiges of the sunlight on his face. "Father or not, I cannot have a link with Sybille. The only other link I have is with my cousin Tristyn."

"Another cousin? Is this on your mother's side as well?"

"No, my father's brother, Marcus. He is one of the few Caskan men I know with three children. His three sons are Diego, the eldest, and Tristyn and Tye. Tristyn and I trained together with my father. He is my age and probably the only reason I did not run away back to Rhys's home when my father made me come to live here with him. Tristyn became the brother I needed. He and I are that close. We spent our childhoods together. He is the only one other than my father who knew of my contact with you."

She played with the sleeve of her blouse. Sybille had been able to donate some clothes to her until they could get her a couple of things. Tabitha found the soft and well-made clothes comfortable. Sybille had also given her a silky shift to sleep in, but Tabitha found herself slipping Luc's shirt on night after night, not willing to give up his scent on it as she drifted off to sleep. She cleared her throat, nervously, wondering how she could casually broach the subject that nagged at her. "So you have no link with any women?"

"Of course I do—one."

She smiled. "I meant other than me."

"No. Once you establish a link, it cannot be broken. So if I were to form a link with a woman, she and I would be unable to find other mates should our relationship not work," he responded, his eyes still closed.

"But is there someone you are…close to? Someone special?" She tried to make the comment as casual as she could, but the words tumbled out in a rush. She felt her face redden at her obvious intent.

He cracked one eye and glanced over at her. "What are you asking?"

"Dammit, Luc. Stop being so difficult. You know damn well what I am asking," she snapped.

He turned, giving her his full attention. Tabitha was caught off guard by the full impact of him, as she always was. "There is one woman who has my attention."

Tabitha nodded. "And is it serious?"

He leaned an arm on the back of his chair, resting his chin in the crook of his arm as he watched her, a slight smile playing about his lips. "You are quite transparent. You know I am speaking of you."

"Well, Luc. We have spent these few days together and…well, we have never even talked about—" She looked away as her stammer began to dwindle. "I guess I am saying we have not even broached the subject of other relationships. I mean, we are friends, right? And it would be natural for us to ask the question. Right?"

His laugh was low and soft. "Why? Will it make a difference? Will it make it easier when you must leave?"

She looked up at him. His expression had lost its humor, and his eyes were intent. "I am not sure that I know—"

"You know damn well what I am talking about." He stood and pulled her up to stand in front of him. "Should we open this door? Should we even begin to explore our feelings? Or should we keep this friendly? Where do we go?"

Luc was the first to tear his eyes away, and he stepped back, leaving her feeling as though a hole had been torn in her. She lifted a hand slightly to reach out to him but let it drop. He was right. They were treading very dangerous ground, and to bring it into the light would only intensify the pain. The casual ground that they had been taking was safer. There were too many obstacles, too many concerns, and too many things to work out. Not the least of them was finding her mother. That had to be her priority. After that she and Luc could deal with the truth of what was happening between them.

He stood for a moment, rigid, his back to her as he stared out at the last dregs of the summer sunlight fading over the trees. Tabitha tried to calm her raging heart; she tried to find some way to break through the wall that he had put up between them. She wanted to reach out, run her hands over his shoulders, and feel the play of his muscles on her hands as she slipped her arms around him. She so desperately wanted to touch him and to be touched, to feel his warmth and strength consume her.

"Stop, Tabitha." His voice was sharp. "I can feel you. Dammit, Tabitha. Please stop torturing me."

She stepped back, horrified that he could sense her desire. She turned to leave, but his hand snaked out and grabbed her. "Don't walk away. I couldn't take that."

She stared at his hand and then at his face. Confusion and pain coursed through her. "Please, Luc. I need to get away from you. I need some space to clear my head."

"No, we need to get back to where we were. We need to be able to find a way to keep us on track. And you need to find your mother. I will help you. I promised you that." He released her arm, dragged his hands through his hair, and released an explosive sigh. "We have to remain focused on why you are here."

"We will. We can." Her voice was soft. She was impressed that she was able to speak at all. "I need you."

He closed his eyes, dropping his head back and letting his breath out in a long, ragged sigh. "And I promised you that I would be there for you. You will not have to do this alone." He went over to the rock wall surrounding the enclosure and leaned his hip against it, one leg propped on the wall. He let his gaze drop as he reined in his emotions. His voice was back to a normal tone when he spoke, no trace of the emotion that they had both just battled. "Tomorrow when our friends and buyers begin to arrive, we will ask them what they know of a stranger who fits your mother's description."

"Will we tell them where I am from? Or where my mother is from?"

"No, we won't. We will tell people you are my companion from school, visiting for a few days." He suggested, "I think it best that as few people as possible know the truth of where you come from. You will be inundated with questions and attention. The truth is, we do not know who your mother is here to see, and by your account, she was not stable upon her return from her time here. We do not know if she or you are in any danger. We have no idea who or what your father is."

Tabitha nodded. "But will I be able to make them believe I am from this world? Will people believe me?"

Luc nodded. "We will tell them you are studying alternate culture. People in that course of study learn the ways of the alternate worlds. They study the media and books available. Most theses involve spending some time over there plus a study of their culture. I imagine you can talk your way through this."

She smiled. "I hope so. But what about the school in your world? What about specific questions?"

Luc lifted a small stone from the wall and hefted it in his hand. "No one will ask you anything too personal or specific. Our people are not known for prying. They will keep their questions general, and that will allow you to remain vague." His mouth twisted in a wry grin. "You will be with me for the next few days, so stay close by. Once people know you are spoken for, most men will remain distant. We are a very possessive race, and getting too close to another man's woman is forbidden."

Tabitha shook her head and laughed. "There you go again with that caveman mentality. I am surprised at your attitude toward relationships."

"Tabitha, you have to understand we are a very passionate race. Women are sacred to us. Once a man and a woman are in a relationship, another man will not approach her. It is a very important aspect of our culture." Luc's demeanor was intent. "I am not trying to say that as a woman you have constraints against you, but once men know you are mine, they will back off from you. It is our custom. Our relationships are precious to us. When a couple is committed, they are equals. Don't get me wrong. I have read books from your history that indicate the woman was considered to be below the man, not able to vote, have a say, or hold an opinion. Our women are often our leaders and always our equals. But the physical bond is sacred. And because our women give birth so seldom and so few children are born, we protect that bond fiercely."

He shrugged, and a smile curved his lips. "I am not trying to alarm you, but you must know that if you are treated with deference by men over the next few days, that will be the basis. And if I have a tendency to be close or to seem to be lingering closely, you will understand."

"Well, that will not make our new pact of personal space and distance any easier," she growled.

He shook his head. "No, it won't, but in light of the gravity of the situation, I am sure we will survive it."

She sighed heavily. "This could get complicated. But you are right. I have to remain focused on why I am here."

He nodded and stretched as he glanced up at the moon that had risen in the night sky. He walked over to her, placed his hands on her hips, and dropped his forehead down to rest on hers.

"With any luck, we will have some direction by the end of the next few days. And with even one clue, we will find a way to find your mother."

She nodded, staring into the amazing blue eyes gazing into hers. She smiled and saw the smile reach his eyes when he smiled back.

"Let's go to bed."

She laughed out loud as she slipped out of his grip, her eyes mischievous. "And there you go, already breaking that first rule. You are out of your mind if you think that it would be as easy as just making that comment! Ha! You are not the first to try. You'll have to be a little more original than that old lame remark!"

He growled at her in mock anger and reached out to swat at her bottom, but she lightly slipped out of his reach and danced through the door into the kitchen, throwing a grin over her shoulder at him.

"You are going to make me crazy," he groaned as he followed her into the house, turning to close the door behind them.

"And to think you have three days of pretending that I am 'your woman'!" she taunted as she took the steps upstairs, turning to stick her tongue out at him as he mounted the steps behind her.

He leaped up two steps with speed that surprised a frightened yelp out of her. Before she could run, he seized her waist between his hands and pressed her against the wall. He leaned over her, his smile devilish. "And I plan on making you pay for that remark in the next three days."

Tabitha laughed, relieved that they had been able to slip back into their casual flirtation. She lifted herself on her toes and placed a kiss on the tip of his nose. "We will see who can play that game better!"

CHAPTER ELEVEN

TABITHA STOOD BEFORE THE MIRROR, READJUSTING her hair and tugging the skirt and blouse into place one final time. Every time she thought her image was fine, she hesitated and did her hair once again or turned this way and that to verify the hang of the blouse and skirt. She wore one of Sybille's skirts, and the length was just a little shorter than she would normally wear. The waist was a bit tight, but the borrowed blouse hung over it to hide any sign that she had struggled into it. She counted herself lucky to be able to get into Sybille's petite clothes at all, but they had been able to improvise.

She patted her flat belly one last time, wishing for her own clothes. But she had to admit that the cut and the feel of their clothing was comfortable and flattering. She adjusted the blouse again, trying to tug the front together just a bit. Her cleavage was showing more than she would have liked, but...well, too late now. Callie was always telling her she should take more advantage of the body she had.

What are you doing?

Will you please stop pestering me? I will be ready in a moment.

How long does it take?

Tabitha went over and flung the door open. Luc was leaning against the doorjamb in apparent frustration.

"Will you please just let me finish?"

Luc sauntered in after her, running an appreciative eye over her. "I am not sure you can get much better."

She could not hide the smile that tugged at her lips as she slipped her sandals on. "I will take that as a compliment."

He grinned and gestured toward the door. "Are you ready?"

She let out a sigh and nodded. "I guess it is time to get this over with."

"Don't be nervous—all will be well."

"If you say so." She followed him out the door and into the hallway.

Luc looked handsome in his dark pants and simple light shirt. She loved the simple and elegant cut of the clothes the Caskans wore.

They made their way through a small group of people nibbling on a spread of food in the large main room. Luc stopped to introduce her to several as they walked through the room into the kitchen. Bertòn approached, his dark good looks set off by the cut of his clothes. Sybille, looking stylish and elegant, finished giving directions about the food arrangements and drinks to the hired people before joining them. Tabitha noted that the people she sent off to begin service all shared her tiny stature.

"Tabitha, you are looking exceptionally beautiful tonight," Bertòn complimented, his eyes drifting over her admiringly.

Tabitha felt a blush sting her cheeks at his open admiration. "Thank you. Sybille was kind enough to share some of her things with me."

Sybille grinned at her. "And you have done a fine job filling them out. You do look radiant. Luc will have his hands full keeping the men from you."

Luc shrugged, leaning over to grab a couple of glasses from a passing tray. "I will stay by her side tonight to make sure she does not get into trouble."

He handed Tabitha a glass and with a hand on the small of her back led her back into the large main room. More people had arrived, and Luc led Tabitha over to meet the newcomers. The men were all tall, lean, and muscular, and each of them shared the same deep black hair and golden complexion of the Caskan men. Most of the women in the group were tall and slender, raven hair falling down their backs in either a dark sheet of straight hair or a long dark braid. The eyes of all of these newcomers were dark onyx. Tabitha noted again that this race of people seemed to be a very attractive one.

And a somber one. Tabitha could detect their pleasure in greeting one another, but their faces showed little emotion, and their eyes held a gravity that she could not fathom. One young woman stood out among them; her soft honey hair and warm golden eyes seemed to radiate among the serious crowd of dark-haired people around her. As she greeted Bertòn and Sybille, her smile was quick and her laughter seemed to fill the air with gaiety. In her arms, a small child clung to her neck, shy of the people crowding around her.

Tabitha watched curiously from beside Luc, taking advantage of the moment before the group noticed her. She thought it amusing that the men greeted one another with a handshake and the women invariably greeted with a hug, but men and women greeted one another with little contact. With the exception of the blond woman, who quickly embraced Bertòn, much to the chagrin of the tall and serious dark-haired man hovering behind her. Sybille glanced over, and she and Tabitha shared a secret smile at Bertòn's apparent unease.

The blond woman caught sight of Luc standing to the side, and her face lit up. "Luc! I did not know you were home! Tristyn does not tell me anything!"

She hefted the child into the arms of the man standing protectively behind her and lifted herself onto her toes to place a kiss on Luc's cheek. The man behind her shared a glance with Luc, and Tabitha could, for a brief moment, see the weary exasperation in his eyes. In just that fleeting instant, she recognized that her identification of their behavior as stoic was actually wrong. These people's emotions were not played out on their faces and expressions when they were sharing raw emotions. In that flash of insight, her perspective changed.

Luc responded with a tolerant half-smirk at the blond woman. "Alena, it is good to see you as well. Still driving my cousin to distraction, I see?"

She laughed uproariously, and the sound took Tabitha by surprise. The Caskan were such a quiet people; this woman must surely be a single bomb in an otherwise quiet existence. As Alena was about to respond, she caught sight of Tabitha. Immediately noting the proximity she and Luc shared, the woman's eyes narrowed as a dimpled grin split her face.

"Well, hello."

Luc began introductions, but Alena shushed him with a hand. Alena's focus on Tabitha had drawn the attention of the others in the group.

Tabitha grinned at the woman, trying to swallow her nervousness. "Hello. Alena, is it?"

Alena smiled at her and gave Luc a sidelong glance. "Yes. And you are?"

"Tabitha Devins," she replied after a momentary hesitation.

Alena took her hand in her own. "Tabitha? How nice to meet you. You are a friend of Luc's?"

"I am," Tabitha responded, putting her arm through Luc's and taking his hand for moral support. "We got to know one another at school."

"Well, that would explain why I have never seen you. It is a pleasure to meet you." Alena grinned.

Luc tugged Tabitha past Alena. "Alena, if I may steal Tabitha away from you for a moment, I would like to introduce her to the rest of my family." He gestured to the tall dark brooding man behind Alena. "This is Alena's husband, Tristyn. And their daughter, Cyra."

I think it obvious to tell you that Alena is human.

Tabitha laughed as she responded, *I did figure that out!*

Tristyn greeted her with a warm nod of his head. "Welcome, Tabitha. It is a pleasure to meet you. Luc has told me quite a bit about you. If there is anything I can do to make your stay with us more pleasant, please do not hesitate to ask." He turned to his daughter, her small arms looped around his neck. "Can you say hello to Tabitha, Cyra?"

The child smiled shyly and tucked her face in her father's neck. Tabitha smiled and Luc grinned at the child.

He turned to the ring of people around them and began introductions. His uncle Marcus stood beside Bertòn. He was more robust than his brother and muscular, his long hair pulled back on the nape of his neck with a single silver clasp. Luc's eldest cousin Diego was Marcus's mirror image, barrel-chested and deep-voiced. His wife, Peri, was tall and slender. Her long bangs brushed her dark eyes. She and Sybille were deep in conversation, but she stopped to greet Tabitha with a warm smile.

Marcus's youngest son, Tye, stood to the back and came forward with a stumble to extend his hand to greet Tabitha. Almost as an afterthought, he sheepishly withdrew his hand and nodded with a shy smile. He tugged a young woman to his side and introduced her as Mia.

Mia stepped forward; her eyes were only for Luc. "It has been a while, Luc." She lifted a gold charm that dangled from a chain on her neck and smiled at him with a challenge. "You can see that in your absence I have been promised."

Luc eyes showed his surprise when he glanced from Mia's smirk to Tye's shuffling feet. "I had not heard. Congratulations to you both."

Mia sniffed, and then she glanced at Tabitha and nodded in greeting. Without a word, she gestured to Tye and walked away. Tye glanced from Tabitha to Luc and seemed about to say something, but with little more than a nod to Tabitha, he turned to follow his intended.

Alena had her daughter back in her arms and a drink in her free hand. She watched Mia stalk off with a small smirk of her own. "Well, I do not believe that went as she intended."

Luc shot her a warning glance. "Gossip, Alena? That is not like you."

She laughed and took a sip of her drink. "No? Then you don't know me."

Tristyn stepped up behind her protectively. Sybille stepped forward and held out her arms to Cyra, trying to coax her from her mother. After a brief hesitation and a little encouragement from her mother, Cyra extended her arms and slipped into Sybille's arms. Sybille's face lit up as she hugged the child to her. Cyra cuddled her head into the tiny woman's shoulder, her thumb in her mouth as she watched people mill about the room.

"How is she?" Sybille asked, a gentle sway in her hips as she rocked the child.

Alena's eyes clouded, and the trace of her smile slipped. "Oh, she has her good days and bad. Today she had a very pleasant day. She spent some time this afternoon with Tristyn riding outside. The sun seemed to do her a world of good." She gently reached out and swept the little girl's dark hair from her brow. She glanced affectionately over her shoulder at her husband. "Tristyn hopes to find her a small, gentle pony tomorrow."

Sybille smiled sadly as she laid her cheek on the tiny girl's head. "Bertòn told me he had a little pony picked out for her. I believe Luc was working with her today, getting her ready for Cyra to see tomorrow."

Alena smiled. "It will make her so very happy if she can have a little pony of her own. Tristyn's horse is so big; it frightens me to see her on his back."

Sybille extended a hand to the young woman and squeezed her fingers. "It is already done. Luc has promised to put some pretty yellow bows in her mane before Cyra sees her. She will love her. He has spent many hours training her to be the perfect little pony for our little princess."

Tears sparkled in Alena's eyes as she smiled at the older woman. "Thank you, Sybille. You have all been so very kind to her. I will make sure to thank Bertòn and Luc as well. It will make her summer so very happy."

Tabitha looked closely at the little girl and for the first time noticed the dark circles below her eyes. Her skin had a sallow pallor, and her eyes were slowly closing as Sybille gently rocked her, as though she could not keep herself awake any longer.

"What is wrong with her?" Tabitha asked quietly, not sure if she was overstepping by asking.

"She is ill. The doctors have done all they can, but the sickness eats away at her. We fear that she may not be strong enough to fight it any longer." Alena spoke softly. All the exuberance that Tabitha had noticed in her seemed to seep out of the woman; her face was a hollow mask of sadness.

Tabitha was perplexed. "If you don't mind me asking, why don't they just heal her?"

Alena turned to stare at her, and Sybille's eyes snapped toward her in alarm. Luc was suddenly beside her, his arm protectively on her shoulder. Tabitha noticed the conversation around them had ceased.

Sybille was the first to break that silence. "They have tried everything they know to do, our doctors." She glanced up to Alena. "Tabitha is from Southern Chandolyn. They refer to their doctors as healers."

Alena nodded and reached for her daughter. "Sybille, do you have some milk in the kitchen? I think it is time that I get her a little something. Perhaps she can lie down for a moment."

"Of course." As Sybille lead Alena to the kitchen, Tabitha turned to find Luc and Tristyn close behind her.

What did I say that was wrong?

Bertòn appeared to Luc's side and asked to excuse him for a moment.

Luc glanced at Tabitha. *I will be right back. You will be all right for a moment? I will explain later.*

She nodded and then found herself standing alone for a moment. The room had filled with people, and they milled about, chatting and greeting one another. Tabitha felt discomfort from the social blunder she had apparently made plus the impact of being alone in a strange place.

"That was an odd comment to make," Tristyn said quietly. She spun in alarm, not having heard him come up behind her.

"I am sorry. I did not mean to offend. What did I say that was so wrong?" She glanced up at his dark, impassive eyes. He was slightly intimidating, this tall, dark man. His good looks rivaled Luc's, but as with Bertòn, his somber demeanor left her feeling slightly unnerved.

"Why did you ask such a question? 'Why don't they just heal her' indeed?" he persisted, ignoring her question.

Luc had told her that Tristyn understood her true background, but no one knew of her ability, so it seemed best to tread cautiously. "I guess I just assumed that with the abilities and magic you have, you would be able to heal."

He led her through the crowd to the large double glass doors that opened to an empty deck and the warm evening air. Tabitha glanced back toward the room, hesitating. Tristyn was, after all, one of Luc's closest confidants and one of the few in this world who knew the truth about her.

He stopped at the railing overlooking the dusky landscape. The moon was rising, and its dazzling face threw a glorious silver sheen over the land before them. Tabitha sipped at her glass as they stood quietly looking over the hillside. The drink was lightly sweet but with a tang. She could not place the flavor, but it was refreshing. She found that only a very tiny sip was enough to give her a feeling of having taking a satisfying drink of water. The flavor tingled in her mouth for a few moments.

"Many years ago, we had healers in our society. They were highly revered and sought after. They kept our people safe and healthy. Women gave birth and the children lived. But some of them began to think of themselves as the salvation of the people. They started to consider themselves the elite and began to charge people more than they could afford. It became that only the wealthy could afford to pay for their services." Tristyn spoke softly. He turned to her, leaning against the railing as he continued. "Even then, sometimes it was not enough for them. They demanded more and more, and they would get it. People will pay anything to save a loved one, after all." She stared at him, holding her breath as he went on. "But not all of them. Many still used their skill to help everyone.'

'But people were angry and many considered healers to be evil, that perhaps they conspired with dark forces—your devil, if you will—for their power. Rumor had it that the healers would heal and then drink their patient's blood, as ridiculous as that sounds. But that was what people were saying. The healers were then treated with fear, and people swore that they demanded the blood of a relative as payment for their services."

"What happened?" Her question was little louder than a breath.

"Many of them went into hiding or monasteries. There they made themselves available to all, but even so, the rumors of blood payment persisted, and people began to fear them. The elite healers were driven out of their homes and killed in public. Stoned. Hung. Whatever the crowd's taste was at that time. And any who tried to stand up for them were considered to be under their evil influence and killed as well. Those in the monasteries were safe for a time, but as the panic over their dark intentions spread, even they were dragged out in the dead of night. Only a carcass was found in the morning." He sighed and put his head down, staring at the tip of his boot as he swept a leaf off the deck.

Tabitha found that she was still holding her breath. "And now?"

"The talent has been destroyed. There has not been a healer born in two generations that anyone knows of." He looked up, and his eyes were intent. "So you can imagine how such a comment would be misconstrued. In your ignorance of our abilities, you can give false hope. If Alena believes that you have healers in Chandolyn, she will do anything in her power to save our daughter. Sybille covered for you, but it is imperative that you tell Alena that there are no healers down there." He watched her, pain evident in his eyes. "I cannot lose my wife to false hope. My daughter's illness has been almost too much for us to bear."

Tabitha let his words wash over her. She now understood why he had brought her out here. She needed to understand the impact of her words. She needed to realize that no question was innocent in this world she did not know.

She inhaled deeply, lifting her eyes to his. For a moment she could see the pain there, the agony of watching his child wither away, knowing there was nothing he could do.

Before she could comment, he spoke again, his voice husky. "I wonder. If you were able to take her back with you, could your doctors help her?"

The question caught her completely off guard. Tabitha stared at him in shock. "You mean to my world?"

He nodded.

"But...but I don't know what is wrong with her. And I do not know if I will be able to return and then come back here again," Tabitha stammered.

"It would be a risk I would be willing to take," he said softly. "If she were healed but had to live elsewhere, I would rather she have a chance at a life rather than keep her here to die."

"Oh, God," Tabitha sighed. Her mind screamed at her to keep quiet, but the pain emanating from the man was almost too much to take. The words slipped out despite her intention to remain quiet. "There is a very simple reason that I asked why you just don't heal her."

Tristyn glanced up and stared at her. His eyes did not register the impact of what she was about to tell him.

Tabitha's inner voice screamed at her, *Shut up! Don't do this!*

"Last week, I found a little stray cat. He had been gravely injured. I took him in my arms. I didn't know what to do to help him. As I sat there, rocking him, my arms heated up, they began to warm up and tingle..."

Tristyn stared at her. He stood straight, and his voice was a hoarse whisper. "Go on."

"I healed him," she whispered. Here she was, telling a man she had known for thirty minutes her deep, dark secret. She looked up, almost afraid to continue. "I don't know how I did it. I don't know if I could do it again. I just know I did it once."

He stared at her in astonishment. The minutes stretched. He opened his mouth to speak and nothing came out. Another minute ticked by. Tabitha hugged herself against a chill in the warm evening air. She dropped her eyes from his shocked expression; her voice came out as a cracked whisper. "I haven't told a soul. I just can't seem to make sense of it. I have tried to ignore it. I have tried to just forget it. But I feel guilt that I could be helping so many people and be doing so much with it..." She inhaled deeply. "But how could I help some and not everyone? I don't know what to do with it. I am afraid."

"Does Luc know?"

She shook her head, fear beginning to clutch at her chest. "I've never told anyone except my cousin. I am so afraid of it. No one should have that kind of power. I can't believe I just told you."

He lifted a hand and then dropped it.

Tabitha let out a brittle laugh. "I need to go home. I am out of my element. I need to go home."

"Please. Tabitha." He gently took her hand, and for a second Tabitha received the fleeting impression of how difficult it was for him to reach out to her. He was, after all, a full-blooded Caskan and he was reaching out to a woman other than his wife. But Tabitha appreciated his touch; the warmth of his hand calmed her and helped to stop her panic.

"Tabitha. Please, will you try again?"

She laughed softly as relief flooded her. "Does that mean you are not going to sound the alarm and have me stoned?"

Surprise flickered across his face. Tabitha was pleasantly surprised to see the briefest smile light his rugged features. "No, of course not."

"Tristyn, I told you this so you would let me try to see what I can do for her. I don't understand it, and I don't know how to control it, but if you will let me try, I will promise you to do whatever I can for her."

He glanced back at the house. The lights cheerily flooded the deck with a warm orange glow. He turned back to her. "Tonight? Will you try?"

Tabitha glanced around. More people had poured into the room, and the gathering was in full swing. "Tonight? Right now?"

Tristyn nodded.

Tabitha inhaled deeply, every fiber of her being screamed out for her to say No and simply run from this place.

She released a long breath and slowly nodded.

CHAPTER TWELVE

HE GESTURED TO THE HOUSE. "FOLLOW ME. THEY ARE down in the library while Cyra rests. I will tell Luc that you are with Sybille and Alena."

Tabitha followed him through the room, trying to stay close behind him while he threaded his way through the crowd. The press of people was unbearable and Tabitha felt the weight of many stares and the open, admiring glances from many of the males in the room. More than once, a man stepped in front of her, blocking her path to Tristyn, but she would skirt them before any comment or conversation could ensue. Her heart began to pound. She was not sure where the panic was coming from, but her feet hastened toward Tristyn's tall back. The atmosphere around her seemed charged.

A hand grasped at her arm, and she spun around with a frightened cry.

"Tabitha, what is wrong?" Luc stood beside her, and she sighed heavily with relief.

"Oh, Luc, I was following Tristyn, and the room suddenly seemed to be closing in on me. I thought I was going to panic."

"I could not sense you."

"I was out talking to Tristyn. I was warm, and he took me outside to get some air. I didn't hear you."

Luc shook his head. "Tristyn was shielding for some reason. I am not sure why. Is everything all right?"

Tabitha nodded. "Yes. He was explaining why my question about healers opened such a sensitive subject."

"Ah. I assume he told you about Cyra?"

Tabitha nodded.

"Where were you going?"

"Tristyn thought I might like some time with Alena and Sybille. They are downstairs with Cyra. The room is getting a little crowded for me."

His smiled and nodded. "I can imagine. The men are trying to determine if the new woman is available. Once I introduce you around, some of that will dissipate. It will give me a chance to talk to a few more people. I will come join you in a while."

She nodded, feeling slightly guilty about hiding the truth from him, but this was not the time or place to start that conversation.

As he brought her to Tristyn, she was aware of a brief communication between them but did not concern herself with what they discussed. Tristyn nodded and then led her through the rest of the crowd to the stairs down to the library.

The atmosphere seemed to lighten as they descended the stairs, and Tabitha took a breath of relief. Tristyn looked back over his shoulder. "Are you all right?

"I am fine. Just got a little spooked back there."

He nodded. "You are an unattached female. Men can sense that, and they are wondering if you are available."

"But I am with Luc. Doesn't that count?"

"You are here as Luc's escort, but you are not Luc's. They can sense an unattached female of age," he explained. They descended the stairs and turned to the right, heading toward a heavy wooden door that she had never seen.

"How would anyone know if I was Luc's or not? I mean—that sounds ridiculous. As long as I have a date tonight, what is all the testosterone about?" Tabitha felt as though she had stepped back into the Dark Ages.

Tristyn turned to her at the door and raised an elegant eyebrow. "You are here as Luc's companion, but you are not physically his."

She shook her head. "I am not following you."

Tristyn sighed and lifted his dark eyes to the ceiling for just a moment. "I assume that Luc told you that our women rarely have more than one child, if that?"

Tabitha nodded. "Yes, like Sybille."

"Well, yes and no. That is for a different reason. Our females have great difficulty conceiving children. It is a sad fact that many do not survive childbirth, and many never regain their strength if they do survive."

"Good God. What are your infants like? Are they gargantuan or something?"

He shook his head. "No, something seems to attack women's reproductive system during the course of pregnancy and childbirth. We do not know what it is. It was not always an issue or we would have been extinct many years ago.

"Some women recover fully, and some never do. My mother bore three children but died soon after the birth of my younger brother. Luc's mother died two years after giving birth to him."

"But wait," Tabitha stopped him. "Luc's mother was human, and you said it was something that afflicts your race."

"It is also so for the human women of this world, but I understand that is not the case in your world. We do not know what the problem is. The healers were able to mediate it while they lived, but in destroying them, we doomed ourselves."

"And what does this have to do with my 'lack of attachment', or whatever you called it, and what these men can sense?" She tapped her foot, irritated with the archaic mode of thought and even more irritated with herself for being panicked by a bunch of men making her feel like a prize cow.

"Men can sense a woman who is yet unclaimed. Of course, they are looking for a potential mate to give them children. An unclaimed woman is rare. When people see one they do not recognize, a lot of interest is generated," he said, looking vaguely uncomfortable.

"What is 'unclaimed'? How do they know if I am attached or not? Does it have something to do with that gold chain that Mia showed us?" She was not sure she was going to like his answer.

He shook his head. "Not really. That has a different significance. What I am referring to is them sensing that you are…umm—"

"What? Just spit it out!"

"Untouched," he said flatly.

"Untouched? What the hell does that mean?"

He squirmed slightly and pursed his lips as though he were looking for the word. "Intact?"

Tabitha stared at him. "What *are* you talking about?"

He opened the door and waved her in. Tabitha swept past Tristyn, annoyance brimming, and then it hit her like a thunderclap. She stopped short and turned to gape at him.

"Are you serious?"

He nodded.

"How in the world does anyone sense that?" Her cheeks flamed as she realized that if that were the case, every male in the room knew she was a virgin.

He lifted one shoulder and let it drop. "I don't know. It is just something we can sense. Perhaps it is instinctive. The need to procreate is instinctive, is it not?"

Tabitha shook her head and stepped into a handsome room lined with books. Long windows faced the back of the house, dark now with the onset of night. Sybille sat on a couch with her feet curled under her facing a fireplace, a cozy fire dancing in its depths. Alena sat perched on a comfortable settee in front of the fireplace with Cyra asleep against her shoulder. A single high-back chair on the far side of the fireplace was the only other furniture in the room. She noticed Sybille and Alena staring at them with confusion.

She dropped onto the couch next to Sybille, burying her face in her hands.

Tristyn shook his head. "She asked why she was creating a stir in the men upstairs. She is unaccustomed to so many men extending themselves to try and determine her status. Luc and I thought it best to get her out of there for a moment so she could catch her breath."

Sybille nodded and smiled at Tabitha. Tabitha groaned. Alena chuckled from the settee across from her, gently rubbing her sleeping daughter's back.

"Oh, just please kill me now," Tabitha grumbled into her palms, dropping her head between her knees in humiliation.

"It is a sweet sentiment. And one uncommon in a young woman your age," Sybille said to the back of Tabitha's head.

Tabitha let out a long howl of embarrassment and heard Alena break out into a delighted laugh.

Tabitha snapped her head up. "It is not that uncommon! I just turned eighteen, for chrissakes. It is not like I did not have the opportunity—I just chose to wait! It is not like I couldn't have..." She found herself sputtering defensively. "I cannot believe this."

Alena smiled. "Tabitha, please do not read too much into this. Your world is very different. We often wed young here, as women in our world have a reduced opportunity to have a child as we grow older."

Sybille was trying to hide a grin as she patted Tabitha's shoulder. "And I am sure that Luc is pleased."

Tabitha stared at her in horror. "Oh God, you could not leave that alone, could you?"

Sybille surprised her by exploding into a delighted laugh. Her amusement was genuine and her laughter was like the peals of tiny bells. Tabitha could not help but join in at the jocularity at her expense.

The group quieted as Tristyn lowered himself to sit on the settee next to his wife. Alena continued to rub her daughter's back. Tabitha watched the shade of sadness slip back across her face.

Tristyn exchanged a glance with Tabitha, and she nodded.

"Alena." He took his wife's hand in his, his eyes intent on her face. "We have something to tell you."

Alena suddenly looked alarmed. She stared back at her husband then over to Tabitha. "What is wrong?"

Tristyn shook his head, speaking slowly to allow the impact of what he was telling her seep in. "Tabitha has shared a very special secret with me tonight. With her permission, I am going to tell you and Sybille. But in telling you this, it is imperative that you understand what we are going to tell you is not something guaranteed. It is unproven."

Alena slowly nodded, her face guarded as she stared at him. He released her gaze long enough to glance over at Sybille. "Please shield yourself from Bertòn."

Sybille looked startled but nodded, and Tristyn continued. "What I am about to tell you may not leave this room, save for with Tabitha's permission. Do you agree?"

The two women stared from him to Tabitha questioningly. It was obvious that they had no idea what had prompted such a request. But they both nodded.

Tristyn nodded to Tabitha, and she haltingly told them of her discovery of her talent and her promise to Tristyn to try and see what she could do for Cyra.

When she was finished, the two women stared at her, a myriad of emotions crossing their faces. Alena could only gape at her, fear, hope, pain, and wonder crossing her expression. She could do little more than nod as Tabitha asked for her permission to try.

There seemed to be little left to do but see what would happen. Tabitha stood, taking a deep breath as she did so. Alena glanced from Tabitha to Tristyn in indecision.

Tabitha waved for Alena to remain next to her daughter. "I've never tried this except one time on a cat. I am not even sure I know what triggers it. If you want to stay where you are with your daughter, it will not affect me. If you think it best that you are not too close to the energy that I use, step away. I have no advice. I know no better than you what will happen."

Alena glanced between her husband and Sybille. "You are the magic experts here. Can I stay, or should I move away?"

Tristyn and Sybille exchanged a glance. "I have no experience with this either. What do you think?"

Sybille considered for a moment and then stood. "Alena, you are human, and as such, you have more to lose. At the very least, Tristyn and I can shield ourselves if need be. Tristyn, you and your wife sit over here on the couch. I will sit with Cyra and Tabitha. Tabitha, should you need to draw strength, draw on mine. I give it to you freely. I can also monitor Cyra. If I detect anything amiss, I will stop you."

Tabitha waited until they had settled themselves before she knelt on the floor near the sleeping child's head. She glanced around the room, absorbing warmth from the fire that sparked and hissed in the fireplace behind her.

"Well, here goes nothing."

Tabitha closed her eyes and sat quietly for a moment, wondering how to summon the healing energy she had once harnessed. Fear and trepidation gnawed at her belly, and she wondered once again about the wisdom of telling them of this ability. That one time could have been a fluke. *Who knows how I did that?*

She inhaled deeply, trying to sweep the fear and insecurity from her mind. But doubts nagged at her, and she dropped her head, trying to quiet her mind and relax enough to focus. Sybille watched, and after a moment she reached out a hand to Tabitha.

The tiny woman leaned forward. "Do you mind if I teach you something?"

Tabitha shook her head, and Sybille smiled. She did not say a word, but Tabitha felt a warm swell of peace and tranquility wash over her. It dipped, and then another seemed to gently bathe her in a serene glow.

Sybille sent wave after gentle wave to wash over her until Tabitha was able to allow the ebb and flow of the hypnotic pattern lull her into a meditative state, her thoughts stilled and her mind relaxed. As she knelt, her body seemed a distant object, and her consciousness rested in a warm and gentle swell of peace. In and out, up and down: she let the familiar memory of listening to the waves outside her window at night form the basis of the tranquil, calm state. All else seemed to fade into the distance. Tabitha was aware of nothing other than the slow beat of her heart and the gentle pull and tug of the ocean swells that Sybille had planted in her mind.

She rested in that place for a moment, letting the days and weeks of stress and confusion ease from her body. She enjoyed the moment of stillness and allowed her mind to luxuriate in the peace.

She let her awareness extend to detect the aura of the sleeping child before her. In her mind's eye, the white outline of the little girl's form lay before her, dark colors swirling through the little girl's organs. The sickness was slowing eating away at the child's vitality and tearing at her delicate organs, stunting them and shutting them down. Her body was fighting the disease, but the cells generated to fight battled her healthy cells as well, and the battle was a losing one. The little girl's strength was waning, and her body was rejecting nutrition in its confusion.

Tabitha felt her fingers tingle. While she let her awareness assess what was happening, her arms began to heat into a searing energy. She lifted glowing hands toward the sleeping child, knowing that the heat she felt was her own, not something that could burn the child's delicate skin. Her hands slid to the child's back. As she made contact, she could feel the leap of the healing energy as it began to seep through Cyra's body. Cyra quietly released a soft noise in her sleep. Tabitha could sense rather than see Sybille reach over and gently place her fingers on the child's forehead, encouraging her to remain in sleep.

She let the warm, pulsing heat begin to seek out and heal the damage to Cyra's organs. She marveled at the ability, not knowing how it happened or how the energy seemed to know where to go. She was simply a conduit for the healing that was flowing through her hands into the body of the child. She had never had any medical training and was sorely limited in her knowledge of the body's functions and abilities, but the healing energy seemed to go where it was needed, leading Tabitha's consciousness along as it circulated through the arteries and blood vessels, seeking out the damage and repairing it. It was slow going, and Tabitha felt her energy levels drop as the healing energy seared through the child's body.

Tabitha pushed through her fatigue, willing the healing to continue. She pushed the flow through the child. As she went from one organ to another, she seemed to be gathering a pool of cells that she swept along from one clean organ to another.

Amazement coursed through her, and she felt a sense of appreciation for what she was able to do. She could not let herself stop. Her fingers trembled on the child's skin, but she ignored them, digging deeper and deeper within herself to find the strength to continue. She started to feel a giddy sense of euphoria; she let the gentle tingling in her mind lull her into a warm state of being. The pleasure she felt in being able to heal the child overtook her as her senses swept the girl's body for any remaining illness. The little girl's aura had changed from a white husk full of dark, swirling illness to a glowing spiral of pastel colors; no trace of the dark browns and blacks remained save for the flow of fluid dripping out of the little girl's nose, draining the disease that had been attacking her. Sybille reached over to swab the nasal fluid from the little girl's lip.

Tabitha checked one final time. All traces of the illness were gone. A pleasant buzz in her brain seemed to grow louder, and Tabitha noticed that the child's pastel aura was the only color she could see. Darkness seemed to be closing in on her from the edges of her consciousness. The pleasant euphoria was evaporating into a slow, steady, spinning void.

Tabitha dropped her hands. The glowing heat left them as she fell forward with a thud, her hands catching her before she tumbled onto her face. She gasped in desperation, suddenly unable to pull enough air into her lungs. Her heart thudded and her head swam. She felt as though she were slipping deeper and deeper inside herself, unable to control or feel her extremities. She was vaguely aware of people calling out to her, but she retreated from them, fearing any touch would make her fall apart. Her limbs were cold. As she fought the grayness that was engulfing her, she could see a tunnel of light that seemed to be slowly growing smaller, replaced by a red glow that was working its way across her field of vision. Her breathing was labored, and a distant part of her mind was surprised that her breath seemed to whistle past her teeth. She backed away from the people crowding her and cowered, snapping at them to stay back.

Her head pounded. A voice seemed to be yelling, but she could not focus on it. She let her head drop back and began to collapse to the floor. Someone tried to come close to her, and she snarled, but it came out as a dull hiss. Her body seemed to be screaming out, and she thought that she could die of thirst that very moment. She had never known such a powerful dryness, but she did not have the strength or the energy to ask for a drink of water. She wet her lips with her parched tongue, but her mouth was so dry that it did little good, and she cut her tongue on her teeth.

As the pounding continued, she tried to lie down and crawl into the blackness. The pounding stopped suddenly. As her eyes began to lose that last vestige of light, she realized that the pounding had been in the room and not in her head. She suddenly felt her body being lifted. She cried out as her stomach lurched, and she fought back the nausea. She cringed; the touch of the hands and arms that held her seared her delicate skin. Waves of need crashed through her. She tried to lift her head but did not have the strength.

She heard voices all around her. One seemed to be right next to her. With an effort, she recognized the person holding her. Her name seemed to echo from a great distance and then a curse followed in an angry, accusatory tone. She concentrated on the low rumbling, trying to remember why it was important not to slip into sleep. But remaining awake was so much effort, and she was so very tired.

Another sound began to intrude on her consciousness. She could just make out the beating of a heart, low and strong. She became fixated on that sound. The low, dull thuds seemed to fill her head and overtake every thought. She could barely think of anything except that sound, which filled her with a gnawing hunger. Her mouth was parched, and the thirst was driving her mad. Red filled her vision. Her tongue tried once again to dampen her parched lips, but again her teeth seemed to be razor sharp. She felt tiny cuts on her tongue. The pulsing heartbeat drummed in her mind. Her breath came in violent gasps, and she felt as though she would die if she did not have a drink of something, anything.

Tabitha, listen to me…Stay with me, please. Tabitha?

Confusion swept through her as she tried to focus. Her mind could not wrap itself around what he was asking her, and his voice seemed to slip away into oblivion, replaced by that strong thud, that steady, strong thud. She could not focus on anything but that sound and her own thirst.

Take from me what you need.

She could not understand, but she felt her head being supported by a strong hand. Suddenly, the strong thudding filled her ears. Her mouth was pressed against it, and she could feel the beat against her lips. As she bit with a sense of urgency, she almost cried out. Then she felt a warm gush of fluid in her mouth. The relief was all consuming. For a brief few moments, all she could do was quench her scorching thirst. The fierce need began to slowly release her, and Tabitha felt the darkness recede and her strength slowly flow back.

CHAPTER THIRTEEN

HER HEART STOPPED HAMMERING, AND HER BODY began to relax. Tabitha continued to quench her thirst, letting the salty fluid douse the inferno that had been blazing within her. The realization that her mouth was fastened on someone's throat began to dawn on her. Jerking back, she cried out in horror, tearing her teeth from skin. She let out a plaintive cry as she saw the bloody gash in Luc's throat. She could do little more than stare in revulsion. She slowly lifted a finger to her own lips, feeling a bead of blood at the edge of her mouth. She fought the urge to lick it away. She touched the twin fangs that were her incisors.

She wailed and tried to escape Luc's arms, unwilling to look into his face and see the expression she feared would be there. He tightened his grip, pulling her closer and drawing her against his chest, holding her in his arms while she panicked.

Her energy gave out quickly and she lay panting in his arms, her head buried against his shoulder. He was sitting on the floor facing the fireplace, and she was cradled in his arms. Once she realized that he was not releasing her, she clung to him, trying to find warmth or comfort for her chilled body. She sobbed into his shoulder. She could not seem to hold back the flow of tears.

When her tears began to dwindle and she started to calm down, her breath was no more than a shaky whimper. She did not want to let go of him and face whatever expression would be in his eyes.

Are you all right now? His voice was the same soft timbre, and she could have wept at his simple question.

How can you ask me that after what I have done?

What you have done is saved a little girl's life.

His head bowed to rest against hers, and his arms tightened around her. Tabitha drew her legs up and curled in the circle of his arms. She sniffed and tried to claim the strength to look up at him, but all she wanted was to stay in his arms.

He held her. No other thoughts were exchanged, and she slowly felt her energy building.

What am I? she whispered to him.

A healer, he answered.

I am a horror.

There is apparently a price to pay for the energy you expend. I would pay it again to save Cyra.

Please don't.

Don't what? Remind you that for the small cost of your dignity, you have saved her life?

It is not that simple.

It is. If you remember that, you will begin to forgive yourself.

How could you let me do that to you?

She felt his breath against the side of her face as he exhaled a low sigh. *You would not have done the same for me had our positions been switched?*

She slowly lifted her face and gazed into the blue ones that smiled tenderly down at her. He knew what to say to cut through all the guilt. As she lay in his arms, feeling the warm beat of his heart through his shirt, she knew she would pay any price if he were in need.

She rested, letting him seep into her. His warmth and presence seemed to penetrate into her core. She glanced down at the twin holes she had torn in his throat; two slim rivulets of blood seeped from them. She lifted a finger and felt a light tingle as she pressed it against his throat. Her finger glowed momentarily, and she felt the slightest twinge of energy as she healed the wounds. When she withdrew her finger from the wound, she saw it was healed, noting with a stab of guilt that two pinhole scars remained.

I am sorry, she whispered.

He seemed amused. *You need not apologize.*

I can't take back what I have done to you.

Well, then you had better make it up to me. His smile turned warm, and his eyes dropped to her lips. He lowered his mouth to hers, and Tabitha reveled in the feel of his lips. When he drew back, she let out a whimper of disappointment.

We are not alone.

In fear, she realized for the first time that Sybille, Tristyn, and Alena were still in the room and had no doubt witnessed her feral survival behavior.

Oh my God. Please, do I have to face them?

"Is she okay?" Alena's voice shook.

Tabitha tightened her grip on Luc, pressing her face into his chest once again. With a deep breath, she released him and sat up, peering over his shoulder at the three people clustered behind them. Alena was just a few feet behind Luc, her hands shaking and her face pale. Tristyn squatted behind her, his dark eyes intent and watchful. Sybille perched on the edge of the settee, seemingly at ease, but Tabitha could feel the tension coursing through the woman, who was ready to leap should there be further signs of danger.

"I am fine. Just a little shaky," Tabitha admitted.

All three of them released sighs and relaxed their positions.

"Oh, Tabitha, thank the stars you are all right! We were so worried!" Alena exclaimed, now leaning against Tristyn, who had lowered himself to the floor behind her.

Sybille reached for Luc's shoulder and peered around at the two of them, inspecting their faces for any sign of trouble. Luc smiled and lifted his chin to her in a simple nod that all was well.

Sybille nodded. "You gave us quite a scare."

Tabitha nodded shakily. "I scared myself. I am not even sure what happened. Everything seemed to be going fine, and then suddenly it was like I had been standing on a paper floor that suddenly gave way, and then the floor below it gave way, and I could not seem to find my way back."

Luc shifted her in his arms and turned so they were leaning against a chair behind him. Tabitha tried to push herself up to peer onto the settee to see if Cyra was all right, but her shaking arms would not support her for long enough. She dropped back into Luc's arms.

"How is Cyra?"

Alena's face brightened, and Tabitha thought at that moment that she had never seen a more beautiful and joyous expression. "She seems to be sleeping comfortably. Her breathing isn't labored, and she seems quite relaxed. Even if you were not able to cure her, the fact that she is sleeping without pain is a blessing to us."

Tabitha bowed her head, emotion overtaking her. She paused for a moment to gather herself. "I believe she is cured. When I started, I could see the colors of the illness and where it was attacking her. Before I moved away from her, I could find no trace of it. She will probably need a while to regain her full strength, but I think she is going to be just fine."

Alena bowed her head. Tabitha heard a soft sob when Alena quietly cried out her relief. Tristyn gently took his wife in his arms. He looked at Tabitha, and, for a moment, the wave of gratitude that poured from him humbled her.

He simply said, "We can never repay you for what you have done for us. I will never forget the toll it took on you. We are forever in your debt."

Alena nodded and lifted her teary face. She opened her mouth to speak, but words would not come. Tabitha reached out and squeezed her hand. No words were necessary; she could see the gratitude and relief on her face.

Sybille leaned over and, with a smile, gently squeezed Tabitha's shoulder. "You have done a great thing. You have given us back our little Cyra. We can never thank you enough. We recognize the great personal cost you expended for her."

Tabitha leaned back against Luc, enjoying the feel of his arms about her as her head rested against his chest. She let out a wry laugh. "Well, maybe you can tell me what happened. Up to the point where Sybille wiped Cyra's nose, I felt like all was going well. After that, everything blurred."

"Of course. Let's get something to warm you."

Alena laughed low, gesturing to Luc's embrace. "Looks like she's already got that."

Sybille chuckled as she stoked the fire, tossing another log onto it, letting the flames lick the fuel. She reached into the fireplace and drew out a glass pot that swung from an iron hook over the flames. She grabbed two mugs off the shelf and filled them. She handed them to Luc and Tabitha. Tabitha reluctantly sat up. Luc leaned back against the chair, Tabitha still curled on his lap, and took the offered mug. His free hand rested on her hip, and Tabitha was all too aware of his gentle touch.

Sybille filled mugs for the rest of them and sat back on the settee, gently sweeping a warm hand along the sleeping child's back.

Tabitha sighed as the drink sent warmth flowing throughout her belly. As she took a second sip, it occurred to her that her stomach was roiling. The memory of what she had ingested threatened to launch its contents from her. She set her mug down, her hand pressed to her mouth. As she tried to rise and race from the room, Luc grabbed her, tugging her back to sit with him. Her eyes were wide with panic as her stomach tried to eject its contents.

He held her arms, and Sybille leaped toward her, placing gentle hands on either side of Tabitha's face. She felt Sybille's consciousness gently ease the raging storm in her belly, and she gasped in relief as her body began to relax once again. Sybille stayed with her until she was sure that the urge had subsided. Tabitha exhaled a long breath.

"I am not sure I will be able to come to grips with this."

Sybille nodded. "Of course you will. You must. It is like any other ability that we possess. Once it has been unleashed, there is little you can do to harness it. You must learn to use it."

Tabitha shook her head. "Not for that price I won't, thank you very much."

Luc lifted his hand to gently rub the small of her back. "You must remember what you gave tonight, the gift of a child's life."

Tabitha sipped at her drink, letting the fluid warm her once again. She wished that she and Luc were alone and all she had to do was curl up in his arms and let her tired eyes close.

Sybille turned to Tabitha. "What did it feel like? Will you tell us?"

Tabitha nodded. "It was as though the energy were flowing through me. I did not know how to direct it or how to heal her; it just flowed through me and began to go where it was needed. I was along with it, watching and expending my own energy to continue it, but I did not seem to be directing it. We worked together when I understood what it was doing. Then I was able to direct it. And I knew that I could have stopped it had I wanted to." She laughed a brittle laugh. "As I was healing Cyra, I felt as though I was doing something right. I felt so good to be able to do this for someone that I became euphoric. I kept throwing more and more energy to keep going, and I didn't want to stop until I was done and she was clean of the mass that I could see attacking her. Now I realize that part of that euphoria may have been coming from my own depleted energy."

Alena nodded. "Perhaps this was something that should have been done in small stages. When you used it that other time, did you have the same reaction?"

Tabitha glanced at her, and Alena bared her teeth to illustrate what she was referring to.

Tabitha laughed weakly, clutching at her stomach. "Don't make me laugh, it hurts. Yes, I had the fangs, but my need did not elevate to that degree."

Luc put his head back against the chair, his eyes on her. "Well, this certainly answers the question about those old legends about the healers."

For the first time, Tabitha noticed that he was pale, and she reached a hand to his face, concern etched in her expression. He shook his head to her silent question but grasped her hand, kissing her palm.

Tristyn interrupted the moment. "It seems that the old legend about healers demanding blood payment was more a physical necessity than a macabre tale."

Sybille watched Tabitha and Luc, concern etched across her brow. "Perhaps if you limit the energy, you might possibly forestall that necessity."

Tabitha tore her eyes away from Luc's intense blue ones and turned back to the others. "I am not sure, but I would prefer to try that instead of tearing out someone's throat!"

Luc grinned, gently rubbing the scars on his neck. “I don’t know. It wasn’t all that unpleasant.”

Alena snorted, rolling her eyes. She glanced at her sleeping daughter, and once again a glow of joy overtook her face. Tabitha knew that she had done the right thing. Anytime she ever doubted, she would remember Alena’s expression.

“So to get back to the evening’s events...” Sybille took the reins of the conversation, shooting her stepson a reprimanding glance. “Once you began to heal Cyra, you seemed to be in a trance. And your hands glowed bright, and you barely moved. You barely seemed to be breathing. Cyra began to wake, and I sent her back to sleep. Were you aware of that?”

Tabitha nodded. “Yes, but that was the last thing I remember until I stopped.”

Sybille continued. “Well, once you completed, your hands stopped glowing and you fell to the side. When you rose, you looked as though you had no awareness of where you were or anything around you.”

Tristyn took up the story. “Alena and Sybille tried to approach you, but you were defensive. You backed up and would not let anyone near. I called for Luc at that point. He was beginning to pound on the door. I had forgotten that I had set a shield around the room; I had not wanted anyone to inadvertently come in while you were healing Cyra. He had been trying to reach out to you and to me and could not get through.” Tristyn shot Luc a glance, a small smile playing around his mouth. “He was trying to break down the door with his hands. He did a fair job of tearing a hole in my shield as well.”

Luc snorted. "I did better than that. Had you been better prepared, I would not have been able to get through."

Tristyn ignored him except for a derisive glance. He continued. "He broke the door open and tore through my shield. If I am not mistaken, his concern for you slightly outweighed his concern for my safety."

Tabitha glanced over and noticed for the first time that even though the door was closed, the handle hung off and part of one side had a long crack. It hung slightly off kilter. She glanced at Luc. He smiled with a slight apologetic lift of his mouth.

"I'm flattered," she said softly. To the rest of the room, she said, "That must have been the pounding I heard. I kept hearing a pounding and thought it was in my head."

"No, it was this one." Sybille shook her head, gesturing toward Luc. "I think I needn't tell you that Bertòn knows something happened. After Luc broke through and saw the state you were in, he asked his father to protect us from any interruption. We will have to tell him what has happened."

Tabitha nodded. "I do not expect you to keep this from him."

As if on cue, the door swung open and Bertòn strode into the room. His face was as impassive as ever, but Tabitha could sense the anger bristling from him. He stopped in the doorway, taking in both the damage to the door and the small knot of people clustered on the floor.

"We have a houseful of guests." His voice was curt. He looked at Tabitha and Luc sitting together on the floor, his hand negligently draped on her hip. Unease seemed to radiate from him. Tabitha did not need any psychic energy to recognize parental displeasure over their proximity. She began to self-consciously move away, but Luc's fingers tightened ever so slightly, stilling her. She glanced from Bertòn to him and saw that Luc's eyes were intent on his father, his jaw clenched. Anger seemed to snap from his eyes.

Alena opened her mouth to speak, an apologetic expression on her face, but Sybille shook her head and then nodded toward Luc and Bertòn.

Tristyn leaned back, his face impassive, obviously unconcerned about the silent argument raging between the two men. He looked at Sybille. "Can we impose on you? I would prefer to spend the night here rather than move Cyra tonight. I would like to let her sleep."

"Of course. I will make up a bed for you here. Our guest rooms are occupied, but you will be comfortable here," Sybille said, pleased to have them staying.

"That is not necessary, Sybille. They can stay in my room. I will not leave Tabitha tonight," Luc said, his eyes snapping away from his father dismissively. Bertòn turned on his heel and left the room, slamming the door behind him.

Tabitha and Sybille both turned to look at him in shock.

I think we had better speak about this before you go ahead and volunteer to sleep with me.

I will not touch you. I just do not want to leave you alone.

But, Luc. I mean, I have only known you for a few days…

Tabitha, I do not want to leave you alone. You needn't share your bed with me, but I will not leave you alone.

Is this to spite your father?

Sybille broke in on their silent conversation. "Luc, did you tell him what transpired?"

Luc shook his head and then stood and stretched. "No, he was not in the mood to listen. He is certain that we are all down here involved in some human drama. When he is ready to listen, I will explain what happened."

Sybille shook her head as she gathered the mugs. "Stubborn fools, the pair of you."

Luc grinned at her, extending a hand to Tabitha. "You would not have us any other way. It makes my departures back to school easier, doesn't it?"

Sybille laughed briefly and responded in a language Tabitha did not recognize. Tristyn chuckled as he assisted Alena to her feet.

Tristyn slid his arms under his sleeping daughter and lifted her up. She released a soft sigh, and her eyes fluttered before she fell back to sleep, her head nuzzled against her father's shoulder. Tabitha straightened her blouse and skirt, running her fingers through her hair.

Luc nodded to the door and led Tabitha, Tristyn, and Alena up the back stairs. Sybille left them to join the remaining guests in the large central room. Luc led Tabitha to her room and left her there with a promise to join her. He returned after leaving Tristyn and Alena in his room, a handful of clothes in his hands. He draped some over the chair and turned to find Tabitha in the middle of the room, looking at him hesitantly.

He grinned at her and strolled to where she stood, indecision dancing along her raw nerves.

"Did you think I would try to take advantage of your physical weakness tonight?"

"I am not sure what to think."

He smiled down at her as he took her in his arms, holding her gently in the darkened room. "Get some sleep. I will leave you be. I just do not want you to be alone tonight."

She shook her head and stepped back from him. "I need to get out of these clothes and wash." She headed for the washroom. "You don't have to stay with me. I will be fine."

He nodded. "Get some rest. I will be back later. I should go see how my father is faring with our customers."

She stopped at the doorway, turning back to him. "Was he terribly angry?"

Luc hesitated at the door and then turned back. "My father's anger was misdirected. He could not understand what would have possessed me to try and tear the door to his library off its hinges while he had a houseful of customers. When he knows the truth, this will all be moot."

"I am concerned about what he thinks. I like your father and do not want him thinking badly of me." She dropped her gaze, chewing on a cheek before commenting. "He is concerned about your feelings for me, isn't he?"

Luc did not respond immediately. The moments ticked by before he told her, "My father fell in love with a human woman many years ago. They married, and she died from a fever when I was very young. Apparently she had never quite recovered from my birth. I don't think he has ever forgiven me for that. And I think he sees some of her in you—your independence, your courage, and your stubborn determination to come here alone to find your mother. He respects you a lot for your bravery. I think you remind him of her."

Tabitha did not answer, and he quietly left and closed the door.

I am sure he is afraid that you will break my heart when you leave, as she broke his.

CHAPTER FOURTEEN

TABITHA WOKE TO AN EMPTY ROOM. SHE GLANCED around and saw no trace of Luc. On the bed, the other pillow was untouched. If he had returned to her room, he had not climbed into bed with her. She had a vague memory of his wolf curled up on the floor, so he must have been in here for Cirrus to have stayed. She felt a pang of loneliness. As much as it had horrified her that he had offered his room to Tristyn and Alena and suggested he and she spend the night together, it had also sent a warm thrill through her body. The thought of his long, muscular body stretched out beside her...Well, she was not sure she could have kept her promise to keep this relationship as close to a friendship as possible.

I am sure he is afraid that you will break my heart when you leave, as she broke his.

Luc's words echoed in her head. She lay back, thinking of them. For the first time in her life, she felt as though someone cared for her, just for her, as she was, with no pretense and no qualms. She had never had a bond like this with anyone in her life. Callie was the closest person to her, and even so she found herself keeping secrets from her cousin. She had not had that relationship with her mother, although she had wanted one. Her mother had kept her and everyone else in her life at arm's length.

Tabitha felt it ironic that the one thing she had disliked the most about her mother was the one thing she had learned the best from her: the talent for keeping people at a distance.

Except for Luc.

He had broken down every barrier, torn down every bit of resistance, and she knew that if she did not get on with her search and find her mother soon, she would be helplessly in love with him.

She recalled the last few months with Greg. They had been going out for two years, but she had never felt for him what she felt for Luc. For two years, Greg had cajoled and begged and waited for her to give herself to him, and she had held him at bay. She had told him she was not ready. She had asked him to wait and he had, mostly patiently, sometimes not so much, but he had waited, giving her the space she needed.

Now she was in a new world, and she was thinking of Luc in a way she had never done with Greg. She wanted to give herself to him—not just the intimacy of intercourse but the intimacy of letting him in figuratively as well as emotionally. She had thought she loved Greg, but she would never allow him close. And he had known it.

After three or four days into a new world, she was already considering Luc in a way she had resisted with Greg.

After a shower, Tabitha dressed in her jeans and tank top, zipping her sweatshirt over her familiar clothes, which Sybille had cleaned for her. She enjoyed being back in own clothes. She slipped her hair into a damp knot and made her way downstairs. She heard voices in the kitchen and walked in that direction. The heavy doors were propped open. Tabitha could see the sunlight streaming in as she followed her nose toward the warm scents of baking.

She entered the kitchen, where a crowd was gathered, some sitting and others milling about with steaming mugs in their hands. Sybille greeted her warmly as she placed baskets of baked goods out on the long table and kitchen island. Baskets of fruit were piled high, and small tables with long cloths on them held appealing displays of Sybille's wares.

Alena was leaning against the end of the island, holding a steaming mug in her hand as she watched over Cyra, who was sitting with a rather impressive mound of fruit and muffins on the plate in front of her,

"Well, good morning!" Alena grinned. "Can I start you out with a cup of javé?

Before Tabitha could respond, Alena grabbed a deep mug and walked over to the fireplace, where steaming glass pots filled with different dark brews were bubbling. Tabitha had become fond of one of Sybille's dark, nutty hot drinks. She had learned that coffee beans were not quite the same as in her world. Their dark drink of choice was a mixture of leaves and a cacao bean that made a dark, hot beverage like coffee but not as bitter. Sybille blended the mixtures with various flavors and brewed them in glass pots over the fire. Tabitha was seriously considering trying to smuggle some back with her when she went. Wendy, the owner of the café she worked for, would flip over it.

The thought suddenly brought Tabitha up. She had not considered for more than a brief moment what was happening back at home. She had selfishly assumed that Trude would cover for her. But she had left quite a few people in the dark, and those people depended on her.

"What has made you look so serious?" Alena asked as she placed the steaming mug in front of her.

"I left home very suddenly. I left a lot of people who depend on me without so much as a word. Not to mention that my cousin, Callie, must be worried sick."

Alena opened her mouth to respond when a shocked voice cried out behind her. "Alena? What have you done with Cyra? Who is this child devouring the muffins?"

Alena lifted a brow as she turned to give her best performance. Peri watched Cyra with amazement as Cyra giggled at her aunt, popping another berry into her mouth.

Tabitha took her mug and drifted over to Sybille. "Have you seen Luc this morning?"

Sybille nodded. "Yes, he was up early and down at the barn with Bertòn. I take it you did not see him this morning?"

"No, I woke and he was gone."

"Ah," Sybille said, but her voice had a tinge to it.

"What?"

Sybille shrugged and her eyes held a twinkle as she leaned in to Tabitha, whispering, "I see you are as you were yesterday morning."

Tabitha glanced down, wondering if the woman meant her clothes, or had she done her hair as she worn it at home? When it struck her what Sybille was talking about, she felt color rise to her face. "Will you stop? I don't even think he spent the night in my room!"

Sybille giggled and opened her mouth to respond, but Tabitha shook a finger at her. "Behave yourself!"

Alena joined them. "What did I miss?"

"Nothing!" Tabitha snapped.

"I noticed that Tabitha seems to have had a good night's sleep," Sybille commented innocently as she hefted another basket of muffins.

"Well, I am sure you were quite tired last night after your ordeal." Alena was nonchalant as she slipped another handful of berries in front of Cyra.

Tabitha groaned. "Can we please stop making my 'condition' a subject of our discussions!"

"Why?" Alena seemed genuinely perplexed.

"Because it's not anyone's business but mine! Can we please talk about something else?" Tabitha snapped. She grabbed a muffin from the basket and began to tear it apart.

"Well, Luc, Bertòn, and Tristyn will all be quite occupied down at the horse auction today. Why don't we head into town? I can show you around, and we can get an idea if anyone has seen your mother. There will be plenty of people there, and it will give you a chance to blend in."

Tabitha pursed her lips. "Even in my apparently unnatural state."

"Sure! People will just assume you are just not interested in men!" Alena announced cheerily as she gathered her daughter.

Tabitha groaned and shook her head. "Great. Whatever. Let's go."

Alena ran upstairs to collect a forgotten item and Tabitha waited in the front foyer, enjoying the morning sun pouring in through the back doors and down from the little atrium at the top of the house. The wood glistened after a fresh cleaning. Tabitha had to wonder how every sign of the party last night had been quietly cleaned up before the morning rush of the horse auction. She wandered around the room, glancing at curios, when the door from the kitchen swung wide behind her. Heavy steps swept into the foyer. She turned quickly, hoping that Luc had been able to break away to say a quick hello, but it was Bertón's dark head that rounded the corner.

"Tabitha, I had hoped to catch you. May we speak?" His deep voice sent a shiver through her when she remembered his anger the night before.

She shrugged and glanced up the stairs, hoping Alena would save her, but Bertòn was already indicating that she should follow him down toward the library.

Bertòn stopped at the library door and stood aside to allow her to enter first. She felt a knot in her belly as the door closed behind him. The jangle of the door hardware slipping free of the latch was an unpleasant reminder that he had been quite angry with them last night.

"Luc told me about last night," he began. "I owe you an apology."

Tabitha nodded, not sure how to respond other than mumbling, "Thanks."

"I don't think I have to tell you how much what you did means to us as a family. The others do not know what has happened, but some noticed the commotion here last night. I am not sure if they have come to any conclusions. We will all keep your talent closely guarded. It is not the time for such an ability to be made public knowledge. We must all consider how to address the gravity of what you can do." He walked over to lower himself into the chair in front of the cold fireplace.

"You have a very special gift. As the leader of the people in this community, I need to know how to react to this. Would you be willing to tell me about the first time you discovered this talent and your subsequent experience?"

Tabitha nodded and, at his invitation, lowered herself onto the settee opposite him, sitting upright and alert on the edge. She spoke slowly of healing the cat and her fear and panic. She told him she had reached out to Luc that morning but had been too afraid to tell him what she had done. She recounted the events of the night before, her face flushing with color as she told him of coming to her senses with her teeth plunged into his son's throat.

He listened quietly, sipping on his javé as he stared off into the distance. Tabitha became silent, swallowing nervously, not sure what reaction to anticipate. Luc's father made her anxious. She waited for him to respond, wondering if he would pass judgment on her behavior after she'd healed Cyra.

He glanced back, his dark eyes revealing little emotion. Tabitha could detect the concern and unease that he emanated. "I don't have to tell you that you took a risk doing what you did. I will chalk up your inexperience to your lack of training."

She felt her ire rise at his admonishment, but she swallowed the resentment. He was right, after all. She had put others, as well as the child, at risk by trying to use a power that she had little knowledge of and even less training in. Her own doubts welled up as she tried to imagine what could have happened as a result of her ignorant use of the magic at her disposal. She tried to respond, but the bubble in her throat choked down her words. She felt tears threaten to spill.

"Tabitha, I think you understand the consequences of what you did. Don't mistake my rebuke for any lack of appreciation. The power you wield is quite extensive. The healing ability has been gone from our world for generations. But I urge you to use your abilities with caution until such time when you can better control them." His voice was direct, and Tabitha recognized the authority of a trainer in his words. She lifted her chin, swallowing back the humiliation of the rebuke, and nodded. She would heed his advice. He was a full-blooded Caskan, trained from birth, a trainer of his people. She would not let her pride keep her from listening to what he had to say.

He nodded, and a hint of a smile played at the corner of his lips. "Good."

As he watched her, his look turned more calculating, and she had to fight the urge to fidget. Finally he continued. "What you have is a very special gift. We are a dying race due to our stupidity and our myopic attitude. We have damned ourselves. Our numbers dwindle, and we are running out of options to save ourselves. I am regional governor for Calais. Marcus, my brother is the provincial leader for all the states within St. Mikel. We meet regularly, all of us, to discuss the war breaking out with the Plain tribes and to discuss options for our race. Some ideas are good, some not so good."

Bertòn shook his head with a sad smile, "Imagine as we have discussed our future and how to save our people that my son has been linked to a woman from another world that happens to be a healer. It is a strange irony to find the last healer of our people and she lives in another world."

"Will you tell the others?" Her voice was a hoarse croak.

"Perhaps. You see, this is not something that affects only you and my son, or even just my family. I am sure that Luc told you that we have not had a healer in many generations. We bear fewer children, and our women often do not survive childbirth. Whatever is infecting our race seems to be gaining potency." He sighed, observing her with hooded eyes. "You understand that you are the only healer we know of in generations."

She nodded as a knot of anxiety began to tighten in her belly.

"We cannot afford to lose the healing line again. Our very survival may depend on the resurrection of your talent."

"When I find my mother, I will be returning home," she replied softly.

"Yes."

"I am sorry, but one person cannot be responsible for saving an entire race." She felt her trepidation shake her voice, and she cleared her throat, hoping for more strength. "I wish I could do more, but I have my own life in another world, and I have to...well, I have to get back to that."

He nodded. "I am not implying we would hold you against your will. Nor am I suggesting you forsake your life for the betterment of our people. This is, after all, not your world. But I will give you some advice and a word of caution: shield yourself well, and do not allow any others to know of this talent. There are those here who would benefit greatly from the use of a healer. My brother and I would never imprison you for our benefit, but there are many who would."

She started to rise but he waved her down. "I have more to tell you. There is a man asking for you down in the village."

"Asking for me?" She was startled. "Are you sure?"

"Yes, by name. He carries a likeness of you with him."

She frowned. "What? A likeness? You mean like a picture?"

"Yes, a paper with your likeness, much like to ones we see in your newspapers."

"Who would be looking for me, and where would he have gotten a picture of me?"

Bertòn slowly stood and extended a hand toward the door. "I would suggest you remain here instead of going into the village until we know who he is and who has sent him."

"Could he be from my mother?"

"I do not know, but I think we need to be safe." He followed her from the room.

She nodded, disappointed about curbing her walk with Alena but nervous at the thought that someone knew she was here and was looking for her.

"I suggest you remain in your room for the time being, away from prying eyes in the house. Our visitors come in for refreshments, and I would hate to have anyone inadvertently see you. I will ask Alena to check around to learn who it is who seeks you." He stilled her with a hand as she started to climb the stairs to the foyer. "Keep yourself shielded, and do not use your link with Luc. You must remain silent until we know if this is a friend or foe."

"Who would be an enemy? I don't know anyone here." Tabitha was irritated about having to hide away in a world where no one knew she even existed.

"You have forgotten that, by your own admission, your mother's sanity was less than stable upon her return to your land. Someone drove her mad, and that someone undoubtedly knows she left with a child." His words sounded so ominous that Tabitha had to check herself from panicking.

"But that was eighteen years ago. How would that someone even know I was here?" she retorted.

"And yet there is a man carrying your likeness asking about you by name," he snapped. "Your mother has disappeared into a world that you do not know. I would imagine a little caution would not be out of line."

Tabitha nodded and turned to head to her room. She could hear his footfalls heading toward the kitchen, and she swallowed her resentment. She had come here on her own, and she was capable of handling herself. Why was she suddenly being sent away like a child who had misbehaved?

She slipped up the stairs, avoiding the people congregating in the large central room. She could feel the flutter of senses as people reached inquiring touches of curiosity toward her, and she felt her anger soar.

Can't these people stop? She was no better off than at home. Instead of gaping stares and pointed fingers, she was faced with constant threads of gentle touches against her mind, wondering who she was. As she took the steps two at a time, she tried to pull herself further into her mind. She raced to her room, slammed the door behind her and slid down to the floor.

CHAPTER FIFTEEN

In a single day, so much had changed. Bertòn was right; she was out of her element. Untrained, she moved among people who had similar abilities and knew how to use them. Who was she kidding? She was no more a part of this world than she was part of her own. Frustration brimmed, and tears spilled down her face. All she wanted was answers; she had wanted to know where her mother had been and how she had given such power to her child. Here she was, in a strange world, among people with amazing power, and she could not even begin to understand how they did what they did, how they controlled themselves, and what they could sense. They all seemed to be able to sense things about her in a way that was unnerving. She was not able to do the same. How would she manage this place if she could not understand the rules?

A tap on the door startled her, and she wiped at her tears. She thought it best if she remained shielded, pretending not to be here. Maybe they would just go away.

"Tabitha?" Alena's voice was soft through the door.

"Oh, shit," she groaned to herself. "Can't you people leave me alone for a second to wallow, for chrissakes?"

"Open the door."

"Alena, can you give me a minute, please? I just need, just need..." she stammered. "Aw, hell, c'mon in." She stood and flung the door open.

Alena looked surprised. Tabitha stood there, arms extended, at the suddenly open door.

"Just come in, but please let me close the door and try and preserve what little dignity I have left," Tabitha snapped.

Alena entered the room, the polish slightly slipping from her cheery demeanor as she eyed Tabitha critically. "Well, with that kind of invitation..."

Tabitha slammed the door behind her. "Don't you start too. I just needed a few minutes away from everyone."

Alena nodded. "You look terrible."

"Thanks," Tabitha mumbled. She turned on her heel and walked into the washroom to splash water on her face.

"Tell me what happened," Alena said from behind her as she leaned against the doorframe.

"Why? Don't you know? I thought everyone in this place knew everything that everyone else was thinking. Didn't Tristyn send you some message to go and try to sooth the crazy person from the other world and keep her from leaping out the window?" Tabitha grumbled from behind her hands as she leaned over the sink, water dripping from her face.

"Nope. Tristyn and I are not linked."

Tabitha glanced up in surprise, her hands half way to her face. The cupped water slowly dribbled back into the sink.

Alena lifted a brow. "I am human, after all. Caskans cannot have links with humans."

Tabitha nodded, placing her hands on the sink. She stared into the water swirling into the drain. "I don't know what I am doing. I don't understand this world."

"Did you expect to?"

Tabitha grabbed a towel; she dried her face and turned, leaning against the sink to face the strawberry-blond woman before her. "I thought that here, I would be where people understood me. I thought that if I found people who shared my power, I would be among people like me and...God, it is so hard! I don't get this! I don't understand this whole thing about what they can sense and what they can shield. Am I shielded, am I not? I have no idea! I can't tell. I just don't get it!"

Alena laughed as Tabitha ranted. "So you come from a world where no one has your ability and you have to hide yourself. And you come here, and they all have it, but since you have always hidden it, you are not in their league. I imagine you would be frustrated."

Tabitha put the towel back and followed Alena into the bedroom. Alena settled herself in the chair and gestured elegantly toward the bed. Tabitha threw herself onto it, not even wanting to acknowledge that what Alena had said was more or less right.

"You make it sound petty."

"It is petty," Alena responded. "To someone who has no such ability. You think *you* are outnumbered—try marrying into them, being the only one without any ability. Talk about feeling inferior."

Tabitha swallowed her resentment and looked at the young woman in bewilderment. "How do you stand it? How do you live among people who can do so much when you are so...*normal*?"

"To them, I am not normal. To them, I am the enigma. I cannot sense other people like the Caskans, so my emotions are evident on my face and in my voice and inflection. I can't just sense them, so I ask. A lot. And it startles them. They cannot predict what I am going to do next, and they don't know what to make of it." Alena grinned. She leaned forward, her eyes shrewd. "If you are at a disadvantage, turn it into your advantage. Don't ever let people think they have the upper hand. I control my surroundings. I may not have their talent, but I can most certainly keep them off kilter."

"Can't they read you?"

"They think they can, but, you see, we have an advantage. We lie. We exaggerate. We cry when we want to laugh, we laugh when we want to cry—we can control what we convey, and they cannot. Their faces remain impassive; their smiles are infrequent because their senses are pouring out of them to one another. They cannot figure me out."

Tabitha leaned forward, intrigued with this new information. "You are serious?"

Alena nodded. "I am. It keeps me sane. If I was forever trying to compete with people born with these abilities, I would go insane. So I have found my own way of keeping things on the level."

"But why did you marry into this? I mean, if you felt like you had to come up with some kind of defense to survive, why did you marry in?"

Alena's mirth turned to a slow smile. "I am telling you what I do to combat feeling insecure against a family of sorcerers. I married into it because I fell in love: hopelessly, passionately, completely in love."

"But if you are so in love, how can you feel like you have to find a way to compete?" Tabitha was confused. "Isn't love enough? Why do you still feel like you have to find a way to make yourself fit?"

"Love is what it is. Don't put such power on it to wipe out the truths around us. The Caskans have power; they were born with it. Humans and the other races cannot compete with that power. Some others have power as well, but none like the Caskans. The truth is, I do not have that power, and yet Tristyn fell in love with me, Tabitha—me, Alena. Not the human, not the non-magic, just Alena. But once we decided to commit to one another, we had to find a way to live with our differences; I had to learn to live with his family. Love is why I do it, but it is not the answer, it is the reason. The answer is to make sure that I feel that regardless of the power they have, it is not something I will allow to be held over me. I will not allow them to control me or intimidate me. I control myself and my destiny," Alena concluded, her feet dangling over the side of the chair. She reminded Tabitha so much of Callie that a pang of loneliness for her cousin swept through her.

Tabitha let this digest, mulling over Alena's tactic. Bertòn had spoken of her with respect and pride when he mentioned her ability to learn things that others could not.

She opened her mouth to respond. Suddenly something Alena said struck her. "Races? Did you say there are other races?"

Alena nodded. "Yes, didn't you know? Humans and Caskans are not the only species on this world."

"What other races? You mean like animals, or what?"

Alena's gaze flickered for a moment, and Tabitha wondered if she was going to respond. After a moment, she said, "No, I mean other races like us. The elves, for one…"

"Elves? Did you say elves?" Tabitha's mouth dropped in astonishment.

Alena nodded. "You didn't know?"

"No! I have never seen an elf! Are there really elves?"

Alena looked baffled. "What do you mean you have never seen one? Sybille is an elf."

Tabitha gaped. She could not even respond as she stared at Alena.

"You really did not know? You have been here for four days, and it never once occurred to you to wonder why she has pointed ears?"

"She has pointed ears?"

Alena let out a laugh. "You have not seen her ears? Well, when you go downstairs, watch her. She does put her hair behind her ears once in a while."

Tabitha was astounded. "Is she the only one? Are they common?"

"Common enough, but not nearly as numerous as the Caskans. They were almost eliminated a few generations ago," Alena said sadly.

"What? Why?" Tabitha gasped.

"They were a competition to the Caskans, who wanted the land but did not want to live with the rules that the elves imposed on their use of the land. It was a massive war, mostly before the humans got here," Alena explained. "The eastern Caskans have embraced a lot of the elves' love of the earth and respect for the land. It was their influence that changed them to not eat meat. The Caskans who live toward the west are more the true original Caskans. They hunt and are more migratory. They do not embrace other races as the eastern Caskans do."

"So the two stay separate? Is there any interaction between the two groups?"

"Oh, yes. They are all still members of the same society. In fact, the Plains tribes are facing some serious drought issues. So the eastern Caskans have been sending food and supplies. There are a lot of talks, as they want to be able to come here to hunt and use our land. But we do not want the sanctity of our beliefs against eating meat to be compromised. I mean, for a race of people that respects animals as brothers to sit back and watch our neighbors slaughter them on our land is a lot to ask," Alena explained.

"Yet they still want to come over and hunt?"

Alena nodded. "And we send food over, fish and vegetables, eggs and milk. We have a lot of seafood from our coastline, but they look at it as charity. I am afraid that another war may be imminent."

"So this is not the paradise I originally thought it to be," Tabitha murmured.

Alena shook her head. "Of course it is not a paradise, but it is our home, and we love it. I would not trade my world for the chaos of yours!"

Tabitha laughed. "Well you have me there. So are elves the only other race?"

"No, there are the Faye," Alena continued. "The Faye are the original magical race of this world, even before the Caskans came over. Legend has it that the Caskans came over from another world and were non-magical. Over time, they lived with and even intermarried with the Faye and developed a new race of magical folk. There are still true Faye out there, but they are seldom seen. No one really knows where they live. People always seek them out, trying to find their villages. But very few ever come back. If they do, they have not found any sign of them."

"Hmm...So how do you still know they are out there?"

"Oh, they come around every once in a while. We will see a representative or two, or a band of emissaries will show up to check in and bring word from their leaders."

Tabitha nodded, amazed at the knowledge she had gained about this new world she was exploring.

Alena sat up and stretched. "But that is not why I came here. Bertòn tells me he asked you to remain hidden from prying eyes. I am sure you are going crazy sitting here, but can you be patient while I check around?"

Tabitha shrugged. "Do I have a choice?"

Alena stood and made her way to the door. "Of course. You always have a choice. We are asking you to let us help you."

"You are asking me to sit still while others do something for me," Tabitha snapped, her earlier anger resurfacing. "I am not a baby. I don't have to remain here locked up while you—"

"Tabitha, listen to me." Alena stood in the open doorway, her voice sharp. "You have two options, as far as I can see: one, you go ahead out there in a world you don't know or understand and try to figure it out yourself. Or two, you wait here while I check out who is looking for you." She lifted an eyebrow. "And that means, yes, laying low and waiting for people to help you."

Tabitha, humbled, nodded slowly. "I am sorry, Alena. I have been left on my own for so long that I am not sure how to even accept help."

"Gracefully," Alena suggested with an impish grin. She quietly closed the door behind her.

Tabitha leaned on the windowsill in her room as the sun began to set in the distance. The afternoon had waned gently into a beautiful evening, and the soft breeze wafting through her window promised a warm night. She deeply inhaled the summer scents that assailed her, trying to differentiate various smells and identify those familiar and those new to her senses. With the forced inactivity, the room seemed to gently squeeze her. She was tired of trying to keep herself occupied while the hours whiled away.

A soft knock on the door broke her reverie, and she jumped from the window toward the door, hoping to finally see Luc. It was, however, Alena who waited outside her door.

"I apologize. That took a little longer than I expected."

"Did you learn anything?"

Alena nodded. "I did indeed. I have some very interesting information. May I come in?"

Tabitha swung the door wide. "Of course."

"Well, I have some good news," Alena began. "I found out who is looking for you, and I also have a lead on a woman who may know someone your mother was here to visit."

"Really? So who is looking for me? I mean, no one knows I came over here, so I cannot imagine who would know—"

"Does the name Antoine Montfort mean anything to you?"

Tabitha slowly lowered herself into the seat behind her. *Of course.* It had never occurred to her that her father would be looking for her. "Oh my God…but how?"

"So you know him?"

Tabitha shook her head. "I have never met him, but I know the name. I just found out recently that he is my father."

It was Alena's turn to lower herself into a chair, her face slightly pale. "Your father?"

"Yes. The woman who gave me the key chain that held the stone that allowed me to cross over worked for him. She told me his name when I went to her seeking information about my mother's disappearance. I just never put two and two together."

"Well, he has his chancellor touring the regions, giving updates on the negotiations with the Plains clans. Do you know who your father is?" Alena's face was hesitant.

"Only the name. Why?"

"Tabitha, Antoine Montfort is lord regent for all of Chandolyn. Just as Marcus is lord regent for St. Mikel."

Tabitha lifted a shoulder. "I had no idea. Quite honestly, it doesn't mean much to me. I only heard his name for the first time last week. But how did he know I am here?"

Alena shook her head. "Jules Moyer, his chancellor and regent, carries your likeness and is trying to find you. Somehow, they know you are here, and unfortunately, someone told them that you were staying here with Bertòn. Moyer approached Bertòn this afternoon. He has asked Bertòn to bring you down to the Village Council this evening."

"My father?" Tabitha inhaled deeply. She was not sure how she felt about this news. She was desperate to meet him but just as anxious to avoid him. Her mother had a tenuous grip at best on her sanity. There were so many questions; she was not even sure where to begin. "I am not sure I want to go down to meet him."

"Well, Marcus and Bertòn will respect your decision. But there is more. I met a man who is traveling with Jules. He tells me that he knows of a woman in the village within Windrift who had a strange visitor whose description matches your mother's. The woman's name is Dedrel. She just happens to live in the village where your father has his estate."

"My mother? Do you think that she was there? Seeing my father?" Tabitha jumped out of her seat.

"We won't know unless we ask. So why don't you plan on heading down to the Village Council after dinner with Luc? We can see what else we can find out." Alena rose. "But be careful. Yet another man is also asking about you. I don't know who that is, and I am not sure what he wants."

CHAPTER SIXTEEN

AFTER A QUIET DINNER WITH LUC'S FAMILY, TABITHA and Luc strolled through the village square hand in hand, peeking in store windows and watching the crowd amble along the square. The town square was carved into the valley between two hills; a cobbled street cut between the rows of houses and storefronts. Tabitha had been amazed when they entered the small, bustling center. From a distance, one could scan the landscape and almost miss the village.

People wandered through the town. Wooden signs hung in front of the storefronts, their windows dressed with displays of the wares inside. Tabitha held onto Luc's hand as she nervously wandered through the throng of people in this strange land. Luc stopped to speak with people, introducing Tabitha and leading her through the village.

People seemed to be congregating toward one large set of double doors built into a long hill, and Tabitha could only assume that was their destination. When Luc led her through the enormous doors, Tabitha was amazed at the cavernous hall that stretched before them. The walls were long, with elaborately carved arches featuring intricate designs of leaves and vines. Pairs of enormous pillars majestically lined the center of the floor, leading toward a large stage at the front of the long chamber. Light streamed in through large glass vestibules sitting atop the hill. The waning sunlight lit the room in pearly gray.

Tabitha stared at the beautiful and spacious cavern, taking in the intricate artwork that depicted animals, plants, clouds, and stars. With every glance she noticed another elaborate carving and yet another colorful depiction of nature at its most lovely.

"This is beautiful," she whispered.

Luc glanced at her and smiled as he led her down the long center aisle. The wood railings on either side of the aisle separated individual boxes containing seats, each a different size and each with a different number of seats. Tabitha noticed brass plates with what appeared to be shapes and symbols etched onto them. She leaned in and pointed curiously.

"Family emblems," Luc informed her. "Each family has one plaque, and each member adds his or her own personal stamp to it. For example, my family's insignia is a mountain with a setting sun. To represent my father's family, we have added his, Sybille's, and my marks. When I marry, I will add my own and my wife's, plus any children we have. When we put together our family tree, it includes the individual symbols of each member, and the crests can be more elaborate."

She nodded and followed him toward the front of the cavernous hall; he stopped next to a small wood railing with a brass plate near the front. The brass plate had a beautifully etched picture of a sun setting over a mountain with a carved wolf howling toward the sky, a hawk soaring overhead, and an elegant fox sitting near the bottom.

"Have a seat," Luc suggested. Tabitha was surprised at how comfortable the wooden chair she chose was.

"How do you decide what to elect as a symbol?" Her voice was quiet in the cavernous room.

He smiled but did not answer. Instead he lifted a hand to greet Tristyn and Alena as they joined them. Bertòn and Sybille also arrived, and Tabitha sat back as Luc talked with his family members. Their boxes, it seemed, were all grouped around Bertòn's, and Tabitha felt slightly overwhelmed at the press of people who began gathering in the hall.

People tried to jostle in and speak with Marcus and Bertòn. Marcus was the governor for the state of St. Mikel, and his brother was the regional leader of Calais. Luc had told her that these were elected positions and that his family had long been involved in local politics. He had started explaining their land ownership and taxation structure, but he had not had a chance to yet explain how people could accumulate or manage their lands and the ownership structure.

Tabitha had to admit that she had listened with less than an enthusiastic ear to the intricate details of their government. Luc, it seemed, had a better understanding of her own world's government practices; he frequently pointed out parallels, obviously thinking that would help her understand his explanations.

What she had gleaned from the discussion was that land was not owned or purchased. Their belief that land could not possibly be owned stemmed from their elfish roots; the idea that one could own land seemed ludicrous to them. People did, however, have the option to choose land that they wished to have under their stewardship as more of a right, and for that privilege they would be taxed on the size of that land. If someone wanted a larger parcel and it was available, they had only to petition for it. As long as they paid the taxes for that land's use, they could maintain their personal use of that land indefinitely. Land use rights were passed down through generations, and if at any time a family or an individual felt that the land was too much, they could opt to turn it back to the collective state. The land would be put up for others' consideration. If someone had built a home on the land, the home was theirs by ownership rights. If they should not require it any longer, the home could be sold.

The room began to settle. Tabitha stirred from her musings as Luc took the seat beside her and Bertòn and Sybille joined them in the family box. Marcus stood at the front of the hall on the elevated platform, and the last conversations dwindled as he waited patiently for silence.

"Welcome all. It is with great pleasure that I stand before you, welcoming another festival and greeting you all. Let us start the evening with a prayer to our One God."

A slim, dark-haired man stood, and the assemblage rose. Bowing their heads, they spoke collectively in a language Tabitha did not recognize. The words were harmonious and their voices songlike in the beautiful cadence of their prayer.

The young man sat when the prayer had finished, and Marcus again took the stage. He began his speech with a welcome and a benediction to the crowd. He spoke of past festivals and of the long history of the festivals as a time for trading, sharing news, and catching up with friends. He introduced their first speaker, a tall, elder woman from a state southwest of them named Vuelac.

The woman stood and began to recite news and updates from the state. She shared a new tax structure and news of the latest elections, as well as innovations and updates on what products Vuelac would be sharing in booths at the fair. Lastly, she wrapped up her oration with an update on an attack on a small village in the west of the state. She gave them details of the attack and the subsequent aftermath for the few survivors.

When she finished, the room remained quiet. She was preparing to leave the stage when a man stood, lifting his hand. Marcus gave the man a nod, and he spoke. "Do you have any clue as to the identity of the attackers?"

She shook her head. "We have clues that we are using to try and determine who did this atrocity. They stormed the homes by night when people slept. No one was even able to sound an alarm. We are sickened by the horror of that night and the pointless deaths. Our people were found lying on the floor, not a mark on them. We don't know how they died. The children are missing."

Another hand shot up, and Marcus again gave a nod.

"Can you tell us what you know of the clues? Any inkling to give us some indication about the perpetrators?"

"No!" Another man stood. "We must not listen to conjecture and speculation. Once they know the truth, they will tell us."

"But how will we know what to look for? What warning signs?" A third voice rang out from the rear of the hall.

Marcus stood and held up a hand. "I agree with Riordan. We must deal with facts only and not be led to assume anything. Once they have enough evidence to point to a certain group, we will be told. We will all hunt them down, and they will face justice."

"Why must we dance around this?" A woman stood, her face alive with fury. "We know who is behind these atrocities! Must we listen to news of the same attacks on yet another evening, of people murdered in their homes, whole villages attacked, and our precious children missing?"

"She is right! We know who is behind this! It is time we band together as a community to protect our own, instead of waiting for these Plains tribes to work their way to our homes and our families!"

People were roused, and voices cried out to be heard; as opinions were bandied, each strove to be heard above the din.

With a great shout, Marcus quieted the room. He bade them all listen to the other states' presentations before passing judgment. He reminded them that this was one update of several to come this night. Once they had word of the other states' conditions and action plans, they would discuss actions.

Luc sat back in his seat, his eyes wary as he listened to the angry outbursts around him.

Tabitha glanced at him. *What are they talking about?*

As I told you, we Caskans are the Coastal people. We live in our communities along the shore; we eat fish, harvest fruit and vegetables. We live in harmony with our world and our animal friends. To our west, the tribes that live along the Plains hunt the large herds of grazing animals; they are nomadic people. They are facing a severe drought. Their herds are dying out from lack of water and food. We fear they will die of starvation. Our people send food and fish. We try to work with them to divert some of our water supplies to them, but it will take years to try and salvage the land. There have been numerous attacks on our outlying villages in the past months, and many believe it is the Plains tribes, tired of our charity, wanting to use our land for themselves.

Do you think that is who is doing this? Tabitha asked.

He shrugged, half listening as the next state's ambassador gave an update on the state's news and political updates. *I don't know. There is no evidence, and no one even knows how they are dying. But many are not waiting to catch the ones committing these acts. Clans of the Plains people have been assaulted in revenge for what was done to our people. It is causing a war between our people. Down in Windrift, your father is acting as a negotiator between our people.*

Is it working? Will there be peace?

I am not sure…

The man who faced the crowd told a similar story of an attack on a village, where the adults were found dead and the children missing. The people of Landor were organizing a guard to protect their borders.

Tabitha listened in horror to the details, alarmed at the atrocities being meted out on the villages on the outer fringes. People around the hall spoke in hushed, alarmed voices and frantic whispers. Fear rooted itself in Tabitha as she envisioned setting out in an unknown world to find her mother. Her impetuous decision to come to a strange world with a very different culture now seemed to have grown out of ignorance. What had she been thinking, setting off on her own, crossing over into a strange world to try and find her mother?

She sat back, her arms wrapped around her torso as a chill swept through her body. The determination and excitement she had felt over setting off in search of the next clues to her mother's whereabouts waned in the face of the truth about the perils of this land. How had she believed that she would be able to wander this land and try and fit in with a world she did not know the first thing about?

A small and wiry man stood, the dark, thinning hair on his head exposing the pointed ears jutting from the halo of his remaining hair. His nose was long and pointed, his lips a thin line. He had quietly conversed with Marcus before addressing the crowd.

He introduced himself as Jules Moyer, the orator from Windrift representing Antoine Montfort, Lord Regent of Chandolyn.

The room grew silent as Jules began to tell the people the most recent news from Windrift and update them on local events. People waited expectantly for news and updates on the status of the negotiations.

"And we have two final issues to address," the small man continued, glancing at his fistful of notes. "I am sure you are all curious about our negotiations between the Plains peoples and ourselves."

A man near the front of the room stood. "You mean *yourselves*. We are not part of these negotiations, so your regent must not be so quick to speak for us all."

Marcus stood, his eyes boring into the man. "Your point is taken, but I advise that we hear what Jules has to say before we pass judgment on what his lord regent has placed on the table. It may well be that a peace settlement is in the works and that peace may yet be secured among our brothers."

The room swelled with rising sentiment, but Marcus cleared his throat with a loud cough, his eyes roaming the room for the people still speaking. Silence once again prevailed, and Jules nodded stiffly to Marcus before he continued.

"Our regent, Antoine, has met with the representatives of the Plains tribes, and the grievances of their people have been made public. I have with me a list of the requests they make of us if we are to continue to help them in their time of need. The list shall be posted at your community gathering hall at the end of this session for all to review. We expect a vote on your level of support and your suggestions at this month's end. We will be hosting a regional meeting of the common lands, and we expect a full debate and a list of your concerns at that time."

Jules paused, and waves of discourse once again rumbled through the room. He lifted his hands and swept them outward toward the room. "I understand your concern, but we will get nowhere without parlay about our mutual issues. You accuse the Plains people of raiding your border areas; they swear innocence and accuse you of harassing their hunting parties and disrupting their progress from one hunting ground to another. These people have every right to pass along our borders, yet they are being attacked and butchered along—"

The room erupted into howls of outrage. People jumped to their feet, bellowing angry retorts in a cacophony of indignation.

Jules lifted a handful of pages over his head, yelling to be heard. Marcus stood, calling for order, but the crowd was beyond reason. The shouts began to dissipate as a group of marshals swept the room, calling for quiet. Jules's voice rang out above the last of the shouts.

"For every accusation of ours against them, they tell of one as violent and as horrific against their people!" he shouted, his face red with emotion as he waved the handful of pages over his head. "Don't you see? This will erupt into a civil war if we do not get some control! This will escalate into a war with no winners! For every act of revenge against them, they will counter with one as deadly and as violent! It must stop! The peace arbitrations must continue!"

The room quieted as his heartfelt arguments began to penetrate their anger. They could now understand. Their enemy was attacking out of revenge, and their allies in the east were apparently taking it upon themselves to seek retribution for each attack.

Marcus stood and nodded to Jules. "I think I speak for us all when I say that we will not harbor any of our own who take it upon themselves to impose justice without proof of the actual perpetrators of a crime." There were murmurs of assent and begrudging nods as people settled their anger and agreed that revenge was not in their natures.

Marcus addressed Jules. "We will, as a community, review your contentions, and we will send representation to the council in one month's time." He turned his gaze to the assembly. "And let no one who does not take the time to say his mind before the assemblage complain once the representatives have gone. The people we elect to speak in our stead must go forth with our collective voices. If anyone remains mute, then be a fool to let others speak for you."

Tabitha watched as the room once again filled with a resounding swell of voices as people began sharing their opinions with their neighbors. She was amazed at the intensity of their voices and the passion these people gave their governing. Her own political experience was minimal, but she knew from watching TV and reading the paper that her world was considerably less passionate about voting. To see such high expectation and demands to be heard gave her pause; she wondered if the democracy in her world back in the Founding Fathers' day had been more like this. She turned to ask Luc a question and found him in a heated argument with Bertòn and Marcus.

She stepped back, letting them have their privacy, not sure what had caused the argument but hoping it was not in some way about her. As she glanced around the room, watching as people spoke to their neighbors and passed the list of contentions around, she noticed that Jules was staring at her intently.

He nodded in her direction. As he disengaged from the group circling him, she was certain that he was going to make his way over to speak with her. She was not disappointed; he began threading his way through the crowd toward her.

Bertòn smoothly stepped in his path and waylaid him as Luc slid up beside her. "Do you wish to speak to him about your father?"

Tabitha swallowed the knot of dread in her throat and tried to croak out a response. When that failed, she switched to mental communication. *Yes. I think that if I want to know the truth, I had best meet my father.*

Luc didn't respond, but he lifted his face toward Bertòn, who was speaking with Jules.

She smiled as she sent a thought to Luc. *Are you two playing defense for me?*

We didn't want you to have to meet the man if you were not ready.

Jules and Bertòn approached Marcus, and Luc guided Tabitha toward the small group. The men watched her approach. Tabitha felt an overwhelming urge to run. As she approached, she was surprised to see how small Jules was in comparison to the two Caskan men standing with him. It was not until she stepped closer that his pointed ears and angled brows revealed his elfish roots.

Bertòn politely introduced him. "Tabitha, allow me to introduce Jules Moyer, Marquis de Windrift. He is a chancellor for Antoine Montfort, the regent of Windrift and our negotiator."

Tabitha murmured a hello, allowing the man to take her hand as he bowed graciously to her. "Well, this is quite a surprise. I had thought that I had weeks of travel ahead of me to find you, and here you are, listening at a village meeting in Calais. I must admit that I am pleasantly surprised to have located you so easily."

"How did you know I was here?" Tabitha asked, and then she saw that he held a picture of her. "Where did you get that?"

Jules glanced down and smiled as he held up the picture to her. "Your father, of course."

"Where did he get it?"

Jules slowly shook his head. "You would have to ask him that yourself. He would like very much to meet you. I have been tasked to find you and bring you to him."

CHAPTER SEVENTEEN

TABITHA STOOD HUGGING HERSELF. THE WARM AIR failed to ease the chill that encased her body. Jules was in the kitchen talking to Bertòn, Marcus, and Sybille. Alena and Tristyn were preparing to leave, and Diego and Peri were gathering their belongings to leave with them. Tabitha stood on the cobbled porch outside the kitchen. Disbelief coursed through her.

My father.

After eighteen years, she at last had a name and an identity. Her father, Antoine, was the lord regent of Chandolyn and the peace negotiator for the Eastern tribes. He was a full Caskan man who had long been searching for his daughter. She had learned that he had recently found out she had crossed over, and he had sent Jules to find her while he made a tour of the various regions.

Her father. It seemed that she was the daughter of a high-ranking official, and he wanted desperately to meet her.

Amazement swept through her. Jules had promised to take her to her father and that he would help her find her mother.

She stood in the evening air, wondering how she felt and how she was supposed to feel. She could not grasp that she had finally found some part of her heritage. She would finally meet her father. The chill swept through her again, but she felt as though she should be dancing with relief and happiness.

"Hey."

She smiled as Luc quietly came up behind her. She did not turn. He slid his arms around her waist, drawing her back against him.

"Are you all right?"

She nodded. Words seemed to lodge in her throat when she tried to express the complete confusion that swelled through her. She did not even know what to say. Was finding her father the beginning or the end? She had no idea. But she did know that her time with Luc was coming to an end. Marcus had tapped him to be on the committee representing the region and to attend the meeting in a month. He was needed here, with his family and people. Jules and his entourage would escort Tabitha to her father. Jules had assured her that at any time, Antoine would have her safely returned to the portal should she wish to return home. All her needs would be addressed.

"Do you want me to come with you? I promised that I would. I will see this through with you," Luc murmured against her hair.

She shook her head. "You have your own life to get back to. You have done so much for me, but now I can go to my father. Jules tells me he will help me find my mother. He has been looking for her himself."

Luc nodded against the back of her head and tightened his grip around her waist. "I don't want you to go."

"It is probably for the best. I need to figure out who I am. I have never known anything about my father, and now I know where he is and that he wants to meet me. It is just unbelievable to me." She turned in his arms. "And I can't be selfish—you're needed here. I will be fine and well cared for. You need to do what you have to do for your family."

He nodded and sighed, placing his forehead against hers, their eyes meeting. "Will I see you again?"

She nodded. "If I have not found my mother, I may still be there when you arrive in a month."

"Will you promise me you will not leave without saying good-bye?"

She nodded, swallowing the lump in her throat.

The moment was broken when Bertòn came racing out of the kitchen, heedless of the door banging back on its hinges. A moment later, Tristyn and Diego crashed through the same door.

Luc's eyes were intent while his father imparted something to him. He nodded curtly and gestured back toward the kitchen. "Get inside with Sybille. We seem to have some trouble brewing."

Tabitha started to open her mouth, but Luc had already stepped forward. Bertòn pointed up toward the sky. "Luc, loop around and see if you can spot them. We will follow on foot."

Luc nodded and jumped onto the stone wall. Spreading his arms, he leaped forward. Without a sound, he transformed into a red-tailed hawk, his long wings sweeping powerfully to drive him toward the sky. Before Tabitha could catch her breath, Bertòn, Tristyn, and Diego jumped the wall, transforming into wolves as they landed on the other side. They sped down the grassy hill, following the hawk's lead, careening toward the forest with astonishing speed.

Tabitha was standing, mouth agape, staring down the path they had taken when Sybille came out and, with a gentle tug on her arm, drew her into the kitchen. The fire had been stoked, and she could hear bustling around the house. The others were on the upper floors, slamming shutters and tugging the wooden outer doors closed across the glass walls that faced the outside.

Peri and Alena entered the kitchen, pairs of evil-looking slim rapiers strapped to each hip, tossing a set to Sybille after the smaller woman slammed shut the last outer door to the kitchen. Jules withdrew a slim weapon and casually placed it on the table before him. Tabitha watched, still wrestling with the image of Luc turning into a hawk before her eyes.

Sybille placed a calming hand on her arm as she passed, twin blades slung low on her hips. She stopped to secure the ends of the scabbard to her legs just above the knees.

"Are you all right? You look a little pale," Sybille quietly asked.

Tabitha opened her mouth but emitted little more than a harsh bark as she turned her eyes to the woman. She shook her head. "What is happening?"

Alena came up to the bar. "Nothing to worry about, just a band of Faye approaching. It is best to be cautious, as they can be unpredictable, and in light of—"

"Alena!" Sybille snapped as she placed a glass of milk before Cyra. The child smiled her thanks and sipped at her milk, her eyes drooping.

Alena slipped her fingers into the little girl's hair and kissed her forehead before shooting a cool eye toward Sybille. "It's best she knows. I do not know why you want to protect her. She should realize the perils of this world."

Jules nodded as he poured himself a hot cup of javé from the glass pot bubbling over the fire. "She is right. As an outsider, we cannot protect Tabitha from the truth of our world. It would be best for her to know what kind of world she has entered. Sooner or later she will find that this world has its own rules. She is no stranger to bigotry and racism."

Tabitha pulled her thoughts back together and stared from one to the other. "What are you talking about?"

"The Faye," Sybille said quietly as she opened a long cabinet and tugged free a long bow and a quiver of arrows.

"What does that mean? I thought they were rarely seen? Are the Faye dangerous?"

Sybille shrugged, her eyes avoiding Tabitha's.

Alena snorted as she came around the island and stood with Tabitha. "They can be and let's just say, they are volatile. They rarely come down to intermingle with us unless there is some problem."

Tabitha could feel the hackles on her neck rise at the cavalier manner of Alena's speech. "And is there some problem?"

"That is what they have gone to find out. The men will see what they want."

"They left here like their tails, pardon the pun, were on fire. What the hell is going on?" Tabitha snapped.

Jules leaned in, his dark eyes narrowing as he watched her. "They have undoubtedly been informed of an outsider. I am sure they are concerned that you have come over."

Tabitha released a long sigh. "Ahh, here we go. And what does *that* mean?"

"It means that the Faye are very concerned about humans crossing over from your world. They have little concern about the ones who arrive here by accident and cannot return, but they take exception over the ones who come intentionally. They are very worried about our world becoming a habitat or an escape, if you will, for people in your world," Jules explained before he sipped from his mug.

Tabitha grappled with the turn of events in the last hour: people turning into animals, a group of magical folk en route with possible ill intent. As confusion swept through her, she lowered herself into a chair, overwhelmed with the questions that spun around her mind. Jules was right. This world had its own rules and standards. This new development lent weight to her sinking feeling that she knew precious little about what kind of place she was dealing with.

"It seems that I cannot escape being an outsider, even here," she stated quietly.

Sybille came up beside her and slipped her arms around her in a warm hug, surprising Tabitha. "You are our friend, and we will not let any harm come to you. But as your world has its own methods of dealing with those who are unknowns, so does ours."

"Imagine for a moment if one of our kind, a magical folk from another world, were discovered in your world. The discovery would send waves of shock and fear through your people, I would think," Peri commented.

Tabitha took this in and nodded. It was true. If her own abilities were ever revealed, she would be put beneath a microscope and studied. Never mind what would happen if someone from another world were discovered.

She sat back, listening for the others to return, wondering what word they would bring when they did come back. She leaned her chin on her hands, weariness creeping over her. She gestured absently toward Sybille's weapons, strapped low on her hips. "So the men leave you here. What happens now?"

Peri slid her pair of rapiers from their sheaves. Tabitha was startled when the rapid flurry of dual blades whirled over Peri's head and in front of her; the air whispered with the spin of the flashing knives. "We protect the home. Every one of us is accurate with a bow and a blade. Should any enemy slip past the men, they will have to deal with us before taking anything from our homes."

"Yet people were murdered savagely in their homes," Tabitha commented.

Alena nodded and spoke quietly. "Keep in mind that magic abilities are an advantage only if you are the only one with them. If your enemy also has the same abilities, they are no advantage."

As the evening wore on and the events of the day began to take their toll on Tabitha, her stress and fear slowly eased into fatigue. There had been no word from Luc's party. Cyra had long since been put to bed. Jules sat by the fire, staring wordlessly into the flames. The other women chatted quietly in the kitchen. The gentle prattle eased her, and Tabitha found the words were bouncing noiselessly off her. Her head dropped into her arms. She noted drowsily that the other women switched between regular speech and another language she could not understand.

As she drifted into light slumber, a dream began to take shape. The foreign language the women spoke became a wall between them. She could not comprehend them, nor could she bridge the chasm that separated them. Their words seemed to tumble away from her and slide into that widening rift between her and the women from another world.

Jules glanced at her from his place by the fire, and in her dream his words seemed to drift toward her. "They have come to speak to you, you know."

Her eyes were heavy, and her head seemed to weigh a ton as she struggled to lift it from her arms. "Who?"

"The Faye."

"Why? Why have they come to speak to me?"

He shrugged and turned back to the mesmerizing pattern of the flames. "Perhaps you should ask them."

Tabitha stared at him as the vestiges of sleep seemed to slip from her. She gently eased up from the chair, observing that the women did not notice her. Her steps were noiseless as she moved toward the door.

She glanced back and was startled to see herself still at the counter, her head resting in her arms, her eyes shut, her face relaxed in slumber. Sybille rose and walked around the island to gently remove a sweater from a seat and drape it over Tabitha's sleeping shoulders before moving to pour herself some water.

"Am I asleep?"

Jules did not turn but snorted quietly. "It would appear so, wouldn't it?"

"How will I find them?"

"They move as the mist. I imagine that since they have come to see you, they will find you."

"How do I get out of here?"

Jules expression was exasperated. "You can no doubt find the turn of mind that will accomplish such a feat."

After his caustic remark, Tabitha gave up and slid toward the door. A feeling of weightlessness seemed to envelope her. She pressed a hand toward the door and found herself sliding through it to the outdoors. She glanced back in surprise at the wooden door behind her that sealed the home against intrusion. Not sure where she was going, she headed down the hill toward the edge of the woods, letting instinct guide her.

CHAPTER EIGHTEEN

AS SHE WANDERED DOWN THE HILL, THE MOON SLID from behind a cloud, and Tabitha noted that she left no shadow. She let her feet pick a trail along the grass, and without a sound she slipped through the still night. In the distance, she could hear a low howl and wondered if that were Luc's family speaking in the dark night as they tracked the trespasser.

Calm overtook her as she entered the woods and continued through the dark trees. It occurred to her more than once to be concerned about finding her way back, but the thought slipped away as she walked deeper into the forest. She was unsure of her destination, but her feet did not hesitate.

The sky lightened ahead. She made her way through a dense group of trees, ducking beneath a low overhang into a clearing. It was not large; a long, dark rock on the far side seemed to dominate the otherwise empty space between the trees. Not sure what had caused her to pause, she walked over to the rock and leaned against it, letting the silence of the forest encompass her and wrap her in stillness. A breeze gently rustled the treetops, and Tabitha raised her face to the gentle wind, slightly amazed that she could not feel the air caressing her cheeks. Apparently that was the way of dreams.

The breeze shifted slightly, and she heard the gentle rustle of trees from her right. She glanced over and realized that the breeze was ushering in a dense fog that seemed to curl from the depths of the forest. She stood, unsure why a chill suddenly enveloped her body. The mist began to enter the clearing and then swept into three long columns. The curl of the mist seemed to solidify, and three human forms began to emerge as gray outlines. Tabitha could distinctly see every feature and detail of the people who stood before her, as well as the leaves on the trees visible through their translucent bodies.

The shape closest to her was a tall woman with light hair hanging in a long braid down her back; her face was both young and old in ageless grace. The two men behind her stood quietly watching, as though on guard. One was tall, his head shaven clean; his features were rough, yet they held a wild beauty. The third was bearded and tall, his eyes masked behind a cloth. Tabitha knew without knowing why that he could see and feel every detail of the clearing around him without the advantage of those hooded eyes.

The woman nodded gracefully to her, her eyes watching calmly. Tabitha stood motionless, unsure what was to happen now. She knew without a doubt that they were the Faye, and she also knew that the pull she had felt was their call to her. She wondered at the wisdom of leaving the house, but the knowledge that her body was peacefully sleeping at the counter in the kitchen calmed that concern. She knew that this meeting was meant to happen, and she knew that she could not have ignored the call to meet them any more than she could ignore the urge to find her mother.

"Are you giving me these thoughts?" Tabitha broke the silence.

The woman nodded and answered in Tabitha's mind. *Yes.*

"Why did you call me here?"

To meet you, of course. We felt you when you crossed over to this land, and we have been waiting for our chance to speak with you. The voice was crystal clear, a high and beautiful tone, like the sound of a perfectly pitched bell in cold, clear air.

"Was it necessary to call them away from the house? Did you think they would try to stop me?"

We did not want their prejudice to color your judgment.

"What is it that you want to tell me?" Tabitha watched the three of them warily. Little emotion was reflected in their lucid faces.

We have a message from your mother.

"My mother? You have seen her? Where is she?" Tabitha's heart leaped at the mention of her mother, and she stepped forward. As she did so, the three of them moved back an equal space, as though to maintain the space between them.

She is home and has asked you to return to your home. She is well, but she is concerned that you might lose yourself in your search for her.

"Why didn't she come to me? Why is she hiding from me if she knows I am here?" Frustration welled up; her mother had once again evaded her.

She knew that the time had come to tell you of your heritage. Your following her here frightened her, and she knows she cannot continue to keep the truth from you. But she wishes you to return, and then she will answer all of your questions. It is not too late for you. Your safety is still assured, but should you continue your quest, we cannot guarantee that we will continue to keep those from you who would do you harm.

Tabitha stared from one to another, amazement and frustration rising within her. She tried to interpret the message and formulate a question, but the message was so convoluted and the words from her mother so vague that she did not know where to start.

"You've been protecting me?"

Should the need have arisen. You are ignorant of our world. Just because you have not yet encountered danger, don't imagine that it will not find you. It is time for you to give up this childish pursuit and return home, before you venture too far into a dangerous world among those who would harm you—or worse.

Tabitha leaned back against the rock, chewing absently on a thumbnail. "Those who would harm me? I don't understand."

We warn you that you are in a place you do not understand, among people who would use you for their own ends. It is time for you to leave before you are further endangered, or worse. You do not understand what is at stake here in this world or what is transpiring around you. The woman's voice was calm and her face was aloof although the message was personal.

Tabitha regarded the three, pursing her lips. "Who am I in danger from?"

No answer.

"Why did my mother send you and not come herself?"

Nothing.

"Why did she hide my identity and my father and this world from me all my life? Why did she slip away yet again, leaving little more than a note? Who is it that I need to fear? Why do I have these powers, and what will become of me when I do go home?"

The three regarded her silently.

Her voice was little more than a whisper. "You come here with only a warning? You will not give me any information?" She shook her head slowly, regarding the still figures before her. Her fear had dropped away, and the frustration over her mother's distance and silence swelled within her belly. The familiar feeling from years of asking questions and only getting blank stares and sad smiles in return, no answers, slipped back into place within her, and Tabitha felt her energy drain.

Her words were tired, their intensity lost in the years of trying to simply get an answer. "Why should I listen to anything you have to say? Because you slip through the night like wraiths, trying to spook me? You come here, whispering about how dangerous it is and that it is time for me to go. Yet you do not offer me one answer or one fragment of truth?" Tabitha paused and stared at the silent group. "I have the opportunity to meet my father. I can finally get some answers from someone. If she will not speak to me, I will go find the answers myself."

You will never find the answers you seek here. You will only find more pain. Your father will not give you truths, only deceit. Please, we ask that you not attempt to delve further into this. Just return home as your mother has asked you.

"So I should just go home and forget that this ever happened? Pretend that I do not need to know of my heritage or the root of these powers." She threw her hands into the air. "Don't you see? No one in my world has such power. No one can do the things I can do. What if I marry? Have children? Will this power be passed on? I can't ignore this. I can't just go home and pretend that everything is normal.'

'My mother is tortured by memories that I cannot even begin to understand because she never once told me one single shred of truth of what happened to her. My whole life has been one dark hole of questions. I feel like I am shouting these questions off a cliff into an abyss. My mother. You. My aunt. If I do not go out there and find the answers myself, I will spend the rest of my life wondering who the hell I am and where I come from."

You will be safe. You have your life in your world. Knowing anything about your mother's past will not change your life.

One more time, Tabitha thought. *Just what I need to hear one more time—that none of it matters.* "How can you say that? You don't know anything about me or my life. I don't know my father or where I was born. I don't know why in heaven's name I can do some pretty incredible stuff with my mind. And let me tell you—people in my world do not have that ability. I am some kind of alien in my own world. If I can understand it, I can start to figure out how to live with it."

It does not define you.

"Yes, dammit, it does!" The three floated backward at her outburst. Her voice was caustic. "Sorry, but it *does* define me. To know where I come from means something to me. Maybe if I had grown up knowing the truth, none of it would have mattered, but I spent my life having information withheld and hidden. Yes, it does mean something to me.

All right, I will return home. If my mother is there, she can come and speak with me. If I don't see her, I am going to my father."

The three stood, their outlines flittering and shimmering in the night breeze. Tabitha leaned back against the rock, regarding them curiously, wondering what their place in this whole scheme was and why they had sought her out. Alena had told her that the Faye did not like outsiders, humans. Yet they had sought her out to give her a message from her human mother, another outsider.

She stood, determined to get some answer from them, when the clearing suddenly seemed to bristle. The three crouched, their faces set in fierce glares. Tabitha stood still, waiting to see from where the threat would emerge.

The night air became still, and the moon slid behind a cloud. Without a sound, three wolves stepped from the woods, their fur bristling, teeth bared. Before she could move, a fluttering sound over her head startled her, and a hawk swept from the dark sky and alighted before her. Luc was suddenly standing with his back to her, facing the Faye. The wolves stepped forward and shimmered into three shapes: Bertòn, Diego, and Tristyn.

Bertòn stepped forward to stand before the three, lifting a firm hand toward Luc. "What business have you here?"

The three Faye relaxed their stances, but Tabitha sensed the waves of wariness that emitted from them. The woman lifted her chin to Bertòn and spoke aloud. "Our business is our own. We do not heed the land laws of your people. As such, we are free to venture where we will. We do not break any rules of our treaty."

"You have beckoned to one within my home. As a guest of mine, she is under my protection. You had no right to draw her from the protection of my home." Bertòn's voice was calm and solicitous, but Tabitha could feel the waves of resentment rising from him.

"She came of her own free will."

The four Caskan men turned startled eyes to her. Tabitha felt self-conscious under their intent stares.

Luc reached out in the silence. *Is this true? Is this your own doing?*

What are you talking about? I left the house on my own. I felt a…umm…I guess a suggestion *would be the best way to put it. But no one forced me.* Tabitha shrugged. *I was curious.*

Luc stared at her for an instant. She sensed his perplexity, but the waves of warmth and calmness he sent her reassured her. He stepped back beside her and nodded to his father. Bertòn's eyes widened as he took in this information, but he turned back to the Faye without further comment.

"Tabitha confirms that what you have said is true. I apologize for the misstep. But I repeat, what business do you have here?"

The woman nodded respectfully to Bertòn, acknowledging his apology. "We have come only to talk with our kinswoman and suggest she leave this place before venturing further from her home. Unrest is upon the land, and it is not time for a stranger to be wandering. I owed a debt to her mother, and I promised to give her daughter a message."

Tabitha stepped forward, and again the Faye moved back. "Kinswoman? Why did you call me that?"

The woman turned back to her. "It is not my answer to give you. You must ask the question of your mother."

Tabitha sighed. "I will not pay any attention to what you have told me. I have had about enough of people telling me what I should and should not do for my own good. If you are not going to give me answers, then get away from me and leave me be."

The woman lifted a hand in supplication and made as though to speak, but Tabitha snarled at her. "If you do not have any answers for me, then we have nothing further to say to one another. I will find the answers myself."

She intended to simply dismiss them, but her anger had taken on a life of its own. With a flick of her wrist, the three Faye suddenly splintered into a million tiny shards of light that flittered into the night sky. She was startled by the suddenness of their flight, but before she could comment, the Caskans were turning to her, away from the shimmering shapes that were just beginning to regroup, their faces reflecting their amazement.

Did I do that? Her thought was a whisper to Luc.

He did not respond immediately. He turned back to watch the three Faye regain their shapes. *Tabitha, how did you do that?*

I dunno. Is that bad?

His faint laugh filled her head. *Remind me not to make you angry.*

The Faye recovered their shapes, and their faces turned to Tabitha. They intently watched the exchange between Tabitha and Luc.

"You are linked?"

"You expect an answer from me? You tell me nothing and you think I am going to tell you anything about me?" Tabitha was incredulous.

Luc sent a quieting thought to calm her before answering the Faye. "We have been linked since childhood. We don't know why. We have only met physically this week. But we have been able to communicate between our worlds since we were both children."

The woman stared at Luc keenly. The information seemed to intrigue her. Tabitha knew that they were sharing thoughts, but she could not get an idea of what they were saying.

"You are blood?" the woman asked.

Bertòn shook his head. "They are not, at least not that we know. We have only recently discovered who her father is, and we do not know her mother. There is no blood relation that we know of."

The woman seemed to consider this. "This is unusual. We have never heard of such a thing."

Bertòn shook his head. "Nor have we. They are the first we have encountered to have this link without having ever physically met."

"He is your son?"

Bertòn nodded.

"You are sure?"

Bertòn's anger rippled. "What do you imply?"

The woman waved off his anger with a hand. "We are just verifying that you know that in fact this is the baby she gave birth to."

"Of course." He was perplexed, as were the others around the circle.

"We ask because two were born to her mother. We do not know where the other has gone."

"Two?" Tabitha gasped. The attorney's comment that day in Boston about her brother slid into place.

The woman nodded. "We do not know where he has gone. We have not seen him since he was a baby."

Stunned, Tabitha leaned back against the rock. "He? I had, or have, a brother?"

She looked up at Luc, and a terrible possibility welled within her breast. *Is that why we are linked? Is he, by some bizarre twist of fate, my brother?* Her stomach knotted as she stared up at Luc. The stunned look in his eyes told her that he was also having the slightest twinge of doubt.

Bertòn shook his head. "Ridiculous. This is my son. His mother died not long after his birth. He is not the missing child you search for."

The woman stared at Luc, her eyes fastened on him intently. He stared back; a frown crossed his brow when, to his amazement, she stepped forward and approached him. She tilted his chin with gentle fingers. Horrified, Tabitha realized she was staring at the twin pricks in his neck, the marks she had left after she had healed Cyra. She had tried again later to heal them, but tiny dark points on his neck remained.

The three Faye stared at Luc. The woman's eyes moved from him to Bertòn and narrowed, accusatory. "What have you kept from us?"

Bertòn stared back and forth in confusion. He shook his head. "What?"

The atmosphere in the clearing had changed, become charged with resentment. Bertòn lifted his palms to the group. "What is the problem?"

The woman rejoined the men. "You have broken a law of our treaty. You know you are required to come forward with this information."

The Caskans exchanged confused looks.

The woman stared at them and gestured to Luc. "If you want answers, we will give them when you come forth with his mate."

"His mate?" Bertòn was at a loss.

"Do not pretend not to understand me. Your son is mated; he is marked as the mate of a healer. How dare you hide such a thing from us? Per our treaty, when one with this ability is discovered, they are to be brought forward. Instead you hide her in your midst and let her mark your son."

Bertòn and Luc exchanged stunned looks, and Tabitha felt her heart skip a beat. Her hands went cold.

Suddenly she jumped up and abruptly found herself in the kitchen, standing at the counter, her body suddenly heavy, her confused mind unable to cope with the intense awakening from the dream. With a cry of confusion, she crumpled to the floor.

CHAPTER NINETEEN

SHE SAT HUDDLED IN FRONT OF THE FIRE, CHILLED AND shaking, a hot cup of tea clasped in her icy fingers. Sybille tried to calm her down. Tabitha had scared the women half to death when she had jumped up at the counter, cried out, and blacked out. Sybille was the first to reach her. She'd helped her into a chair as Tabitha shook, terrified by the vivid dream. Her teeth chattered, and Sybille had rubbed her legs and arms, trying to warm her up while Tabitha tried to quiet her rapidly thumping heart.

"I had the most intense dream..." Tabitha's teeth chattered as she spoke.

Sybille hushed her and rubbed her back to warm her. "All is well. You are here with us. We were watching over you."

Tabitha lifted haunted eyes, unsure whether she had indeed dreamed the encounter. She had never been able to leave her own body, depart, and wander around at will.

Alena, her eyes creased in concern as she crouched in front of Tabitha, encouraged her to drink more tea. "All is well. The Faye have left, and the men return even as we speak."

Tabitha nodded. Looking around, she noticed Jules watching her with an unusual glint in his eyes. He did not comment, but as he watched her struggle with her shaking limbs his expression seemed knowing and thoughtful.

Peri went to open the wood doors when the sound of footsteps approached. Bertòn was the first to enter the room, his face a mask of fury as his gaze snapped from one to the other. Luc, Diego, and Tristyn walked in after him, haunted expressions on their faces.

Sybille stood. "What happened?"

Bertòn shook his head and with an abrupt bark dismissed the question. "Was a fruitless search."

Jules stood, his eyes reflecting an understanding of the tension in the room. "If the crisis is past, I shall retire for the evening." He turned to Sybille. "Thank you for your gracious offer of a place to sleep." He then turned to Tabitha. "I must meet with Marcus tomorrow. Will you be prepared to depart the following morning? Can you be ready?"

Tabitha nodded. As Jules left, she warily watched the occupants of the room. Something had happened out there that they had not wanted to talk about in front of Jules. Fear gripped her belly as understanding slowly took root and reality began to set in. They all stood quietly as Jules's steps echoed toward the sleeping quarters upstairs. Tabitha closed her eyes tightly, praying that it had been a dream.

"What happened?" Sybille hissed.

Bertòn strode to the fire and crouched in front of Tabitha. "How did you do that? How did you learn that separation?"

"Oh, God, tell me it was a dream...Please do not tell me that it actually happened." She moaned, dropping her head into her palms.

It was Diego who quietly told them that the four of them had been drawn to follow the Faye and what transpired after they entered the clearing and located the three apparitions.

The room grew silent, and Tabitha inhaled deeply, trying to find the will to raise her head and face their eyes.

She slowly stood and turned to face the seven faces that were watching her intently. Her voice was a shallow whisper. "I take it that this is not a normal occurrence."

Bertòn shook his head. "It is not something Caskan people can do. The Faye have mastered it, but we have never been able to do it. And you seemed to be able to do it with little or no training. Have you done such a thing before?"

Tabitha shook her head. "Never. And I have no idea how I did it. I fell asleep, and then in a dream I spoke to Jules. He told me that they were looking for me. When I asked him how to get out of the house, he told me he thought I could figure it out. And I just seemed to be drawn to that clearing. But no one forced me. I went because I could. I wanted to know what it was I was looking for."

Luc lowered himself onto a stool, his eyes haunted. He glanced at Sybille and Bertòn. "What of the other thing?"

Sybille lifted an inquisitive brow, and Diego stepped forward to glance at Luc's throat. "So that is how Cyra was suddenly cured. It was a miracle indeed, but who?"

Sybille and Diego exchanged a look, and Peri stared at each in turn. Diego shared what had transpired in the clearing, and Peri stared in shock at Luc. She too leaned over to observe the dark twin marks on his throat. "By the One

God, when? What happened? Luc, is this true—a healer? You have been marked as her mate? But...Oh my God..." Her dark eyes stared at Tabitha, her mouth open in shock.

Diego turned to her as well. "Tabitha?"

Tabitha slowly nodded, not seeing any sense in keeping this a secret from them. They obviously realized she was the one. Her voice once again dropped to a whisper. "I had no idea that I had marked him in any way."

Diego shook his head. "I don't understand. You two have not, well, been 'together', yet she marked you? That is the stuff of legends. Couples marking one another as mates—that happened in centuries past. I do not understand. Why and how did Luc get the marks on his neck?" His face remained impassive, but Tabitha could sense his embarrassment as he struggled to put into words what he was thinking.

"You forget your legends of healers, Diego," Bertòn commented, his voice taking on the confident resonance of a trainer. "Think back to what you have known of healers. The legend spoke of the healers taking the blood of their patients or relatives. It was one of the reasons for eradicating the healers."

Diego and Peri looked between them, unsure what it was that Bertòn was telling them. Tristyn spoke next. He told them of his meeting with Tabitha, her admission about her ability, and her willingness to try to help Cyra. He told them of her healing capability and described the evening's events when Tabitha used her life energy to heal Cyra in one sitting.

"When she finished with Cyra, we could see that she was struggling to stay conscious. She would not let any of us near her. She did not seem aware of where she was or what had happened. When we tried to approach her and help her, we saw her fangs. Luc was the only one she would let near, and he bade her to take what she needed from him. It was not until she had been replenished that she became aware of what she had done. As you can imagine, she was quite horrified herself."

Luc nodded. "It is a price I would pay again for Cyra's life."

Peri turned to stare at Tabitha. Her face revealed little emotion, as was the way of the Caskan people, but Tabitha could feel the shock she emitted as Peri stared at her. Tabitha felt she had to say something. "I had only used the power one other time, to help a cat that had been injured in a fight. I was holding him, and suddenly my hands warmed up, and it just started. I remember becoming aware again after he was healed. I was dying of thirst. I was simply terrified over what I had done."

Diego sat on a stool next to Luc. "By God," he exclaimed, "a healer. A healer?"

Tabitha nodded.

Bertòn scratched his head, rose, and went to get himself a mug of javé. "Luc told me the following day. We all felt it best to not share this, as a healer has not been heard of in generations. We would not even know what to do with one, especially one from another world. Tabitha has the responsibility and the right to go home when she has found what she needs. It would not be right of us to assume she will stay here for the good of our people. She has her own home and her own decisions to make. We must leave it to her to decide what we should or should not do with this information."

Luc spoke next. "And what of tomorrow? You think the Faye will not go to Marcus and demand he tell them who the healer is? What will we tell him?"

Bertòn pursed his lips, and his eyes grew distant. "I don't know, but I suggest we think of something to placate them so Tabitha has the chance to do what she must do. We cannot let them take her. If they find out the truth, they may not let her return home."

Tabitha lifted her eyes to him. "You think they would try to keep me?"

He nodded. "Think. What would your government do if they found someone with that capacity? Would they just let them return, or would they try and maintain them, try and harness that ability for the good of their people?"

Tabitha stared from one to another. "They would force me to stay? Can they do that?"

"Any of them could, yes. The point is, we must find a solution in the meantime. We can find some way to placate them. Knowing that you and Luc are linked, it will only be a matter of time before they put the pieces together and figure out that it is you. They know your mother. We must assume they know who your father is. I would imagine that few would assume a half human could ever have the healing ability," Bertòn commented, rubbing his hands over his face.

Sybille spoke. "Bear in mind that the fact that she is half human does not diminish her abilities. Luc is also half human, and he has as strong an ability as any full Caskan."

Diego nodded. "And what of their question about her brother? Is it possible, in any way, that Luc and her being linked has something to do with Tabitha's missing brother?"

All eyes turned to Bertòn. He shook his head. "I cannot even begin to imagine how they could possibly be linked. There were no strange circumstances behind Luc's birth. Yolanda did not give birth to two children. I admit that I was not present when she gave birth, but I have little doubt that Giselle, her sister, would certainly have mentioned that. And Yolanda did live for two years after giving birth to Luc. I was with her all that time." He glanced at Tabitha. "And you are several years younger than Luc. You have described your mother—she is not my wife."

The room was silent as they all wrestled with the information and the knots of the puzzles.

Tabitha finally stood. "Well, we are not going to figure this out tonight. I am so tired of thinking that I want to sleep on my feet."

Sybille nodded. "I can imagine. Separating from your body is said to be very exhausting."

Tabitha glanced up in surprise. "You cannot do that?"

Sybille slowly shook her head. Tabitha glanced from one to another, and they all shook their heads. She exhaled and sank back onto the stool. She lifted haunted eyes to Bertòn. "How is this possible?"

He slowly smiled, shaking his head. "You, Tabitha, are one of the greatest mysteries I have come across in my life. If I had a week to spend with you doing nothing but exploring your talents, I would perhaps be able to give you an answer."

She saw Luc staring into the fire, his eyes distant. She reached out a gentle thought to him, and he glanced up and smiled.

"I want to go home. They told me my mother was home. I want to go home and try and get some answers from her. If she is not there or if she does not speak to me, I will find my father," Tabitha stated. "I can leave in the morning, cross over, and be back tomorrow night in time to leave the next morning with Jules."

"I will take you to the portal in the morning," Luc pledged.

Will you come with me? The question was silent and pleading. She knew that in light of what he had found out tonight she was asking a lot, but she wanted him with her as she faced her mother.

He glanced up in surprise. She could almost see his thoughts racing as he considered. A slow smile lit his face: *Yes.*

CHAPTER TWENTY

TABITHA AND LUC STOOD AT THE SHORE, LOOKING OUT over the dark ocean waves crashing toward them. The lights of a late fishing boat twinkled in the distance. Tabitha breathed a sigh of relief to be home. Luc stood beside her, his thoughts silent as he stared out over the familiar ocean pounding the beach at his feet, yet a world away. They had spent the day preparing Tabitha for her journey to meet her father, and by the time they arrived at the portal, the evening was creeping across the land.

"It's getting late. Let's head up to the house. I want to see my mother. I can get some clothes and call Callie," Tabitha said quietly. She led him up the beach toward the house. She had given him the stone and told him to hold onto it in case something unexpected happened. No matter what happened, he had to be able to get back to his world.

They climbed the hill toward the house, and Tabitha gestured for Luc to wait for her at the top of the stairs. She looked at the dark house.

It is too dark; there should be some lights on.

Perhaps no one is home. She could sense his apprehension as he waited behind her, quietly watching the dark windows.

Wait here.

You should not approach the place alone.

She did not bother to turn as she climbed the remaining steps to the house. *I am better alone. If anything is wrong, I will know right away.*

She approached the back deck of the old house, peering toward the back door and kitchen windows. Nothing—no lights, and all was quiet. Her belly tightened as she stared at the empty house. Then she crept toward the garage and noted that Trude's car was gone. She entered the garage and flicked on the light. On tiptoes, she felt along the small sill of the I-beam for the hidden key. Once she had it in hand, she noticed her mother's car, dusty in the far bay. Her bike rested on its kickstand where she had left it.

She shut off the light and closed the door behind her. Throwing caution to the wind, she gestured for Luc to join her as she headed for the back door of the house. He stepped onto the deck as she was opening the door and looked up at the old Victorian in wonder.

It is so exposed.

Come on in. Let's see if we can find where Trude went and if my mother is here.

He grunted as he looked dubiously at the house. *I have seen pictures of these structures; it does not seem safe to me.*

He entered the kitchen with her and looked around curiously while Tabitha flicked on the lights. She headed to the kitchen table, looking for any note or clue about where Trude had gone. The light flicked off and she spun around, only to find Luc, his hand on the light switch, flicking it back on and then off again.

"Will you stop that?"

"Why does this control the light over there? We have to touch the light. How does this happen?"

She rolled her eyes. "For God's sakes, Luc, let me see where my aunt is, and then I will answer all your questions."

He nodded and continued to explore the kitchen. He was opening cabinets and looking curiously at the microwave when Tabitha found a note with her name on it. As she snatched it up, Luc let out a groan. She turned to find him picking up Trude's clown cup from the dish drain.

What would anyone want with this garish thing?

She could not contain a laugh. She went to the refrigerator and grabbed two bottles of water. She handed one to him as she opened the note. She read her aunt's words.

"Dammit!"

Luc turned startled eyes to her.

"She is not here…Goddamn her for having them lie to me." Tabitha waved the note angrily at him. "It seems that Trude has gone to the mainland to try and find some psychic who says he can speak to other worlds. She is trying to find me and my mother and hopes this guy will help her."

"And your mother?"

"She has not been here. Trude left this morning, and my mother had not been home," Tabitha snarled. She threw the note on the table in disgust. "How could they have lied to me? Why would she tell them to tell me she had gone home…"

Luc stopped his exploration and turned to watch her. She chewed on her bottom lip as she tried to figure out what her mother had gained by lying to her. She must have known Tabitha would return when she discovered her mother was still missing.

A thought occurred to her, and she turned haunted eyes to Luc. He leaned back, silently waiting for her to follow the thread of thought. "They said she was home..." She lifted a hand to her mouth. "What if they did not mean *this* home?"

"Meaning?"

"Maybe she is home, but home is not here." She stared blindly at the shadows slipping across the yard. "Luc, they called me 'kinswoman'. And they said she was home. I just assumed they meant here. But wait—that does not make sense. She is my aunt's sister. I mean, she is human, born here, right?"

He did not respond. Tabitha gripped the back of a chair, conflicting thoughts racing through her mind. She could not make heads or tails of what she was thinking; every thread of an idea ended in a question, a question to which she had no answer.

She shook her head. "I don't know. I just do not understand how I can be related to them and they would tell me she is home. Where is that? I just do not understand."

He shrugged and lifted the note toward her. "What else does it say? Your aunt has gone off to find some psychic? Someone to help her contact you?"

Tabitha groaned and nodded. "Oh, Trude, what were you thinking?"

She took a long drink of water and noticed Luc, leaning against the counter, was doing the same and watching her.

"What does that mean? She is looking for someone with a connection to someone in my world?"

"It means she is probably going to some quack psychic who is going to charge her a small fortune to tell her that they cannot contact us." Tabitha shook her head. "I swore I would never do to my family what my mother did, but the first chance I get, I take off on them."

She sighed and threw the note on the table. "I am no better than she is. I felt justified by my anger to leave my aunt here to try and make excuses for me."

"A quack psychic? What is a quack psychic?"

She dragged her hands through her hair in frustration. "I am making a mess of everything! I am leaving my life here to fall apart, and I have dragged you with me! I don't know what the hell I am doing."

She groaned and fell back into a kitchen chair. "Why am I so damn obsessed with finding a woman who does not want to be found? Maybe I should just stop this, call Trude, and stay home. I can just get on with my friggin' life."

Luc stayed quiet when she rose and began to pace the kitchen. "I don't know what I am doing, Luc. I don't know why I want so badly to find a woman who barely gave me any attention growing up. She barely spoke to me or listened to me. She was so wrapped up in her own little world that I was just an annoyance in her life, someone in her way, and probably someone who kept her from just going back to your world with my father." She turned to him, her silver eyes welling with tears as she searched for answers. "Do you think she would have stayed there if it weren't for me?"

He put his water down and slowly walked over to her, placing his hands on her shoulders and forcing her chin up so their eyes met. "I cannot answer that anymore than you can. There is only one person who can give you those answers, and she is back in my world. If you need to know, then find her."

Tabitha stared into those incredible blue eyes, getting lost in them as he placed her ravings into perspective. She nodded.

"Okay, let's do what I came here to do and then get back. I need to make some calls, and then we can go."

"You are not leaving to meet your father until morning. Why not stay here? You can get some rest and be among your own things for a night. We can return in the morning." He opened the refrigerator. "You can show me your world."

He closed the door and reopened it again. "Does that light always stay on?"

Tabitha hung up the phone after speaking with Trude, tears pouring down her face. Trude had cried when she heard Tabitha's voice. After Tabitha told her what she was doing and that she was going back, Trude had begged her not to go, or at least to wait until she got home before heading back. Tabitha calmed her and promised to be careful. She told her she had friends who were helping her and that she would be gone again in the morning.

She tugged a tissue from the box and wiped her eyes. Luc sat across from her, the chair turned around, his arms crossed over the back. He watched her.

"Is she coming back?"

"No, she is in Rhode Island. She won't be able to get here in time, and it is just as well. If I see her, she will try to convince me to not go back."

He nodded and sat quietly while she tried to gather herself to call Callie. He extended a hand and drew out a tissue and then another one, a slight frown crossing his brow. Tabitha finally grabbed his hand with a chuckle.

"Will you stop?"

"You have the strangest things here."

"If you want to see strange, we should go shopping. You would lose your mind in a hardware store."

She took a deep breath and a long drink of water and dialed Callie's cell. Callie answered; Tabitha could detect the hesitancy in her voice as she recognized the number.

"Trude?"

"No, Cal, it is me, Tabs."

"Tabitha? Oh my God, is everything all right? How is your mother? Trude has been so bad about telling us anything. My mother is frantic! Is she okay? You're home? Oh, God, tell me she didn't die! My mother would never forgive Trude if she died and she wouldn't tell Mom what hospital she was in!"

"Cal, Cal, calm down! What are you talking about? Hospital?"

"Yeah, hospital. Didn't your mother try to commit suicide? Where are you? You are home, right?"

"Suicide? Are you kidding? Who told you that?" Tabitha demanded, the horror of the lie inciting her.

Callie was silent for a moment. "Tabs, what is going on? Where have you been?"

Tabitha ground her teeth. "What did Trude tell you?"

"That Doni had tried to commit suicide and she was in a hospital in Boston, but she wouldn't tell us which one. She told us that besides you, they wouldn't allow any visitors and that your cell didn't work there." Callie sounded confused and frustrated. "Tabs, what is going on?"

"Where are you?"

"I'm at Outriggers. I am working tonight. Come in. I need to find out what the hell is happening up in that house."

"I can't." Tabitha glanced at Luc, wondering if she should take him out and show him some of the town. "Callie, can you come up here after work? I can tell you everything. I don't want to talk over the phone."

"Sure, Tabs. Let's see…It is six now. I can be there about nine."

"Okay. Listen, I think I am going to head into town for a little while. Call my cell if you get out early. "

"'K. See you in a bit."

Tabitha ended the call, staring at the phone in her hand. She replaced the receiver and turned to Luc. "Trude told them that my mother tried to commit suicide and that I was at the hospital on a death watch. And that no one could visit or call me."

"It seems the lies continue," he responded, his chin resting in his arms as he studied her. "How much will you tell her, your cousin?"

Tabitha shook her head. "I don't know. I really don't know. I guess I will tell her the truth, but I am not sure how much. I am not sure how much I believe, to be frank with you."

He remained quiet while she sat staring at the floor, her thoughts distant. She glanced up at the clock and stood. "We have a couple of hours before Cal gets out of work. Let's go into town so I can show you a little of this world before we go back."

Luc stood and stretched, his eyes glancing down at his attire. "Will I pass for someone from your world?"

Tabitha assessed him. He was wearing a soft, fitted collarless white shirt with several buttons at the top undone, a pair of faded pants, and work boots. He looked incredible; the clothes accented his muscular body and golden skin. She reached up and brushed his hair into some semblance of order.

"I think you will drive the women in town fairly wild."

"Great. Wild, I can handle."

She let out a laugh before she grabbed her wallet and her mother's keys. "We'll take Mom's car. It'll be quicker. I really don't want to run into anyone. I am glad that Cal told me the story of where I'm supposed to have been. It will make it easier in case we see anyone. We'll just grab something to eat and walk around so you can see a little of the town. I am sure we can be covert."

He shrugged. "It's your world—lead on."

Tabitha punched the garage door opener and then she headed for the driver's door, lost in thought. She swung her purse into the car before she noticed that Luc was not following her. She saw him standing in the middle of the garage, staring at the car, a doubtful expression on his face.

"What?"

"We are going to get in that and ride in it?"

"It's a car. If you have seen newspapers, you must have seen pictures of cars."

"Yes, but I had not thought I would have to get in one."

"Just get in, you big baby."

He seemed unconvinced, but with a huff, he walked over to the car and opened the passenger door. "You sure this is the only way to get there? I can follow you." He lifted a brow questioningly.

"That would be awesome. Just fly behind me, drop down in the parking lot, and change from a hawk into a gorgeous six-foot man from another world. Sure. That would be covert," she exclaimed sarcastically. "And speaking of covert, just when did you plan on telling me that you could shape-shift? Is that a little tidbit you forgot to mention?"

He looked thoughtful before responding. "Oh yeah, I had planned on mentioning it, but maybe that little detail about you being a healer and needing to suck blood from me in order to keep from dying in my father's library drove it out of my head. Sorry, I guess I forgot."

She stared at him in amazement. Her mouth dropped open, and she sputtered, trying to get out a defense. "I cannot believe you! I mean, you are saying that…"

His lips curved into a lazy smile. "Yes, I am saying I kept my shape-shifting from you as you kept your healing ability from me."

She glared at him, ticking her nail against the roof of the car.

Luc broke the silence. "So...you think I am gorgeous?"

"Get in the damn car before your head doesn't fit."

They drove along the shore road, the evening sun twinkling off the waves as another perfect Porta Negra summer day came to a close. Tabitha noticed that Luc had his arm resting on the open window, looking slightly more relaxed.

"Do you have to go so fast?"

"I am barely going the speed limit" She glanced over at him. "If you were on horseback and cantering along here, you would be enjoying it."

"Not if I was at the mercy of you directing the horse," he muttered. He jumped and grabbed at the dashboard.

They'd had quite a struggle back at the house when she had started the engine. He had jumped from the car with amazing dexterity, refusing to get back in while the engine was running. She had calmed him down and persuaded him that this could be a once-in-a-lifetime opportunity, and he had relented.

Now he glanced over at her. "This is unnatural."

She could not help but laugh. "Oh, yes, and in my world, you flying down in the shape of a hawk is not terribly natural. Driving is much more so. I wonder what the humans who cannot shape-shift would think of having a car at their disposal."

"Alena has no trouble getting around."

"She is married to Tristyn. I would imagine that she gets irritated with asking him to assist her."

He grunted but did not respond.

"Is shape-shifting your only option for travel?"

"No, we also use a technique called journeying. If I want to get to the shore, I can will myself there and there I am."

"Ah, very convenient for Alena, I imagine?"

"Tristyn can take her anywhere she needs to go."

Tabitha scoffed. "Don't you see? She is at his mercy. What if she just wants to go there alone? What if she doesn't want to rely on Tristyn to get here where she needs to go?"

"She has other options. Trust me, Alena is a headstrong woman. Don't mistake her humanness for any kind of weakness. She has Tristyn on a fairly short leash, and he is well aware of it."

"Ha! That is funny..."

"What?"

"C'mon! She has Tristyn on a leash—you know, the wolf thing? Never mind."

He grunted again, relenting. He glanced around the car, taking in the instrument panel. "I must admit, I would not want to see her get her hands on one of these."

Tabitha laughed. "What other shape can you do? Any one you want?"

"No, it takes years of study to shape-shift into an animal. We chose one, maybe two. As a child I started as a wolf. That was my father's shape. He is originally from the northern clans, and they often shaped wolves because they could travel great distances and also hunt. I chose to shape a hawk as I got older. The allure of flying was too great to not take advantage of."

"And your father, does he shape more than the wolf?"

"No, he considers most other animals beneath his dignity," Luc commented.

"And Sybille?"

"Sybille is a different story," Luc replied evasively.

"Why do you always get elusive when I ask about Sybille?"

"I don't. It is just that asking about people's talents is a bit of a breach of courtesy. We do not normally ask about people's abilities."

"Why is that?"

"Well, it could mean that you are looking for their weakness."

"Ah, okay. Is that why you did not tell me about shapeshifting?"

Luc sighed as he stared out at the sparkling ocean. "Maybe. It has only has been a few days that I have known you. It is not like I am going to let you know everything that I am capable of— Hey! Hey! What are you doing?"

Luc pushed against the dashboard in alarm.

"What is wrong with you?" Tabitha asked as she swung the car into a parking spot.

"I thought you were going to hit that car!" Luc exclaimed. He got out of the car as soon as it stopped. Tabitha got out and saw him looking at the cars next to them. "Did you have to park so close?"

Tabitha glanced around the packed public lot. "Yes. It is the only way to make sure everyone fits."

He stared at the cars filling the parking lot. "There are so many! I cannot even imagine all of these cars driving around at once. How many people belong to this many cars?"

She smiled. "Luc, to tell you the truth, this is only a small percentage of the cars on the island right now."

He stared at her and shook his head. They walked to the sidewalk; the car beeped as she locked it with the remote. The sound startled him, and he glanced back at the car. She led him toward the quaint cobbled streets of the island center. As they turned the corner onto Main Street, he stopped for a moment, staring in amazement at the number of people bustling along the streets. Baby carriages jockeyed for space on the sidewalk; people walking dogs tried to dodge large groups of families; others window-shopped, reading menus and glancing at the assorted shop windows.

"Welcome to my world," she muttered as she led him down Main Street, trying to skirt the tourists who meandered down the crowded sidewalks. She led him along the twisting street, and he stared at the crowds and the mass of humanity that jostled past him.

She ducked down a side street and led Luc through a knot of tourists gaping at a street performer. They skirted down an alley and emerged onto a busy side street. Tabitha wove her way through the traffic, tugging Luc behind her.

"Doesn't that red hand mean 'don't walk' across the street?"

"Amateur," she grumbled. She pulled him into the next alley, and they cut through an apartment complex walkway.

" 'Lessees only? No trespassing'?" Luc asked. "If I am not mistaken, these signs have no meaning in your world?"

She chuckled. "You have to learn the ways of a very different world here. We consider most of our signs more as suggestions." He looked at her with skepticism and she laughed. "Okay, we learn which ones to ignore and which ones not to."

They emerged close to the waterfront, and Tabitha led him to a tiny restaurant at the corner, where a simple wood sign hung over the door.

"Where are we?"

"At a restaurant," she responded. She opened the door and led him into the dark interior. "We can get some dinner."

He glanced around as they entered, his gaze curious as he took it all in. She waved hello to the hostess and gestured to the deck. The hostess smiled and nodded, and Tabitha leaned over the hostess station, grabbed two menus, and tugged Luc out to the deck. She spotted a table in the corner and led him over to it.

"Do you want to explain all of that gesturing and arm waving? Is it some sort of restaurant language that one needs to know to get seated?" he asked as he sat.

She laughed. "No, I know the hostess. She was seating someone else, so she just told me to grab a menu and seat ourselves."

He nodded, leaning forward to take in the sight of the people bustling on the street below them. Cars passed by, the sounds of horns and the occasional screech of a siren erupting as the evening tourist business got in full swing. The red traffic light below them flicked back and forth, allowing cars to pass until the intermittent swell of pedestrians halted the pattern to cross the road. Luc watched this dance of humanity with amusement.

Their waitress brought glasses of water, and Tabitha waved a hand at her question about other drinks. She studied the menu while Luc stared at the tourists meandering in and out of the shops.

"It is like they have no purpose," he murmured.

She glanced up. "They don't. This is a vacation for most people. They do not have anything more to do than wander through the shops and look at trinkets. It is why people enjoy wandering the center at night. They check out the stores, stop for a drink, get an ice cream, and people-watch."

"I will take your word for it."

She turned back to the menu, looking for simple suppers. She had considered stopping somewhere for pizza or something quick, but she knew that Luc had never eaten any kind of processed foods or additives. She was not sure how his body would react to the influx of chemicals a pizza would give him. The restaurant she chose was one of the simplest in town, offering some organic meals.

After dinner, she decided that the best thing to do would be to walk back to the car through town to give Luc the opportunity to see her world, if only for an evening. She hoped to avoid running into anyone. They crossed the street and walked along the waterfront, watching the people pass and enjoying the warm summer evening. They passed an ice cream stand. Luc stood watching as people got cones through the window.

"Do you want one?" she asked.

He shook his head. "Just taking this all in. You have no idea what experiencing this is like. I told you we get newspapers on occasion, and we have studied your culture. But to see your people in everyday life is incredible."

She slipped her hand into his and pulled his arm around her waist. "Who knows?" she commented as he turned to look at her. "Maybe when this is all over you will want to spend some time over here. Learn more about us and study our culture?"

His smile was slow and lazy, and he tightened his grip on her waist. "I am thinking of taking up one particular avenue of study."

She smiled at him, enjoying his flirting. The warm summer breeze tugged at his hair, and Tabitha leaned against him, reaching to lift the hair from his eyes. Her fingers curled in the hair on his nape, pulling him down to her—

"Tabitha?"

A cold dash of water could not have ruined the moment more effectively. Tabitha turned guiltily from Luc to see Greg standing a few feet behind them. She observed the flash of pain in his eyes as he absorbed the sight of their close stance, Luc's hand on her waist, her fingers tangled in his hair.

"Greg. Hi. Umm, let me introduce you."

She stood back and glanced between the two men. "Greg, this is Luc DesChamps. Luc, Greg Doherty."

They exchanged a handshake. Luc's smile was enigmatic, but she could see the flash of understanding in his eyes.

"How is your mother? I am surprised to see you. I heard that your mother was not doing well. When did you get back?"

Tabitha inhaled as she prepared to live the lie that her aunt had painted for her. "This afternoon. I am going back in the morning. I...umm...just had to come back for a few things."

"Hmm. Strange. I would have thought that Sean would have seen you on the ferry. In fact, he didn't see you the night you took off either. And he was working the ferry then." Greg's stance was confrontational, and he eyed Luc with ill intent.

"No, he would not have. I went and returned by a private boat." She felt a twinge of guilt at how easily the lie slipped from her mouth.

"Ah." He nodded his head in apparent understanding, but Tabitha knew he was not buying her line. "Seems strange—and convenient."

Tabitha replied, "Yes, it was. Luc's family owns a boat, and he was able to help."

Greg shifted his gaze from Tabitha to look Luc full in the face. Greg shrugged. "Yeah, lucky for her that she had someone that could do that for her." His gaze shifted back to Tabitha. "You must have been relieved to have someone you could turn to when you needed them."

"Greg, don't do this. It is not about you."

"No, don't worry about it. So tell me, how did you two meet? Seems that having spent the last two years with Tabitha, I would have heard of you. But maybe not if you just met." Greg crossed his arms across his chest, and Tabitha bit down in irritation at his implication.

"Quite frankly, it is none of your business. I was seeking some answers about my mother's past, and Luc's family was kind enough to help. As for you and I, we agreed to ditch. Anything going on with me has nothing to do with you," she ground out between clenched teeth.

Greg nodded. "You're right. It isn't. But then again, you made sure that not too much *was* my business when it came to you." He stepped back, pain evident on his face, and Tabitha felt a cruel jab of guilt. "I was hoping to get hold of you to see if there was anything I could do for you. I am sure you got my voicemails. Obviously, you are well cared for."

He turned and, with a curt nod to Luc, stalked off. Tabitha hung her head in shame.

Let him go.

I have hurt him, Luc. It was never my intention.

Let's go back.

CHAPTER TWENTY-ONE

THE NIGHT WORE ON AS THEY WAITED AT TRUDE'S home for Callie to arrive. Luc was engrossed in flipping through the TV channels. He never stayed on one long enough to absorb the show, just flipped through the multitude of choices in fascination.

Whoa! What is this?

She caught a glimpse of naked flesh as a couple wrestled in bed. She glanced at the guide along the bottom of the screen.

You are watching the soap opera reruns. It does not get more explicit than that.

Does it have to? I am watching two people…

Luc, you are watching two people acting. They are pretending. It is not real.

He seemed perplexed, his brows knit, as he watched in apparent disbelief. The show flipped to a commercial about laundry detergent, and with a grunt, he continued his exploration.

She wandered out to the deck, the sound of the TV a dull buzz as she stared out at the darkened ocean. Her mind scrambled over the events of the last days.

She turned back to the house, watching Luc through the window. He was perched on the coffee table, amazed by the plethora of TV shows and sheer visual overload. She smiled as she watched him.

God, he is gorgeous, she thought to herself. For a moment, she let her mind wander along, imaging herself falling in love with him. But he was from another world, with power that he used with an amazing dexterity. He could shape a hawk and a wolf and apparently move himself at will to other locations. He was a wizard, a sorcerer, a man with power that she could not even imagine, and that frightened her. Even as he sat, mesmerized by the news, she watched him with a mixture of awe and fear. He was everything she could hope for, a friend, a confident, someone who understood what she was and what she could do. And he had promised to teach her, to show her training he had mastered.

She had spent a lifetime in fear of her talent, afraid of what she would unleash if she should try and investigate its full potential. And here he sat, ready to teach her, in her living room, remote in had, watching some foolish commercial for a vaginal cream, his brows knit in apparent confusion. She could barely contain the bubble of laughter that threatened to escape as he changed the channel again with a shake of his head. He glanced up. Seeing her through the windows, he put the remote down and came out on the deck to join her.

"You had enough?"

"I am amazed. With all that, how do you possibly choose something to stare at? How does one decide what to watch and what to miss?"

She laughed. "You would have had to grow up with it to understand. Suffice it to say that there is not all that much once you actually start watching half the stuff on there."

He nodded, leaning against the deck rail. "What were you thinking about out here?"

"Everything. Nothing." She barked a short, brittle laugh. "How do I even begin to explain to Callie what has happened in these past days? And where do I go from here?"

He glanced up, watching the headlights that lit the front of the house and then slid to light up the garage. "If I am not mistaken, looks like it is time to figure that out."

Tabitha walked over to the top of the stairway as Callie flew out of Derek's car, the door still open as she ran up the stairs to throw her arms around Tabitha's neck. The two girls clung to one another for a few moments. Tabitha heard Derek's footfalls as he climbed the stairs behind Callie.

Callie exhaled as she hugged Tabitha tightly, and then she stiffened. Without letting her grip loosen, she whispered in Tabitha's ear. "Oh my God, Tabs, who is that?"

Tabitha laughed and pried Callie's arms away, stepping back. Derek swung her into a bear hug while Callie stood, staring, her mouth slightly agape, at Luc.

Tabitha stood back with a smile. Holding Callie and Derek's hands in hers, she turned to face Luc.

"Callie, Derek, let me introduce Luc. Luc, this is my cousin Callie and her boyfriend, Derek."

Luc stepped forward, extending a hand to each. Callie smiled, staring back and forth between them.

Tabitha waved toward the kitchen. "You had both better come in. This might take a few minutes."

"I can't believe this." Callie shook her head as Tabitha finished telling her about the past few days.

Tabitha glanced at Luc, who leaned against the counter, arms crossed in front of him.

Should I tell her more?

It's your secret to tell, he responded. *But I ask, is there anything to gain from telling her more?*

No, why overwhelm her? I just wanted her to know where I have been and that I am looking for my mother. Someone should know, just in case...

He shrugged, remaining quiet. Tabitha was aware that his dark and quiet presence made Callie and Derek nervous. He had stood like a dark sentinel, leaning against the counter, watching and listening as Tabitha relayed her experiences since she had left Callie so many days ago. Callie glanced uneasily over at him. Luc stayed quiet, letting Tabitha tell her tale.

"Tabs, this is so unreal. I am sure that tomorrow morning I am going to wake up and wonder if this was all a dream." Callie's eyes were wide open in disbelief. Derek remained quiet, skepticism written across his face.

"This is a little odd," he said slowly. "I am not so sure that this all makes sense." He gestured to Luc. "And you are telling me that he lives in that place? Some other world?"

Tabitha nodded, and Derek leaned back in his chair, watching Luc warily. He pursed his lips. "Hey, no offense, man, but I am having trouble swallowing all of this. I mean, how do we know that he's not some guy who slipped you some crazy-ass shit and you have been having one wild hallucination?"

Luc was silent before responding, his body seemed relaxed but Tabitha could sense the wary alertness in him. "I would think less of you had you believed all of this without question. Tabitha wants someone to know where she is as she searches for her mother." He lifted his chin to indicate Callie. "She did not want her cousin to suffer as she had suffered, wondering where her mother had disappeared to."

"Tabs, are you telling me you are going back?" Callie was concerned, her eyes shooting uncertainly between them.

"I have to. Except for finding the place where I think she went, I have nothing else. I need to find her and my father. I need to know what went on and finally put some of these questions about myself to rest," Tabitha told her. She paced the kitchen; Luc's edginess was affecting her, shooting nervous energy through her.

"But you have discovered where she went, and you know why you have your abilities." She gestured to Luc. "From his people. Obviously your mother found her way over there somehow and must have fallen in love or met someone. And decided to stay..."

As Callie looked back and forth, Tabitha could sense her cousin's fear of Luc and her trepidation that Tabitha would go back with her mysterious dark stranger and never return.

"And you think I plan on doing the same?" Tabitha finished softly.

Callie lifted one shoulder, her eyes welling as she stared back at her. "Tabitha, don't go. Let Doni find her own way home. Just leave it be. Please."

Tabitha shook her head and walked over to Luc. She slipped into his arms and leaned back against him, turning toward her cousin. "I can't, Callie. I finally know a way to find all those answers that I have been looking for. I can finally find out. These people understand me; they know the power that I am struggling with—they understand it. They can help me to meet my father and to learn to control this, before I do some real damage the next time I lose my temper." She pulled Luc's arms closer around her to ward off a chill. Her voice shook. "What if I had not aimed at the china closet that night? What if I'd damaged something closer to Trude? I was so angry. What if I had hurt her? What happens if I lose my cool at someone driving in traffic? If I don't learn more about this, I could do God-knows-what harm."

Derek shrugged. "Would not be a bad talent to have in Boston traffic."

Luc chuckled. In a more somber tone, he addressed Callie. "Tabitha is not coming back to stay. She has intended all along to return. But with a little more time, she can get the answers she seeks. And maybe come back with some peace."

Callie watched as Tabitha glanced up at Luc, her smile warm. His eyes glowed as he winked at her. Some of her fears were slightly alleviated, but the connection and the warmth she saw between them left her wondering if Tabitha would be able to tear herself from the handsome man now holding her. For the first time in years, she understood what Tabitha had been saying about Greg. She finally saw that Greg had not been right for her. But this man, his arms around Tabitha, her body nestled against him—he was a different story. And that frightened Callie more than anything else.

She finally released her worries and smiled at her cousin. "Okay, Tabs, I will be behind you one hundred percent. Do what you gotta do. But before you head off, you have to tell me more about this world. What is it like? What can these people do? I mean, do you walk around with wands and fly on broomsticks?"

Luc lifted an elegant eyebrow. "What?"

Tabitha laughed. "I do not imagine your reading of the classics has enlightened you about our world's more recent stories of wizards and strange worlds."

Luc exhaled. "Broomsticks? I cannot even imagine how one would ride a broomstick. I have seen references to your witches. I can assure you, no one I know has ever ridden a broomstick."

Callie grinned. "So what can you do? Can you show me a trick?"

Tabitha winced, and Luc sighed. *A trick? Is she serious?*

Tabitha grinned up at him. *Come on! Remember that they have never met someone like you. She is not asking you to per-*

form, only to show her something. They have never seen real magic.

How about you?

They know I can do something— at least Callie does, and I guess that Derek does now. But you— if you can do something to convince them, maybe they won't think you are some bullshit artist.

He groaned. *What is a bullshit artist?*

She laughed and stepped back from him. *Just an expression...*

He sighed and nodded toward the door. "Follow me."

Callie and Derek followed him out to the deck, with Tabitha trailing behind. Luc did not look pleased. He shot Tabitha an irritated glance as he stepped to the edge of the deck.

Derek watched warily, holding Callie by the waist as he tugged her back. "What are you going to do?"

Luc glanced back at them and snorted derisively. "You're expecting a cloud of smoke and some dramatic gestures? Just watch."

Luc stepped onto the deck railing and lifted his arms. The change into a hawk was almost instantaneous. With a powerful thrust of his wings, he propelled himself upward and soared toward the sky. They could see his dark silhouette against the deep violet of the waning evening. He circled the house once and dropped gracefully to the ground, changing shape as he landed. He did not look pleased when he slowly climbed the steps to the deck. Tabitha smiled at him, but she could sense his unease at having to perform a "trick" to prove his legacy.

She turned and saw Callie and Derek staring at him, mouths wide open. Derek slowly lowered himself into a deck chair, still staring at Luc. Callie's gaze shifted between Luc and Tabitha as she struggled for words.

"Adequate proof, or do you require something more substantial?" Luc growled.

Derek slowly shook his head, closing his mouth. "I have never seen anything like that..."

"Oh my God, this is real," Callie murmured. All her life she had known about Tabitha's abilities. They had always been simple, like easing the soreness from her feet or small telekinetic tricks. But this! What Luc had done...She could not believe that she had just seen him turn into a hawk. She slowly turned to Tabitha. "Can you do anything like that?"

Tabitha shook her head.

Luc dragged one of the patio chairs around and swung onto it, his arms folded along the back. "Tabitha has some amazing abilities, from what we have seen of her potential this week. But you have to realize that I have been trained since birth on how to focus what I have."

Derek leaned forward, his elbows on his knees, his gaze intent as he stared at the other man. "That was amazing. Can everyone in your world do that?"

Luc shook his head, slowly relaxing. "People in my world, much like yours, all have different abilities and talents. What we can learn and how diligent and focused we are during our training all play a role in what we can do. Like yourselves, it is difficult to gauge one talent against another because we all learn differently and have different aptitudes."

"But can everyone change shape? What else can you do? Can you read minds, disappear?" Callie stepped forward, hesitation and fear reflected on her face.

Luc lifted his hands and rocked them to and fro. "Some can and some cannot, for a variety of reasons. Not everyone feels comfortable with it. Some people would rather not shape-shift, and others cannot grasp what it entails. But since my father was a clan of shape-shifters, that was something I was taught young. The southern clans are not as adept as shape-shifters. But they have the blood of the tree sprites and water sprites, so they find it more comfortable to shape water or trees. I find it easier to take the shape of an animal. I could not imagine shaping water. I can't understand it. But I guess if I had been brought up learning the principles, I may have mastered it."

"Tree sprites? Water sprites?" Callie sank into another chair, her fear turning into wonder. "What are those?"

Luc seemed to relax as the focus switched to his world, not his talents. His comment earlier about not showing one's abilities haunted Tabitha. She realized what he had done for her and smiled as he described his world.

"A wood sprite is a form of an elf that can take the shape of a tree. They do not become a free-standing tree, but they can…Let me think how to describe it. I guess you could say they sink themselves into the tree. And a water sprite, the same thing—they can sink into a spring or a lake or stream and I guess lose themselves, become the water. I can't explain how it is done because I have no aptitude or understanding. But I understand it is fairly common in the southern clans."

"The sprites and elves exist in my world, along with the Faye. Many years ago, humans began to come into our world, sometimes whole villages. In time, the races intermarried and formed new races. The Caskan, which is what I am, are descendants of the Faye and humans. The southern clans are descended from the Faye, but they also have tree-sprite and water-sprite blood in them. It seems that only true Caskan descendants can shape into animals; the others seem to be able to shape into water or trees or wood."

Derek shook his head in amazement. "And you have humans there as well?"

Luc nodded. "People still suddenly appear. No one knows why. For some reason, most cannot cross back over. Many of us can, using the type of stone that Tabitha has. I must admit that the human population is probably a very small percentage of our world. Most are either full magical or a partial descendant of some mix."

Callie and Derek quizzed Luc, fascinated, and Tabitha found herself learning much more about it as he spoke. When Callie began yawning and Tabitha felt her eyes drooping, Derek stood.

Callie rose, her eyes huge as she stared at Tabitha. "I am not going to cry..."

Tabitha smiled. "I will be back before you can miss me."

Callie swept her into a hug. "I miss you already," she whispered against her hair. "Promise me, please promise me you will be careful and you will come back."

Tabitha nodded and bit back tears when Callie finally released her. Derek lifted her off her feet in a growling hug. As he put her down, he turned to Luc.

"Take care of her."

Luc nodded. Callie and Derek left with a last wave, and Tabitha watched the tail lights head down the hill. "I hope we did the right thing by telling them everything we told them."

"Do you have any reason not to trust them?"

She shook her head. They headed into the house, and Tabitha locked the door behind them. She showed Luc to a spare bedroom and then showered. She lay on her bed, the window open, remembering the night not many nights ago when she had lain in her bed and reached out to Luc. So much had happened since then that she could barely believe it had only been a matter of days.

Exhaustion began to overtake her, but she could not seem to relax. She lay, heavy with weariness, her mind swirling with questions and thoughts.

Luc?

Hmm?

You sleeping?

No.

Do you know my father?

Only what I have heard about him. He is the governor of the state that my uncle and cousin live in. They know him quite well.

What do you know of him?

She heard him sigh. *I am trying to remember.*

She rose from her bed and went down the hall. With a slight tap, she opened the door to the bedroom he was using. He lay atop the bed, his clothes still on, his arms folded beneath his head. He glanced over at her and gestured to the bed. She grabbed a blanket off the chair as she passed and climbed onto the bed beside him, curling against him.

The windows were opened wide in there as well, and she could hear the gentle sweep of the tide as the cool sea air slid over her.

"I know my uncle thinks highly of him. He has a great land parcel and has set aside much of his property for smaller homes for people who might struggle to have one of their own. I understand that he has been searching for a way to cure the disease that seems to be gripping our race and killing our women and children," Luc commented.

"He is trying to negotiate a peace treaty, isn't he?"

Luc nodded, and she leaned her head on his shoulder, gazing up at his profile as he spoke. "Where they live runs along the Plains clans' land, so they are close to the stretch of land where they migrate. The clans have customary places where they summer and winter, so I imagine that over the years he has become familiar with the people who live alongside his lands. Perhaps that is where he started? And as the tensions rose, I believe that he began setting up meetings between the clan elders and our own. Marcus has on occasion traveled down for them."

"And now it will be you?"

He exhaled. "Yeah, apparently it is so. I will have to spend the next several weeks meeting with committees from all the communities in Marcus's territory to establish the concerns and issues that I have been designated to represent."

"Alone?"

"No, I will be one of a committee of four. Each of us will represent one portion. I would not have time to travel to the entire territory."

"And then you will come to Windrift?"

He smiled. “I will. And will you be there? Waiting?”

She shrugged. She was comfortable against him, his warmth warding off the chill of the night air. “I don’t know. I will have to see how meeting him goes. Jules tell me he has been looking for my mother as well. I guess whoever gave him that picture of me must have told him that she was there.”

“Who do you think gave him that picture?”

She blew out her breath. “I don’t know, but I have my suspicions.” He glanced at her, and she rose onto one elbow. “I have been trying to figure that out. I can only come up with my aunt Trude. I try not to think about it too much, because the question of what she knows and her involvement staggers me, and I can only handle one focus at a time. Right now I have to remain focused on meeting my father. I can find out what he knows, and that might determine where I look next. Maybe he can shed enough light on all of this to allow me to get back to my life with some feeling of closure. Maybe when I find out what he knows, it will be enough for me, and I can just leave my mother to do whatever she wants. But Trude must have known who to give that picture to. She had to have contacted someone.”

“Or maybe the lawyer that you met contacted her after you left?” he suggested.

“Maybe.” She thought that through for a moment; it seemed to fit. “But if she had spoken to that lawyer, why would she be with the psychic in Rhode Island, trying to get a message to me? Why not just give the message to the lawyer? She had to have known that by giving her the picture, someone would be looking for me.”

The questions piled up. Tabitha dropped her head back on his shoulder. Her mind was overwhelmed, and she found herself unable to think straight, never mind formulate another theory. Luc lay quietly while she struggled through her thoughts. When she put aside the questions she had for Trude, the answers she wanted from her father came cascading, an avalanche of inquiry. She shook her head as though to dispel some of it, but then the questions the meeting with the Faye had brought up seemed to engulf her.

Shhhh. Stop thinking.

I can't, Luc. I do not even know…

Shhh. Get some rest. Let me help you.

He shifted onto his side so he was facing her. She held back a nervous giggle, but he shook his head, placing a finger on her lips. She felt him wash over her mind with a warm and peaceful hold. She fought, slightly alarmed by the sense of him taking control of her, but he gently eased her panic. She once again let the slow sweep of peace and calm wash over her. She began to realize he was not exerting himself but simply projecting, and she began to relax. With a soft sigh, she closed her eyes, and with the sounds of the waves and his gentle encouragement, she slipped into sleep.

CHAPTER TWENTY-TWO

TABITHA EYED THE COFFEEMAKER SPECULATIVELY AS the early sunlight twinkled off the ocean into Trude's bright kitchen. After so many days of drinking javé, she was not sure she could choke down coffee made in the dilapidated old coffeemaker from Trude's canned coffee grounds.

She glanced up toward the second floor. She heard the water running as Luc showered and wondered if she had time to run to the cafe and grab a half-decent cup of coffee for them. With a groan, she shoved the glass pot under the running water, opting for homemade. She was measuring out the grounds and daydreaming about getting Trude a coffeemaker made in this millennium for Christmas when a sharp rap at the back door startled the coffee can out of her hands.

6:15? Really? Who would be at the door at 6:15?

She grabbed a dishtowel and headed for the back door, swinging the old mini-blinds aside as she peered out onto back deck. Shock and trepidation shimmied through her body. Greg stood rocking from one foot to the other, waiting on the back deck.

"Oh, shit!" Tabitha groaned. She wondered if it would be possible to pretend she was not home, but he had spotted the swinging blinds. His hand was already reaching to rap again on the old door when she snatched it open.

"Greg? What are you doing— Hey!"

He shoved the door open, shouldered his way into the kitchen, pushed her aside, and slammed the door behind them.

"Just shut the hell up and listen to me for a second," he snapped.

"Greg, if this is some kind of—"

"Tabs, this is no kind of anything right now, so just shut up! I am only here because Callie called Derek and he called me," Greg snapped.

She gripped his arm in a panic. "Is something wrong? What? Why didn't she call me herself?"

"Because she and her family have been spending the better part of the night sitting with the Island police and the FBI. She was able to get the hell away and call Derek from the bathroom on the phone Roni keeps hidden there." He shook his head. "I don't know what the hell is going on here, and I don't know what you told them or where you have been, but some serious shit is starting to hit the fan around here, and apparently your mother is in the middle of it."

Her mouth went dry and her head began to spin. She didn't even know what to try to comprehend. "What? I— What happened? Is Trude all right? I don't understand. What has happened?"

"Trude is fine and with the FBI in Boston right now. Apparently they have transported her from Rhode Island and have her in for some questioning about your mother." His eyes were hard and challenging as he folded his arms across his chest and regarded her. "So do you want to give me some hint about what the hell is going on and where you have been? I am guessing the whole suicide watch and your mom being in a hospital in Boston is just another load of bullshit? Just asking."

She could hear Luc's steps as he trotted down the stairs, fresh from his shower and oblivious to the drama unfolding in the kitchen. She and Greg turned as Luc came around the stair banister, passed through the living room, and headed toward the kitchen, his hair still wet at the ends, tugging his shirt over his lean waist.

Luc stopped when he saw them standing across the kitchen from one another. Tabitha exhaled, knowing there was no way to soften the blow. Nothing had happened last night between her and Luc, but the look on Greg's face seared pain through her emotions. It would be pointless to even try and comment at this point, and she refused to try. A thousand different excuses bubbled up, but she squashed them down. When all was said and done, maybe this was what they needed to end the cycle she and Greg both knew they were going to slip into.

Tabitha drew her hands through her still-damp hair and groaned, staring at the ceiling. "Greg, you have to tell me what the hell is going on down at Ell and Frank's. Why did the police show up? I mean, why after all this time are they suddenly looking for my mother? It is not like we did a missing person—"

He cut her off sharply. "Well, this time they found a body, Tabitha."

She dropped her hands. "What? A body? Whose body did they find?" she whispered. "Is it my mother?"

Greg shrugged. "They don't seem to know. It seems that this body was found down in the Hollow and has been down there for—oh, I don't know—twenty years, give or take? Seeing they just found it last night, it will probably be a while before they know."

"Twenty years? How can that be? Who could it be? I mean, my mother was the only one who disappeared, and she returned," Tabitha stammered.

Luc walked into the kitchen. "No one else disappeared? Your mother was the only one?"

Tabitha nodded. "Yeah. I mean, the island has all these legends about people disappearing from the Hollow, but my mother was the only one in recent history."

Greg glanced at Luc and then back at Tabitha. She could not miss the tightening of his jaw as he averted his eyes. "Yup. She was. So the question is, who is the dead chick and where is your mother?"

"Oh my God, I have no idea," Tabitha moaned.

"So you don't know where she is?" Greg demanded.

Tabitha shook her head. "I was looking for her with Luc's help, but I have not been able to find her."

Greg nodded, lips pursed. Tabitha could still see tension coursing through him. "They have not come up here yet because when they came to the house, you were not here and no one had seen you for days. They went to get Trude to ask her where your mom is and where you are. I guess they want to know if any of you might know why another body might have been found down in the Hollow. From what Callie tells me, they are getting a search warrant signed right now so they can come up here and search the premises for any clue about where any of you might be."

"Oh God...We have to get out of here," Tabitha gasped.

"So where is this so-very-convenient little personal boat that you have been using? You might want to trot on down and climb aboard while you can, because it is not going to be long before they start fanning this search out." Greg's voice was clipped in a desperate attempt at casual.

"Did you say the body was found down in the Hollow?" Luc asked quietly. He glanced up and caught Tabitha's eye. "The same place where we arrived?"

Tabitha's hands flew to her mouth. "We can't go back down there! There must be police all over the place!"

Greg looked from one to the other. "What do you mean? What 'place' you arrived? I thought you guys were going back in Mr. Convenient's boat? Callie told me to get you out of the house to someplace where you could get back to searching for your mother. How the hell could you have come through the Hollow? It's not like there is any canal or anything. It's just a friggin' swamp."

Luc ignored him and turned to Tabitha. "We can get through undetected if you get me there."

"How you going to do that?" Greg demanded.

"Luc, we have to know who that body is. I mean, Doniella Devins disappeared twenty-two years ago. What if that is Doniella Devins?"

Luc stopped and stared at her. "But then—who is your mother?"

"That is the question, isn't it?" Tabitha murmured.

"I don't know what the hell you guys are talking about, but I've got a fishing boat to catch, and I am not going anywhere near that body. I am here to get you out of here. If the FBI stops you now, you'll never get out until they do all that DNA crap and figure out where your mom is and where the hell you have been." Greg pushed away from the counter. "So if you want a ride before the cavalry shows up with a search warrant, let's go. Otherwise, I am out of here."

Tabitha grabbed the coffee pot and dumped the water, shoving the grounds into the trash. "Luc, get upstairs and grab the wet towels. It can't look like we were here."

She wiped the pot as fast as she could and shoved it back into its cradle.

Greg stood at the door with his hand on the knob, watching Luc slip up the stairs. "What the hell, Tabitha? They are going to figure out you were here. It's the FBI, for chrissakes. You think you are going to fool them?"

"No, but at least I don't have to be obvious," she grunted as she swept up the coffee grounds she had dropped when he knocked on the door.

"How long you been banging this guy?" Greg asked quietly.

"Shut up, Greg," she snapped.

"No, seriously. I mean you guys seem pretty tight for someone you only met recently," he sneered.

"We are not talking about this." She lifted a hand. "I am getting out of here so I can find my mother and straighten this out."

Greg lifted a defensive hand. "Yeah, whatever. I told Derek I would give you a heads up and give you a ride where you need to go, and then I am done." He turned back as Luc was coming down the stairs, and his voice dropped. "How many friggin' people do you think saw you and lover-boy in town last night? Won't be long before people start coming forward to say you were on-island."

She spun. "You know what? You are—"

Luc came into the kitchen with the towels in his hand. "Enough. Stop the arguing so we can get out of here."

Greg drew himself up to face Luc. "Hey, this is none of your concern. You can just shut the hell up."

Luc ignored Greg and deposited the towels in her arms before he yanked the door free from Greg's hand. "I am pretty deep in this myself. I have a lot to lose." He glanced at Tabitha and gestured out the door. "I do not know your world well enough to be able to talk myself out of it. Let's go."

Tabitha nodded and shoved Greg out the door in front of her.

"Your world? Where the fuck you from? Mars?"

"I am going to check out what is going on. Go to the edge of the Hollow, the path we took to get out, and wait for me there. I can see if we will be able to get through."

"No, Luc, we can't split up."

"It will take only a moment, and then we will have a better idea of what we will face. Wait at the path." He slid the stone from his pocket and pressed into her hand. "Take this. I will meet you at the path."

Luc stepped to the edge of the deck. As Greg opened his mouth to comment, Luc stepped off the edge, changed into a hawk, and drove himself toward the sky. Greg stopped and dropped his jaw, his lips moving without sound coming out.

"Yeah, Mars—they do that a lot up there," Tabitha grumbled as she propelled him toward the driveway. She stopped short when she saw it was empty. "Where is your car?"

Greg snapped himself back to reality and pointed through the woods. "Just over the there. I didn't want it in the driveway in case they showed up with that warrant."

They both jumped off the deck and ran into the woods, shoving the branches and brambles aside as they wove through the underbrush.

"How did he do that? What have you gotten yourself involved in?" Greg demanded.

"I didn't get myself involved in anything!" Tabitha snapped back. "My mother dragged me into this craziness, and I brought Luc along with me. If she had been truthful with me all along, I would not be in this mess right now. God, Greg, whose body is that down there? Are they sure it is twenty years old?"

"Hey, all I know is what Callie told Derek last night, and she did not have long to talk. How do I know how they figure out how long it's been there? Besides, your mother was the only one who had gone missing, and when she showed up again, she wouldn't say a word. I imagine they have some questions for her," Greg responded as they approached the concealed car. He emerged from the brush and headed over to the driver's door.

"Who's car is this?" Tabitha asked as she tugged open the passenger door and tossed the damp towels on the back seat

Greg dug the keys out of his pocket. "Marcy's. Mom's got mine."

"Shall I ask how long you've been banging her?" Tabitha shot back, her voice dropping to mimic his tone.

"Shut up. I will drop you over at the Hollow, and then I am gone. I do not want to get sucked into this three-ring circus of a life you have pulled out of your ass." He started the car and began to turn around, only to jam it into reverse and ease back into the brush again.

"What?"

"Two unmarked cars just pulled into your driveway. Shit. They are going to hear us pull out." Greg exhaled.

"Give them a second to get out of the car. We'll be down the hill before they can even get back to their cars." Tabitha turned and craned her neck to see through the short but dense woods that separated them from her driveway.

"Yeah, great plan. What the fuck, Tabitha? He turned into a fucking bird."

She let out a long breath. "Would it help to know that I have some abilities as well? I have no idea why, and I have no idea how to control them. I need to find my mother, Greg, and find out what happened. I need to know what I am."

"Why didn't you tell me?"

She let out a caustic bark. "Really? Just share something like that?"

He shrugged. "I might have surprised you."

He began to pull out and gently ease the car down the lane. She murmured, "Oh, I *know* I would have surprised you."

Greg dropped her off at the closest corner of the Hollow, along the path where she and Luc had emerged yesterday. He watched her get out and then leaned over the seat, staring at her through the open window for a few long moments before shaking his head and mumbling a quiet, "Be careful."

She nodded and slipped into the brush as he pulled away. She found a spot off the path and crouched, waiting for Luc to reappear.

Tabitha? You down there?

Yes, where are you?

I have something to show you. Hold onto something.

What does that mean?

Her world began to spin, and she saw what he was seeing as he circled the dark swampy area in the depths of the Hollow. She clutched a branch in front of her to keep her equilibrium as she witnessed what Luc was observing.

There is a Faye down there among the humans.

A Faye? Are you sure?

Yes, he wears a shield as do they, but he is not in their designated attire.

A shield? What are you talking about? Designated attire? Oh! Oh, you mean he is not in a uniform; the shield is a badge. So he is wearing a badge, but he is not in a police uniform?

Luc circled slowly overhead. Tabitha's stomach did a slow turn when he dipped and soared closer to the activity.

There. Do you see him?

Tabitha caught her breath. She recognized the man who had tried to take her off the ferry so many days ago.

Luc, that is the man who tried to kidnap me when I was coming back from Boston. He tried to stop me from leaving the boat. Kayle was able to intervene. She paused, remembering the argument between Kayle and her aunt she had overheard. *Kayle said something about him not being able to come onto the island for some reason. I remember them saying something about something weakening.*

Luc released her. As her senses returned to the damp ground of the Hollow, she heard a flutter when he landed on the path. She peeked through the bushes and stood as he approached.

"I believe they may have been talking of the net around the island," Luc commented.

"Net? What net?"

"There is a fairly intricate power net around the island. However, it has been weakened." He tugged her onto the path and led her down toward the portal. "The enforcement personnel are not in this area. We should have safe access to the portal."

"Enforcement personnel." Tabitha chuckled. "That is funny."

Luc shot her a grin and a shrug. He looked more relaxed now; it appeared they'd be able to cross back over. "So who is Kayle? You mentioned him both in regards to your mother and to saving you from the Faye."

"He's a local fisherman. I haven't got even the slightest clue what he has to do with my mother or a net or how in the world he was able to get me away from that guy. All I know is I woke at home and he was downstairs talking to Trude. He said he expected me to sleep until morning. I cannot even guess why he would have thought that or if he had something to do with my mother's disappearance."

"Is he Caskan or Faye?"

"Kayle? How could he be? I mean, he is just one of the local fisherman," Tabitha retorted. As the words left her lips, she knew that she had no way of knowing. "I have no idea. At this point, I am not sure about anything."

The path took a turn, and Tabitha nudged Luc toward the left, where the granite outcropping and the portal waited for them. The lightening of the woods was an indication that the portal stone was just ahead. Tabitha reached into her pocket and verified that the stone was tucked safely there.

The trepidation she felt about stepping back into Caska was tempered by the reality of what was exploding here in her own world. Luc was obviously more at ease as he stepped toward his home and away from the craziness she had dragged him into.

In a couple of days she would meet her father, continue to look for her mother, and then figure out what to do next.

"Just ahead," she murmured as they emerged onto the large granite platform. Tabitha stepped forward and slammed into his back. "What—? Oh."

There, in front of the portal, stood the man from the ferry. Fear ran alongside irritation as she stopped beside Luc, watching the grinning man regarding them.

"I have been waiting for you," he commented.

"So it seems," Luc responded. "Why?"

"Well, I assumed you'd be back this way. Once I saw the former boyfriend hightail it to the house, I knew it was only a matter of time," the man responded.

"Hightail? Does he shape shift?" Luc seemed confused.

Tabitha shook her head. "You have been watching us?"

"Of course. I did not need to act unless you tried to leave. I need to keep an eye on you." He wandered in front of the portal. "Now that the barrier is dissolving, we can all come on the island. It will be much more convenient."

"The barrier? Is that what kept you from coming on-island before?" Tabitha asked.

He nodded. "With your mother gone, the barrier has been disintegrating." He grinned at Tabitha. "I am surprised that she left you unattended for so long. Our gain."

"I don't think you understand. We are crossing back over. I am going to find my mother," Tabitha retorted.

He grinned. "Well, that can be arranged. I can take you over, and yes, we will find your mother. But we are not going over here. Another portal off-island lands us in a more…convenient place for me."

Tabitha shook her head. "What is the difference? I mean one portal or the other?"

He must not have a stone. Tabitha shot the comment to Luc. *He is right in front of the portal. If he had a stone, it would have flared up by now.*

"We will go to the portal that I choose," he responded as he slipped a sidearm from its holster. "And you two will come with me."

He glanced at Luc. "Mr. DesChamps, I assume you have enough knowledge of this world to know what this is?"

Luc nodded. "I have seen one similar. When you press something, a little flag pops out that says Bang."

The man's smile turned ingratiating. "Funny. So I wonder if you took the opportunity to see the morbid find we made down here?"

Luc shook his head. "We are only trying to get back to Caska. I have no interest in delving into whatever is transpiring over here."

"Interesting. I would have thought this particular find to be very much in your interest," the man responded.

Luc seemed perplexed, and Tabitha waved a hand at the man in annoyance. "We are going back. I don't understand why you think we will return with you."

"Because you are a little too valuable to leave running around to get into more trouble. You are getting a whole lot more attention than you should. The people I work for would like to see you contained until we can determine what to do with you," he responded.

"And who is it that you work for?"

He grinned. "Well, come along with me and you can meet them!"

She shook her head, and Luc shifted his weight. Before she could respond, Luc sent her a quick thought. *He is right in front of the portal. You have your stone?*

Luc, he has a gun, and it is pointed at us.

To the man, she said, "I will make a deal with you. We will all return through this portal, and then when we get there, we can discuss where it is you think I should be going."

He shook his head and waved the gun, indicating they should separate. "No, we do this my way. The two of you will accompany me off the island to another designated portal. If you do not, remember the protective net has been released enough for us to be able to come on-island. Your family is still here, after all, aren't they?"

Tabitha felt the color drain from her face.

Well, that clinches it. He is coming with us. You ready?

Luc! What are you going to do?

I am taking him with us. You are the one with the stone, so when I move, grab the stone and hold on!

Before she could respond, Luc leaped forward and dove straight down, the sudden explosion of movement startling the man. The gun wavered, but before he could aim, Luc grasped him in his arms and drove him backward toward the portal.

Come on!

Tabitha grabbed the stone and dove forward, reaching for Luc when the portal flared in a bright ring before them. She felt herself tumbling as she clutched Luc's shirt. The men wrestled in a tangle of arms and legs, both shouting. With a sickening thud, the three of them hit the ground.

Tabitha rolled away and turned to watch as the man and Luc grappled. The man leveraged Luc off him and rolled over until he was straddling Luc. His arm lifted to strike, but a long, cold blade suddenly appeared before his face, the point inches from his nose. Both Tabitha and the man looked up to find Peri standing there, legs apart, her rapier at the ready.

"You may want to rethink." Peri spoke quietly, her dark eyes intent on the man.

"Yes, my wife is in less than a pleasant mood and is just looking for someone to cut." Diego approached the group on the ground. "I would prefer she chose you rather than me."

Tabitha exhaled in relief as she watched Luc's family approach and drag the man off Luc. She and Luc were offered hands to pull them up, and Tabitha found herself embraced in a warm hug from Sybille.

Luc glanced over and grinned at her. "My father knew we were approaching, and they were waiting for us. We just had to get him over here to receive their help."

Bertòn clapped his son's back and gave Tabitha a warm nod. "Welcome back. I trust your visit home was a pleasant one."

Tabitha sighed. "I wish it had been more productive. It opened up more questions than answers at this point."

"Well, let us get you both back to the house. Jules is awaiting your return, and I believe Marcus would like to speak to this gentleman."

Diego held the man's arms, and with a nod to Bertòn, the two took a step and vanished.

"Where did they go?" Tabitha was unprepared for the sudden disappearance.

"I imagine Diego took our friend to see Marcus. Let's go back to the house and get cleaned up. I could use some clean clothes," Luc commented, brushing off his pants.

Bertòn, Peri, Sybille, and finally Tye all stepped forward and disappeared, leaving them alone in the glade on the other side from the Dark Hollow in her world. The sun was rising over the ocean. She knew where she was in relation to her world, but here, it was different. Her home was not nestled among the pines up on the rocky coast on Shore Road. Shore Road did not exist here.

The mystery was clearing slowly, like the morning fog that hugged her island home. The breeze of knowledge had begun to clear the wispy gray vapor, but in its place lay a puzzle more intricate than she thought she could ever hope to crack. And a woman's body, left so many years ago in a shallow grave, was the latest addition to the murky mystery.

Her mother had disappeared twenty-two years ago, and now, finally, after eighteen years in a dense fog of confusion, Tabitha knew where Doni had gone. She knew where she had been born, and she knew where her abilities came from. But those answers came at a cost. She prayed they had removed the threat to her family by bringing along her abductor.

She was in Caska with Luc, and her father awaited her. By discovering where her mother had gone, she had leaped off the ledge and landed on the first step. Now it would take another leap of faith to go to her father against the advice of the mysterious Faye.

As Tabitha unraveled her mother's tangled web of deception, each strand she tugged opened a door to another bevy of questions.

One at a time. All she could do was tug one string at a time. And at the end of the next one was her father.

She glanced up to find Luc waiting, watching her as she stood lost in thought.

"You ready?"

She reached for his hand and laughed. "That is a loaded question."

The End

If you enjoyed Dark Hollow,

Follow Tabitha's adventure in Dark Legacy Book 2 in the Hidden Heritage Series